BATU KHAN

THE CONQUEROR OF EUROPE

A Historical Novel

SAM DJANG

Batu Khan: The Conqueror of Europe

First Edition, 2023

Published by Brave Future Books

Copyright © 2023 Sam Djang

Copyediting, interior design and layout, and proofreading by Joanne Shwed, Backspace Ink (backspaceink.com)

Cover design by Rick Schroeppel, Book Cover Design (BookCoverDesign.us)

This is a work of fiction. Names, places, characters and incidents are primarily real based on extensive historical research on the life and history of Batu Khan. The author has added elements to fill in gaps not recorded in history, and these are either the product of the author's imagination or are used fictitiously, and any resemblance to actual persons, living or dead, business establishments, events, or locales is entirely coincidental.

Library of Congress Control Number: 2022919028

ISBNs: 978-0-9970263-2-0 (paperback)
        978-0-9970263-3-7 (hardcover)
        978-0-9970263-4-4 (e-book)

Printed in the United States of America

CONTENTS

CONTENTS

CONTENTS

CONTENTS

CONTENTS

Preface

The emergence of the Mongol Empire in the 13th century was the turning point of human history. The dramatic change in the human world after this turning point was a positive one, especially for the Europeans. This is my belief.

Before the Mongol Empire, there was no communication between the east and the west. At that time, the world was wide. Many different forms of natural barriers—rivers, mountains, deserts, impenetrable dense forests and enormously wide plains—were between them, and they didn't have any reason to cross over all of them. Communication and the exchange of ideas could now be possible after the emergence of the Mongol Empire. Gun powder, paper and compasses were introduced from the east to the west, and the concept of chemistry, astronomy and mathematics was transferred from the west to the east.

Before the Mongol Empire, it was very dangerous or almost impossible to travel from the city of Venice in Italy to Beijing, China, which was a trip that Marco Polo's father Piccolo and his uncle Maffeo frequently made. After more than 20 years of staying in China, Marco Polo, who travelled to Beijing with his father and stayed there under the protection of Kublai Khan, finally returned to his home in Italy and began his storytelling, which influenced all of Europe.

PREFACE

Marco Polo's well-known book, *The Travels of Marco Polo*, inspired many young men in Europe at that time to go to the east to find the riches and gold that Marco Polo described. Marco Polo's story influenced Europe inwardly and outwardly. Inwardly, it ignited the new Renaissance wave; outwardly, it motivated many men who were seeking adventure and fortune. At age 14, Christopher Columbus was one of the young men who was inspired by Marco Polo's story. His introduction of the existence of a new continent to the Europeans was a great event as everyone knows. All these were chain reactions related to Marco Polo and the Mongol Empire.

Batu Khan was the front-runner by breaking the wall between the east and the west, yet his story has not been told often to the public, which motivated me to write about it. All these stories were written based on the most trusted histories. When different theories related to the same event conflicted, I picked the most probable one based on my common sense. The only fictionalized areas in this book were episodes written for the purpose of connecting stories and making the reading smoother.

The descendants of Genghis Khan

The descendants of Genghis Khan are many, yet only the names that appear in this book are listed for the readers' convenience.

2ND GENERATION	3RD GENERATION	4TH GENERATION
1st son Juchi	Orda	
	Batu *(founder of Golden Ordu)*	Sartaq *(2nd khan of Golden Ordu)*
	Berke *(3rd khan of Golden Ordu)*	
	Seiban	
	Tangut	
	Sinkur	
2nd son Chagatai	Moetuken	Buri
	Baidar	
3rd son Ogodei *(2nd khagan)*	Kuyuk *(3rd khagan)*	
	Koten	
	Kochu	Shiremun
	Kadan	
	Qachar	
	Qasi	

THE DESCENDANTS OF GENGHIS KHAN

2ND GENERATION	3RD GENERATION	4TH GENERATION
4th son Tolui	Monku *(4th khagan)*	
	Kubilai *(founder of Yuan Dynasty in China, 5th khagan)*	
	Hulegu *(founder of Il Khanate in Persia and the Middle East)*	
	Arigh Boke	
	Bujek	

CHAPTER 1

The beginning of the new beginning: the fall of Samarqand

Genghis Khan advanced toward Samarqand, the capital city of the Khwarazm Empire. Samarqand—a city with a population of half a million—was a political, commercial, cultural and industrial center for the empire. It was also grand in scale and magnificent.

The buildings were built with red bricks and marble, and creamy tiles covered the bricks to make them clean and bright. In the downtown area and marketplace, stores carrying luxurious foreign goods and merchandise from all over the world lined up endlessly, and inns and theaters for travelers were everywhere. Blessed with warm and pleasant weather, neighboring areas of Samarqand were filled with numerous varieties of fruit trees, including date palm trees, figs, pomegranates and quinces, and the vineyards and watermelon fields spread out endlessly.

The watermelons—a specialty of this area—were highly popular because of their great sweetness and less fiber than the others. The city exported a large amount of watermelons each season to satisfy the demand from faraway countries. When exporting to faraway places, they put these products into wooden boxes filled with heat-resistant and shockproof materials.

The Persian poets praised this beautiful city:

Samarqand!
The jewel of the east!

Full of grace of God,
It is the hometown for angels.

Sweet wine rains,
And the wind is full of fragrance.

The earth is musk,
And the gems are rolling everywhere.

Where is the Garden of Eden?
It is Samarqand!

Samarqand was guarded by 60,000 Turks and 50,000 Tajiks, totaling 110,000 men. They were the elite troops of the Khwarazm Empire. Their generals—Alper Khan, Shaik Khan and Bala Khan—were the best among them and major role players in building up the empire.

One evening, a man galloped his horse at full speed toward the main gate of Samarqand. His hair was disheveled, and his clothing was torn to ribbons. He was the Tajik soldier who had escaped from Bukhara and one of a few survivors of the garrison there. He was ushered in front of Sultan Muhammad II and, panting, he told him what had happened in Bukhara.

"They burned Bukhara! The city is completely destroyed and leveled. No more garrison. They collapsed and all were slaughtered."

Sultan Muhammad II was shocked. He thought the Mongols could not break the Syr Darya River defense line so easily and, even if they did, it would take a long time for them to get to Samarqand. Now that Bukhara was in their hands, he was surrounded! He was in danger of the supply line from the west. He was still intent upon repairing the rampart of Samarqand, and it was not over yet!

Sultan Muhammad II decided to escape to the west with the excuse that he had to bring more troops from the west. His transparent lie left only one man who could dare to resist his escape plan: his firstborn son Jal-al-Addin. He was one of only a few heroes of Khwarazm; however, he also had to flee to the Hindu Kush, the 500-mile-long mountain range west of Himalaya, once his father had left there.

Genghis Khan's first army group arrived at Samarqand with their 70,000 levies in front of them. A levy was a selected group of laborers from surrendered enemy soldiers or citizens who pledged to fight for the Mongols, although they were not allowed to have weapons or horses. All the while, Genghis Khan was in close contact with the other three army groups and knew their exact locations, movements and situations.

CHAPTER 1

Only a half day after his arrival, Chagatai, Genghis Khan's second son, and Ogodei, Genghis Khan's third son's second army group, also arrived with their 20,000 levies. For a day, Genghis looked around the outside of the city, and the following day he created complete encirclement.

The city of Samarqand had enough stored provisions for 600,000 people, including the garrison, to use for several years. They thought they could resist and hold the city for at least a year; however, it fell to the Mongols in just five days!

First, Genghis had the levies fill the deep moat around the rampart. The levies completed their job using nearby dirt and rocks. On that first night, when the moat was completely filled, the Mongol troops commenced a surprise attack. The rocks, which were shot by the catapults, began to break down the buildings and houses, and the naphtha flames lit up the city like daytime.

As the Mongol troops approached the rampart with their 3,000 ladder carriers, they greeted them with showers of arrows; however, the ladder carriers were designed and equipped with an anti-arrow system. The Mongol soldiers began to climb the rampart using the ladder once they got there. The garrison soldiers tried to push away the approaching ladder carriers with long logs, yet some of the Mongol commandos were already on the rampart.

After fierce man-to-man fighting on the rampart, the Mongol commandos successfully occupied one of the main gates. Knowing that they had lost one of the main gates, the leaders of the Khwarazm garrison tried a full-scale counterattack. They opened the other gates and came pouring out of the city with 20 armed elephants in front of them; however, it turned out to be a damn fool tactic. Being attacked by showers of arrows, the intolerant elephants stepped back or turned around, trampling their own soldiers. The Khwarazm soldiers, who were pouring out of the gates, fell down in great numbers and were crushed. The dead bodies of the Khwarazm soldiers covered the field outside the city, making it hard for the Mongol soldiers to move around.

The following day, the leaders of the city gathered, discussed and decided to surrender. The citizens of Samarqand were not very loyal to Sultan Muhammad II, just as he deserted Samarqand quickly for his own safety. The Mongol troops broke down the rampart first and then attacked the citadel where the defiant Alper Khan and his 30,000 troops were hiding. Three days later, the citadel was taken and the 30,000 troops were annihilated. At the last moment, Alper Khan tried to escape with his 1,000 suicide soldiers; however, most of them were massacred and only he and a few survivors made their way to the west.

Genghis Khan issued an order of evacuation of all citizens from the city. They needed to be screened. The whole population of Samarqand was evacuated to the field. The Mongol soldiers entered the city and killed tens of thousands of disobedient people who were hiding in the ceiling or the sewers in spite of the evacuation order.

Then the Mongol officials began the screening and selection of the citizens. The first group of people selected included leading figures connected to the Mongol Empire and cooperative officials, and second were engineers, technicians and artisans. Their numbers came up to 50,000. Among the rest, 30,000

CHAPTER 1

levies who pledged their allegiance to the Mongol Empire were selected. Next, women and children were selected.

Among the rest of the male population all the defiant, disobedient ones, and some who had refused to convert were executed. The selected citizens were imposed with 200,000 dinars of war support money, and two men—Siqa-al-Mulk and Amid Buzurq—who had pledged their loyalty to Genghis Khan were installed as chief administrative officials. Genghis appointed Yalavachi as the governor of Samarqand and left several darughachis (supervisors) there.

Genghis Khan organized the pursuit of Sultan Muhammad II, who had fled before the fall of Samarqand. For this mission, 30,000 elite troops were selected and two commanders named Jebe Noyan and Subedei Bagatur were appointed. They were ordered to chase down Sultan Muhammad II to the end of the world.

CHAPTER 2

The last of Sultan Muhammad II

Jebe and Subedei continued to chase down Sultan Muhammad II with their 30,000 cavalry men. It was early April 1220, after the fall of Samarqand, of which garrisons—110,000 of them—had perished, leaving the fate of the citizens—a half million of them—to the victor's hands. Genghis Khan found that Sultan Muhammad II had escaped on the pretext that he would summon more troops, regroup and come back.

A deed is not glorious until it is complete!

Jebe and Subedei were told to discuss everything with each other when they had to make decisions. When it was hard to agree, Jebe would take the lead.

After crossing the Syr Darya River, they began to sweep over area after area with earth-shaking hoofbeats and roaring sounds, like a tempest. It was the first step of the fantastic, long march of 8,000 miles, unparalleled in human history, and took more than three years.

The first city they encountered was Balkh. At the time, Balkh was not a city of resistance. Being surprised and over-whelmed by the superiority of the Mongol troops in every aspect, the leaders of Balkh decided not to offend them but to cooperate with food and water as demanded. They accepted, without resistance, three darughachis (supervisors) that Jebe installed. Jebe learned that the sultan had left there a few weeks prior. Jebe rushed to continue the chase after picking up several guides from the residents. Later, this city turned to Jal-al-Addin, the firstborn son of Sultan Muhammad II, and became rebellious, which drove them into a horrible disaster.

The vanguard of the chasing troops arrived at the city of Zava, which was on a vast, open field with a protective ram-part and three citadels within the city, built of strong, dried mud. The residents began to shake in fear of the approaching huge group of men and horses that were coming from the east, making thunderous, earth-shaking hoofbeats and huge clouds of dust rising into the sky. They closed their city gates firmly and were on high alert.

The Mongol troops arrived in front of the main gate and urged them to open it and surrender. The leaders of the city had an urgent meeting and decided not to surrender. Since the Mongol troops were in a hurry chasing the sultan, they intended to pass over; however, when the last cavalryman holding the banner had passed their gate, they began to hoot and ridicule, hitting big drums and tabors, which were small hand drums that made a high-pitched sound when used.

They invited their own tragedy. They humiliated Genghis Khan's banner! The returned Mongol troops attacked the city and the three citadels. After three days, the city fell to the Mongols, the entire population of 20,000 was slaughtered and the ramparts and citadels were leveled. The city was burned to the ground, leaving no trace of the man-built city. It was the first blow of the chasing troops, and it was fierce.

In June 1220, Jebe and Subedei's troops arrived at the city of Nishapur. Jebe urged them to surrender by sending an envoy into the city. Like Balkh, Nishapur was also cooperative by accepting Jebe's demand. Jebe left three darughachis in this city with a rolled-up written decree and an al tamgha, which was an official seal, that said:

God's power on Earth,
Khagan.
The land from sunrise to sunset,
Has been bestowed on him.
From God.
A new order and new world,
Will be created.
This is the will of the supreme being.
The ones who follow this,
Shall survive and thrive.
The ones who stand against this,
Shall be perished.
Until the end of time.

CHAPTER 2

The Mongol chasing troops hit Juvine, Tus, Radkan, Khabushan, Isfarayin and Adkan, one by one. Darughachis were left in the surrendered cities, otherwise, they were completely destroyed along with their entire population.

Jebe and Subedei's troops arrived at the city of Damghan, which was located at the eastern end of the Elburz Mountains, around the southern end of the Caspian Sea. The Mongol troops entered the heart of the past Persian Empire. Having known of the Mongol troops' arrival, the aristocrats and leaders of the city fled into Girdkuh, the strong fortress nearby. Girdkuh was on top of a high mountain, and it was one of the strongholds of the Assassins, a branch of Islam.

The Assassins were a group of Shiites who rose in revolt, declaring religious reform. Since they were not accepted in mainstream Islam, they retreated into the mountains. They built fortresses on top of the high mountains in many places and retired there, waiting out their days. They dealt with their enemies not by routine warfare but by an individual hitman or teams of them. In normal times, they contemplated life, raised sheep and goats, drank grape or honey wine, wrote poems, painted and danced to music.

They called their leader Hassan Sabba, which meant "the old man on the mountain." Hassan Sabba used to come down to the villages, tempting young ones aged 12 to 20 and taking them into the mountains to brainwash them. He used to tell them things after giving them hashish, a strong hallucinatory drug:

The utmost beauty in life,
Is to give your life to God.

The ultimate goals of the mortals,
Are to get eternal life in heaven.
Kill the enemies of God,
That is the way to please the divine being.
Put your life on God's altar,
That is the sure way to heaven.
Ten thousand different kinds of flowers,
Ten thousand different fragrances.
Ten thousand beautiful lasses and women,
Are just for you and waiting.
Ten thousand different kinds of pleasures and happinesses,
Will be with you in eternity.
So, you are in heaven.

The young ones, under the influence of hashish, left Hassan Sabba with only one short dagger in their clothing and committed murders. Their success rate was so high that many monarchs and religious leaders fell victim to their plots. The area under their influence was from Turkey to the east and Syria to the west, and the targeted monarchs and religious leaders even had to wear their armor to bed. They were called assassins because they committed murders under the influence of hashish. They could not be removed because their bases were located on top of high mountains, which other troops could never approach.

Jebe and Subedei dispatched 3,000 commandos to take the Girdkuh fortress while the main troops headed for Damghan.

Damghan was taken after seven days of resistance, and all 50,000 residents were slaughtered. Meanwhile, the leader of commandos, who was headed for Girdkuh, selected 500 out of 3,000 mountain war specialists and let them climb the mountain at night. They successfully reached the top of the mountain and crossed over the rampart with a rope ladder. They opened the gate for the main troops and took control of 2,000 enemy garrisons. All the members of the Assassins and the garrisons were beheaded, and all the aristocrats from Damghan, who were hiding there, were arrested. Those who were cooperative and provided valuable information were saved, and the others were slaughtered.

The Mongol troops continued to take Samnan and Khuvar, massacring all the residents there, and proceeded to Ray (Teheran), which was the biggest city in the region and the industrial center, especially for pottery and ceramics. This city was also completely destroyed and a great number of the residents slaughtered.

From there, the Mongol troops learned that Sultan Muhammad II had fled to Hamadan, the city between Ray and Baghdad. The Mongol troops advanced toward Hamadan. Ala Adduala, the ruler of Hamadan, opened the gate and surrendered to the Mongols. He supplied food and clothing and accepted the al tamgha, Genghis Khan's seal. Jebe installed three darughachis there, yet they did not find the sultan.

Ala Adduala said, "He escaped to Mazandaran about three weeks ago. His family members and concubines are staying in Mazandaran; however, on the way to the city, about 30,000 of his loyal troops were stationed there to guard the city. The name of the spot is Sujas."

Mazandaran was a city located close to the southwestern end of the Caspian Sea and about 200 miles from Hamadan to the north-northeast. At the time, when Sultan Muhammad II was escaping from Samarqand, he dispatched urgent messengers to the city of Urgenchi, where his family members and concubines were staying, and moved all of them to Mazandaran. Mazandaran was in the westernmost territory of the Khwarazm Empire and close to the border with Shirvan (Azerbaijan).

The Mongol troops clashed with the sultan's 30,000 troops at Sujas. The sultan's last defense line was broken down. Dozens of arrows coming from the Mongol archery unit were responsible for the deaths of the two commanders of the defense troops. Beg-Tegin Silahdar and Kuch-Buga Khan and their troops were completely destroyed. The Mongol troops advanced toward Mazandaran, stepping over the dead bodies of the Khwarazm soldiers that were strewn across the field.

Upon receiving the news that the last defense force had been destroyed, Sultan Muhammad II summoned Nazil Addin, the governor of Mazandaran, as well as his loyal servant.

"Take my family members to the two fortresses of Larijan and Ilal and put half of them in each. Kill all the hostages we are keeping."

In Mazandaran, they were keeping about 150 hostages, who were taken by the sultan while he was conquering many different areas. They were sons or brothers of the monarchs of the various areas he had conquered. Nazil Addin, the loyal servant of the sultan, tied the hands and feet of all the hostages and threw them into the river. As the urgent report came in that the Mongol troops had arrived outside the city, the sultan hurriedly left the city after asking Nazil Addin to take good care of his family and concubines. Before leaving, he accepted some advice from Nazil Addin.

"Sultan, change your clothing. You never know if the Mongol spies are already in the city."

Nazil Addin brought him a set of dirty, lousy clothes that he had taken from a beggar. The sultan, after looking at the tatters, nodded and changed his gold-embroidered silk garments with those of the beggar's. He also changed his turban, which was decorated with gems and peacock feathers, to that of the beggar's. He hurried out of the city with only two servants.

His escape was immediately reported to Subedei by his spies. Subedei rapidly dispatched a chasing unit. When the Mongol chasing unit arrived at the seaside of the Caspian Sea, the sultan, in a small fishing boat, was rowing away from the shore with his two servants. The Mongol chasing soldiers shot arrows as they galloped along the shoreline; however, the fishing boat was already out of range.

Nazil Addin rushed out of the city with about 400 of the sultan's family members and concubines and put them into the two fortresses Larijan and Ilal. Subedei immediately chased them and surrounded the two fortresses. Since the fortresses were firmly built on a high mountain, Subedei reinforced the encirclement instead of attacking directly. They held out for two weeks; however, since they were running out of drinking water and began to die of dehydration, Nazil Addin gave up. He descended the mountain and surrendered.

Sultan Muhammad II's sons and grandsons—about 60 of them—were all beheaded. About 200 of his wives and concubines and about 50 of his daughters were sent to Genghis Khan in Talaqan after all sorts of humiliation. Among them was the sultan's old mother Terke Khatun, who at one time was considered a heroine in their world. After they were taken to the Mongol mainland, they were forced to live the lives of slaves.

As for Nazil Addin, he was flayed alive by a skillful butcher, and his flayed skin was used to cover a dummy made of barley straw in front of them. They took over the city of Mazandaran, which was the last stronghold of the Khwarazm Empire, beheading 100,000 of its resisters. This meant the complete fall of the Khwarazm Empire.

But what happened to Sultan Muhammad II? After he left Mazandaran, he escaped to a tiny island in the Caspian Sea. It was an uninhabited island with rocks that were covered in seagull droppings. The sultan's two servants made a hut with small pieces of wood and dried weeds that they collected. After they used up all the food they had brought, they had to fish to survive.

The sultan held out there for some time; however, he fell into intense grief when he heard the news from a nearby fisherman who had come across to the island. All his male descendants had been killed, and his wives, concubines and daughters had been taken to some other place after many humiliations. After all that, a few weeks later, he died of a disease—possibly acute pleurisy—caused by emotional hardship and malnutrition. The man, who at one time had an empire with vast land, more subjects than stars in the sky and hundreds of concubines, died in beggar's rags, in his hut on a tiny island where the cold wind never ceased to blow.

Before he died, with his two eyes staring into space, he shouted, "Ah! Where are all my subjects? Where is my great land? Now I don't even have a piece of land for my own body!"

His two servants tried to bury him, but they could not dig a hole deep enough to bury his body because, after a few inches of digging, they hit a rock. They left the island after covering his dead body with gravel and small stones.

It was January 1221—nine months after the Mongol chasing troops had been dispatched.

CHAPTER 3

The conquest of the Georgia Kingdom

That winter, they experienced very heavy snow. The great plain of Mughan, which was close to the western shore of the Caspian Sea, was covered with white snow. From there, they could see the faraway horizon of the great Caspian Sea. On the vast plain covered with snow, countless yurts—the Mongols' unique, dome-shaped felt tents—were spread out, forming a city.

Jebe and Subedei passed the winter there. Neither men nor horses could move freely due to the snow piled up to human height. In the meantime, they sent mountains of war booty to Genghis Khan in Talaqan. They were not to leave until they confirmed the death of Sultan Muhammad II. In February 1221, the two servants who had been with the sultan until his last moment were captured, and the death of the sultan was confirmed through them.

Subedei dispatched an urgent messenger. The arrow messenger—the nickname of the urgent messengers of the Mongol troops—ran 1,200 miles in seven days, arriving at Genghis Khan's main camp with Subedei's letter. Subedei was reporting to Genghis the complete conquest of the western Khwarazm and the death of Sultan Muhammad II. At the same time, he was reporting the political climates of those areas, including the possible supporters of Jal-al-Addin, who was still alive at that time, in the remaining Islamic world. He also put down his opinion about the future movements of their troops and asked for approval. Subedei, the great general, had sharp eyes, and his judgments were accurate. He was already looking to the far-distant future of the Mongol Empire.

Genghis Khan's answer was this: "Advance to Russia!"

In the spring of 1221, Jebe headed for Iraq. In the region of Ardabil in Iraq, a man named Ai Baba organized troops, and then attacked and took Hamadan, the city that had previously surrendered to the Mongols, and killed three darughachis there. Ai Baba also imprisoned Ala Adduala in a small castle in Girit. Jebe surrounded Hamadan again and attacked and successfully recaptured the city. Ai Baba, the head of the rebels, tried to surrender, but it was not accepted. He lost his head along with several hundred of his followers. Next, Jebe advanced toward Ardabil, the place where the revolt began, and completely destroyed and slaughtered the whole population after taking the city. Ala Adduala was reinstalled as the governor of Hamadan.

Jebe and Subedei headed for the north from the southwestern region of the Caspian Sea. They crossed the northern border of Khwarazm, stepping into Shirvan. The Mongol troops took Maragha and Nakhchivan, massacring the resistant residents. As the Mongol troops surrounded Tabriz, their capital city, Ozbeg, who was the atabeg (ruler) of Shirvan, came up to surrender. He sent tuzghu, the symbol of their ruler, a great amount of gold and treasures, 10 of his envoys and 20 of their beauties.

Upon facing 10 of their envoys, Jebe drew his scimitar (curved sword) and cut off one of their heads, which fell to the ground. Since they could not be fully trusted, it was an example and a warning. Ozbeg's request for surrender was accepted, and Tabriz was saved. Ozbeg became the last king of Seljuk Turkey.

The Mongol troops advanced toward Arran (now Armenia). From there, it was a Christian world. As the Mongol troops were approaching their capital city of Bailaqan, the Armenian ruler as well as garrison chief Vardan closed the city gate firmly and ordered his garrison soldiers ready for defense battle. At that time, Arran belonged to the powerful neighboring Georgia Kingdom as a vassal state.

On top of the city wall, Vardan was watching carefully approaching, mysterious, unknown troops with his high-ranking subordinate soldiers. Approaching men and horses, who were making golden dust clouds that covered the southern sky and earth-shaking, thunderous hoofbeats, turned their majestic scenery into a fearsome one.

One of Vardan's men shouted, "Look! They are holding a cross!"

Vardan carefully watched the approaching front group. He confirmed that one of them was holding a large cross, and the front lines of cavalrymen were holding a large shield painted with an image of a cross.

CHAPTER 3

"They are Christians!" Vardan thought as he put his falchion (a single-bladed, one-handed sword) into the leather sheath on his sword belt.

The huge group of men and horses stopped at some point, and three cavalry men galloped out from their group and approached the main gate. They were all holding large, rectangular-shaped red shields with white oblique cross marks on it, and one held a banner with a Christian cross.

One cavalry man in the center shouted in Armenian, "We are Nestorian Christians! We came from the east. We destroyed the Islamic Khwarazm Empire. We are on the way to join the crusaders! All we need is some water. Allow us to get some water!"

The Nestorian church, or the church of the east, was a branch of Christianity that arose around the fifth century in Constantinople and transferred to the east through Persia, Transoxania, central Asia and China. They were expelled from mainstream Christianity due to their beliefs, which were treated as heresy. They refused to believe the Virgin Mary as the mother of God and Jesus himself as merely a human body imbued with the Holy Spirit, by will. Among the Mongols, many of the descendants of the Kerait tribe were Nestorian Christians. The Mongol society was under the freedom of religion.

Vardan didn't know what to do.

One of his assistant captains commented, "They put an end to Seljuk Turkey by conquering Tabriz. It happened not long ago."

Vardan shouted to the messengers, "That's fine! But I limit it to only 100 men and horses. Bring the largest water bags you have," and he opened the gate.

Sometime later, about 100 men and horses came in through the gate. They were all carrying two large bags on both sides of the horses. Suddenly, just after they passed the gate, they transformed themselves into combatant soldiers. They were Mongol special-unit commandos and, inside their leather bags, they were hiding all sorts of weapons.

In a blinking moment, they subdued the front-gate garrison and opened the gate wide for the main body of the Mongol troops. There was some fierce street fighting; nonetheless, the conquering procedure was an easy one. All the defiant soldiers and citizens were massacred, and the cooperative ones and the ones who pledged allegiance to the Mongols were saved. Vardan was executed due to his lack of cooperation.

The Mongols declared Arran as a new Mongolian territory and left three darughachis there.

The Mongol troops continued advancing, stepping into Georgia, which was another Christian kingdom located just south of the Caucasus Mountains. At that time, Georgia was at the peak of its power and wealth, and its knights were known to be invincible. Their knights were wearing protective, metallic tunics and coifs and, on top of them, they wore metal armor. Once they put on their armor and helmets and shut the visors for the eye opening of the helmets, not even a single arrow could hurt them. They were armed with long, heavy spears, swords and huge battle axes.

CHAPTER 3

George IV, the Georgian king and commander of their troops, faced the Mongol troops with his invincible armored cavalry. The knights—10,000 of them—in their protective armor and helmets proudly marched toward the Mongol troops. They even had heavy coverings on their horses. Behind them, about 20,000 foot soldiers followed like their shadow. They faced each other at the field of Tiflis.

After careful evaluation of the enemy's power and situation, Subedei said to Jebe, "I think we need to separate the knight troops and foot soldiers first."

Jebe agreed. For a brief moment, they made their battle plan, and the battle began.

King George IV thought the Mongol troops, whose main weapons were bows and arrows, could never defeat his knight cavalry who were protected by metal armor, which was believed to be arrow-proof. But it was a mistake. The Mongol arrow could penetrate their armor.

Later, days after this battle, the Mongols developed a more powerful arrow, replacing the arrow tip with a much stronger metal and a different design. The Georgian's armor was quite effective against the smashing blow with a scimitar but not with the Mongol arrow.

After their commander's charge order, the Georgian knight cavalry dashed toward the Mongol troops like a huge, rolling rock. Subedei, who was acting as the vanguard, immediately ordered his troops to retreat. For a while, the knight cavalry chased the Mongol troops; however, their horses could not catch up with them because their horses were carrying heavy armor, about 150 pounds of weight, and the soldiers.

Once the knight cavalry passed a certain spot—an area sided by heavy woods—they were suddenly attacked by unknown troops from both sides. They were Jebe's ambushed cavalry group. At the same time, Subedei and his troops turned around and began a counterattack. It was a hand-to-hand combat. The knight cavalrymen in heavy armor could not move as fast as the Mongol soldiers, who were wearing very light, leather armor.

The Mongol soldiers used spears with hooks or lassos to take them down from the horses. Once they fell to the ground, they could never remount them. The Mongol soldiers attacked the enemies' armpits with a scimitar or a spear where there was no protection from the armor. The grounded Georgian knights, mostly after losing their helmets, were killed by smashing hits with maces or battle axes on their heads and faces exerted by the Mongol opponents.

After completely laying down the knight cavalry, Jebe and Subedei's joint forces turned to the Georgian foot soldiers—20,000 of them—that were still 10 miles away. They cut them down like weeds with a scythe. The dead bodies of all 30,000 of both the knights and the foot soldiers were strewn across the field. They couldn't create a synergistic effect of a formidable combination of horsemen and foot soldiers in case of a man-to-man ground combat. Thus, the Georgia Kingdom fell to the Mongols.

The Georgian king escaped with very few retainers; sometime later, he died from the wound he got on his chest during the battle.

CHAPTER 4

Into the Russian steppe

Jebe and Subedei crossed over the Caucasus Mountains by way of the gate of Derbent and the pass of Bab al-Abwab. Now they were in Europe. Jebe's and Subedei's eyes met with magnificent images of the vast steppe of the Kipchak. It was February 1222, and the field was still covered with snow. The beating sound of their horses' hooves on the vast ground dispersed through the snow, which absorbed the noise. The sky was deep-sea blue, and the land showed horizons in all four directions. Nothing was different from their homeland on the Mongolian plain.

It had been two years since they began their mission and expedition. Their strong life force, their traditional culture that any place could be their home once they set up their yurts and their philosophy that they wanted to die on the battlefield all contributed to their strong mental immunity against the hardship of the long march. Their thousand-year-old traditional belief engraved in their bones—that a man will be born in a yurt but should die on the battlefield—was the most important. This was their mental background as warriors directed their movements and actions.

INTO THE RUSSIAN STEPPE

Their best friends and companions—the Mongol horses—had extraordinary toughness, resilience and life force like their owners. They threaded their way through the battlefields and stepped over immensely long distances. The Mongol horses, which did not need particular feed unlike others, could eat snow and ice and had instincts to find their own food.

As soon as Jebe and Subedei stepped into the vast plain of the Russian steppe, they were greeted by four, not-so-friendly, different types of tribes in this area. They were Kipchak Turks, Alans, Lezghians and Circassians. They claimed it as their own land and became hostile to this uninvited guest.

The truth was that they were informed by the secret messenger sent by Rashid, who was the chief of Derbent, warning that the Mongols were approaching and explaining what had happened in the Khwarazm Empire, Arran and the Georgia Kingdom. When the Mongols arrived at Derbent previously, they made a deal with Rashid. If they supplied enough fodder for their horses and 10 guides, they would just pass by without destroying it. The Mongols needed their cooperation. The deal had been met; however, Rashid had deep relations with the people on the Russian steppe, and many people from those regions were living in Derbent. So, he double-crossed the Mongols.

He gathered 10 would-be guides and secretly told them, "Do not give them the best way. They should suffer. Anyway, they are our enemies." Then, he gave them a dark hint. "It would be a pity if anything happened to your family in case you ignore my words."

CHAPTER 4

When the 10 guides were sent to the Mongols, Jebe drew his scimitar and cut off one of their heads. It was a warning.

Three days after their departure, the Mongols faced three to four different routes in front of them. Subedei interviewed each of the guides separately.

After, Subedei said with Jebe, "They had been told from Rashid not to cooperate with us. One of them confessed."

They shared their opinions for some time and then organized four different groups of reconnaissance units. Each unit was composed of 100 soldiers, and they were supposed to pre-step each respective route with the guides who recommended it. This should have been done before the main troops stepped in.

About seven or eight days later, they all came back, and Subedei got the report. Three out of four routes were considered inappropriate or even dangerous for the large army to step into. Only one route had a possibility and was considered relatively safe. All of the nine guides were summoned in front of Subedei and divided by the route they recommended. Eight out of nine were the ones who recommended the wrong track. They were immediately executed on the spot. The only one left, who pointed to the right direction, was surprisingly a boy about 15 years old.

"What is your motivation to help us?" Subedei asked.

"I want to be a soldier."

Subedei heard this through an interpreter and continued. "You don't have your family in Derbent?"

"No. My father died a few years ago, and I don't know where my mother is. I am living with my uncle's family, but I want to be on my own."

"So, you want to join us?"

"Yes." The boy gave this answer without hesitation.

Subedei gave it a little thought and said in an encouraging tone, "Your wish has been granted. Be a good one."

Subedei gave an instruction to the captain to put the boy in the interpretation and pacifying unit.

The first group encountered by the Mongols were Kipchak Turks. The Kipchak Turks were called Polovtsy by the Russians and Cumans by the Hungarians. They were the most furious and powerful among the four groups and nomadic in nature like the Mongols. The total combined forces of all four groups encountering the Mongols were 50,000. Among them, 35,000 were Kipchak Turks; however, they were moving individually, not in one group. In normal situations, they were not the groups that got along with each other.

Koten, the chief of the Kipchak Turks, sent his brother Yuri and son Daniel to stop the Mongols. Yuri and Daniel, with their 35,000 warriors, moved toward the northern end of the pass of Bab al-Abwab (gate of gate) where the Mongol troops were stationed. The pass of Bab al-Abwab, as its name implies, was an immensely tough and dangerous route, which the Mongols had just crossed. The snow on the route doubled the danger, and the Mongols had to lose many of their belongings.

Jebe and Subedei sat down and discussed this situation.

CHAPTER 4

Jebe said, "According to our sentry unit's report, the Kipchaks will be arriving here soon. They are outnumbering us. Let's talk about what we have to do with them."

"This is not a good location to have a large-scale battle," Subedei answered. "We just passed Bab al-Abwab, and it's on our back. It's just a one-day walk. In case we must retreat, it could be trouble. We must make them retreat at least one day's marching distance."

"How can we make them retreat without fighting?" Jebe asked.

"I think, in this case, a fake tactic could work. And, since they are outnumbering us, it should be a surprise attack. If we destroy the Kipchaks, the other three won't be trouble to us. And the other three groups are on the way but still far away. But time could be on their side."

They talked until late into the night, making a detailed plan. The great psychological warfare began.

The following morning, they organized a special pacifying unit of 30 messengers who could speak Kipchak Turkish. The Mongolian language and Turkish were very similar because both languages shared the same root. Even their ancestral roots were very close, and the original home town for the Kipchaks was central Asia. Their ancestors emigrated from there hundreds of years ago. In many cases, they were categorized as the same group of people, like Turko-Mongols. Among the Mongol soldiers, the Naiman descendants were of Turkish origin.

The pacifying unit carried 200 high-quality, gray-colored stallions, which the nomadic people valued as symbols of good luck. They also carried nine large chests full of gold and silver coins. The frontmost messenger was carrying Genghis Khan's banner, or tuk, which was made of nine different horses' tails. There were two different kinds of banners—one with a black tail, which meant war, and one with a white tail, which meant peace. They were carrying a white banner.

Enkh, the chief of the messengers, was ushered in front of Yuri and Daniel.

After formal greetings, Enkh spoke in fluent Kipchak Turkish. "Greetings! I am here to convey warmest greetings from our generals Jebe Noyan and Subedei Bagatur. We are here to chase and terminate our enemy, the Khwarazmian Sultan Muhammad II, and now that mission has been fulfilled. We are on our way back to the homeland. We are very careful not to give unnecessary worries to peaceful people around here. We just want to pass through. That's all we want."

Koten's brother Yuri gave a careful look at Enkh and asked, "Where did you learn our language?" He was impressed by Enkh's fluency in their language.

"Turkish language and Mongolian are very similar, and probably we share the same ancestry. Actually, many of our soldiers are of Turkish origin. They are excited to meet their ancestral brothers but not as an enemy. There's no reason to fight each other. Brothers to brothers."

Enkh repeatedly used the word "brother" and showed the gifts he brought.

"This is just a small token to show our warm friendship as brothers," he continued. "Our lord Genghis Khan has a great plan to open a trade route between the east and the west. When that moment comes, we can help each other build up riches together. That will be the great future investment for both of us."

Yuri, budging his fat body, repositioning his buttocks in the chair to make it more comfortable, could not hide his excitement—not by mutual investment in the future but by the gifts the Mongols had brought: enormous amounts of gold, silver and fine horses.

He said to his nephew Daniel, who was sitting next to him, "We don't need to bleed. Just let them go. I think they are no threat to us. What do you think?"

Daniel, without thinking, nodded to his uncle. Both of them seemed to be astounded and exhilarated deeply due to the enormous amounts of gold and silver that they had never experienced before. The agreement was made.

The Kipchaks began to retreat through the same route on which they came, on the same day. That night, the Kipchaks celebrated for what they had achieved and had a feast. The Mongols secretly followed them all through the night without getting noticed, and at dawn they commenced their surprise attack.

The Kipchaks were completely destroyed. Most of them were killed, and the rest of the survivors ran away in every direction. Yuri and Daniel, who were still drunk after the previous night's feast, were also killed, and the treasure chests as well as the gray horses were all retrieved.

The Mongols turned their direction to the west and easily destroyed the remaining three tribes: Alans, Lezghians and Circassians.

CHAPTER 5

The Venetians

From that moment on, the road was opened to the Mongols. Nothing could stop them. Jebe and Subedei were well aware of their mission. Their expedition started with pursuing Sultan Muhammad II, and that mission had already been fulfilled. Now they were on a new mission: reconnoitering the European lands for a future conquest.

Jebe and Subedei arrived at the coast of the Black Sea. They marched along the coastline, looking at the dark blue water, and finally arrived at the northern area of the Sea of Azov. From there, they divided their troops into two groups to cover a wider area. Jebe moved along the Don River, and Subedei went in a southwestern direction, following the coastline of the Sea of Azov. Of course, communication between the two groups was well conducted by sending and receiving the arrow messengers every day.

About a day after their individual expeditions, Subedei encamped in an open area some distance from the Sea of Azov. In the middle of the day, Subedei got a report from the captain of the sentry unit.

CHAPTER 5

"A group of three people is asking for an audience, my commander. They say they are representing the city of Venice."

"People from Venice! Where are they now?"

"They are in the guest tent, waiting for an audience. We have already frisked them. They are clean. Let me have your order for what should I do with them, my commander."

In the war camp, the supreme commander's security measure was heavy. Nobody was allowed to keep their weapon in the commander's tent other than commander himself.

"I will see them in my main tent. I need a recording officer."

Their meeting was arranged almost immediately.

Subedei's round-shaped main tent was built with grayish felt and was large enough to accommodate about 20 to 30 people. Inside, at the center of it, was a large-size, round-shaped bronze furnace, about 4 feet in diameter. It had a bulky shaped body with three short legs and, inside, a stack of dried horse droppings was burning. Just above the furnace, at the vault of the tent, was an opening to the outside, which seemed to be mainly for egress of the smoke for ventilation. The commander's seat was in the northernmost part of the tent. To the left and right, wooden chairs and benches lined up alongside the wall toward the southernmost flap door. At the outside of the tent, just in front of the entrance, two guard solders were on duty with spears and scimitars on their waists.

Subedei was using this tent mostly for official meetings and sometimes for guests' receptions. He was sitting on the northernmost chair flanked by two captains on each side whose main functions were reconnaissance, intelligence, espionage, infiltration and pacification. Next to them, to the east side, two recording officers were sitting next to each other. Their job was to take rapid notes of every conversation shared by all the attendants in Uighur character. Later, after the meeting, they compared notes and generated the perfect one.

"Greetings! My name is Giovanni, and I am representing this group and my city of Venice."

Anybody who spoke was supposed to stand up and speak loudly so that everybody in the tent could hear. For this meeting, two interpreters were on duty to convey the accurate meaning of the words. First, Venetian—a dialect form of Italian—was changed into Persian, and then Persian was changed into Mongolian.

Giovanni continued. "We are here to give our warm greetings and to find a way to establish a cooperative, friendly relationship between the great Mongol Empire and the city of Venice. This is for our mutual benefit and prosperity."

At this point, Subedei returned a welcome remark. "We welcome you in the name of our supreme leader Genghis Khan and the great Mongol Empire. The Mongol Empire is always ready to welcome friends who want to share mutual friendship. I am absolutely sure that there are ways we can help each other."

"We are merchants," Giovanni added. "We make our living by selling, buying and trading goods and merchandise. Sometimes we do fine and are well off, and sometimes not. We import goods from many different parts of the world and export to many other parts of the world. Our trade routes are mainly maritime ones, but we also caravan on the land."

CHAPTER 5

At that time, Venice was the final destination of the silk road, and they were accumulating enormous riches through selling silk, cotton and spices to all of Europe.

Subedei remarked, "The ideology of the Mongol Empire is to open the communication and trading route from the land of sunrise to the land of sunset, and so unite the whole world in one unit in the expectation of spurring the speed of development of the human world. Based on our necessities and pursuance, I see that the agreement of cooperation and mutual support is already halfway done." After these words, Subedei let out a big guffaw.

"Our city of Venice with 150,000 people is a commune," Giovanni continued, "so we don't have a king. We simply elect a representative when we need one. Our citizens are from many different parts of the world."

Giovanni waited a moment to make sure that the two interpreters were following and doing their job right.

"We thought we were on the way to building a trad-ing empire," he continued, "but things didn't go the way we wanted. Our trading rival—the Genoese—frequently invade our territory and attack our trading posts. We are trying to find a solution for this trouble because this is a matter of Venetian survival."

Zorik, a commander of 1,000 men in the Mongol army and a spy chief of Jebe and Subedei's expedition troops, was sitting next to Subedei and asked the Venetian a question.

"So, how can we help each other?"

"We don't have enough military power," Giovanni responded. "We simply have a public safety unit or a civil militia to keep the peace among our citizens and in the city.

To keep and protect our properties and our future, we need friends to cooperate and support each other."

After these words, there was a momentary silence in the tent.

Subedei said, "I appreciate your honesty, straightforwardness and open-mindedness. But can you tell us more in detail about anything you want or a specific need you are facing?"

"At the southern end of the Crimean Peninsula, there's a trading post named Soldaia [Sudak]. We consider that post to be very important in every aspect, and now the Genoese are holding it. We absolutely cannot allow our rival to control it alone. We will lose a big chunk of our trading route and our influence in the trading world."

After these words, Giovanni sat down on his chair.

Some moments later, Subedei asked, "If we take Soldaia from the Genoese and give it to you, what can we expect in return?"

At this question, Giovanni stood up again and made two deep bows. "Whatever you say—as long as it is within our reach."

A moment later, Subedei eyed him carefully and said, "What we need is a detailed, accurate map covering all of Europe, a list of kingdoms, the size of their troops and possibly their population. Do you think you can do that for us?"

Giovanni made another deep bow. "That won't be an easy job; however, it is not impossible for people like us, who are travelling around all the time. If you can give us three months, we will bring you an answer."

Subedei nodded slowly in agreement.

CHAPTER 5

After three months, the Venetians came back with the information they had promised. They brought a fine, detailed map of Europe and a list of all the kings of each nation, their relatives, their lineage, the current and maximum number of troops and even their personalities and hobbies.

Subedei was satisfied. An extensive spy network was built with the Venetians as the leader. This time, Giovanni brought seven more Venetian officials who represented different areas of the city of Venice. The official agreement as well as the treaty was signed between the Mongol Empire and the city of Venice, and they became allies. The agreement was that the Mongol Empire would help the city of Venice to secure their trading posts and to build up their trading empire by suppressing or destroying their rivals. In return, the Venetians would help create and maintain Subedei's extensive spy network in Europe. The Venetians stayed in the Mongol camp for five days. During this time, they built up frameworks, outlined the spy system and detailed every important corner.

When all was done satisfactorily, Subedei dispatched 2,000 cavalries under the commandership of Zorik. Subedei thought that was enough. Zorik marched with some of the Venetians as the guides and attacked Soldaia and easily subdued them. All disobedient residents were executed, and the Venetians claimed their post. The Mongols carried enormous war booty from there and returned.

CHAPTER 6

The battle of the Kalka River

Koten, chief of the Kipchaks, tried to persuade his son-in-law Mstislav Daring (Bold), the prince of Galicia. "The Mongols are conquerors! Not just a large group of raiders or plunderers. They will take over your land and enslave you and your people very soon if you do nothing now."

At the time, Russia was divided into eight principalities. Each principality was ruled by its own duke, and they were independent of each other. The eight principalities were Kiev, Chernigov, Galicia, Smolensk, Rostov, Suzdal, Novgorod and Vladimir.

"I lost my son and brother along with my 35,000 men," Koten continued. "They are killers, warriors and a different breed!"

The Kipchaks were nomadic people like the Mongols. They didn't self-produce all the necessities from their own, so they had to attack and plunder neighboring, sedentary people to satisfy the minimum. The Kipchaks were a headache to the princes of neighboring Russian principalities.

CHAPTER 6

Prince Mstislav Daring's marriage to one of Koten's daughters was understood as a largely political motivation to reduce or minimize the headache by building up a blood relationship between the two groups. Many of the Russian princes were relieved when they got the news that the Mongols had destroyed the Kipchaks rather than be alarmed or worried; however, when they got the second news that the Mongols crossed the Dnieper River and approached the further western Dniester River, invading deep into the Russian territory, they began to think differently.

Mstislav Daring asked Koten, "How many men do you think we need to meet the Mongols? How many are there?"

"I think there are about 25,000," Koten carefully answered. "But I have to remind you that they destroyed our coalition army with Alans, Lezghians and Circassians—a total of 50,000. You might need much more than that."

Mstislav Daring gave this a little thought and murmured to himself, "If that is the truth, it's beyond my limit. I have to contact the other princes to join us."

Mstislav Daring, the duke of Galicia, was the first one who took action. He was an undaunting and audacious man, which is how he picked up the nickname "Daring." He had some notable battlefield experience too.

He immediately contacted his son-in-law, Prince Daniel of Volynia (the same name as Koten's son Daniel but a different person), to assemble the army and convince the other princes throughout Russia. Soon, he got answers from the princes of Kiev and Chernigov, Prince Oleg of Kursk and finally Grand Duke Yuri of Suzdal. Grand Duke Yuri sent his nephew, Prince Vasilko of Rostov, as the commander of a contingent.

Their total number reached almost 80,000, which Mstislav Daring speculated and desired.

Their temporary gathering place was the island of Khortytsia.

On the other hand, Subedei was becoming aware of the Russians' movement through the reports from scouting units covering every direction. He immediately dispatched an arrow messenger to Jebe, who was stationed west of the Don River, to regroup. Their two army groups' rendezvous locations were west of the bank of the Kalka River. It was a small river, narrow and shallow for most of the area, and the soldiers could cross the river on horseback.

Subedei's message instructed them to gather in the shortest possible time to avoid a possible multipronged Russian attack—especially for Subedei's group. The distance from the Dnieper River, which was Subedei's current location, to the appointed Kalka River was about 150 miles. Subedei needed time. Until the two army groups rejoined, Subedei alone could be vulnerable and dangerous. He summoned Hamabe, who was the commander of 1,000 men and in charge of the rearguard unit.

Standing face to face, Subedei looked into Hamabe's eyes and opened his mouth heavily. "How long have we been together? So many years! Today, I must give you the most serious and dangerous assignment, which I have never asked you before. Hold the enemy line as long as possible, so that we can earn the time to rejoin our other group. Your role is crucial in this battle."

Hamabe bowed deeply. "Commander, they will cross the line upon my dead body! All of my 1,000 warriors will share my destiny. I am already envisioning my commander's tremendous victory. Leave that to me."

The first runner of the Russian army was Mstislav Daring's Galicians and Volynians. They arrived at the island of Khortytsia in the Dnieper River by 1,000 galleys from the north. They had been waiting for some time for the other army groups' arrival, but there was no centralized leadership system among them. All the principalities were independent of each other, and rivalry was the main mentality among them. It was unfamiliar to them to get together and erect a centralized commandership.

They had created a war council though, in the city of Kiev, some time ago. About 20 princes attended but nonetheless ended up with no agreement. Fierce arguments between the two princes erupted and remained through the end of the war. Mstislav Romanovich III, the prince of Kiev, insisted that he should hold the supreme commandership of the entire Russian army because Kiev was the capital city of Russia; however, Mstislav Daring had a big say too. He was the most war-experienced prince among the others, so it was practical that he should be the one.

Mstislav Daring dispatched 10,000 of his soldiers across the Dnieper River, targeting the Mongol rear guards at the opposite bank. Until that time, Mstislav Daring didn't know that Subedei's main body of the troops had already slipped out. They tried to cross the river by boats, intending on a landing operation. The Mongol soldiers poured fire arrows to the galleys, and soon many of them caught fire and burned.

THE BATTLE OF THE KALKA RIVER

The deathly accurate shots from the Mongol side killed the Russians even before their landing. The Russians retreated and reinforced their ships by covering the hull with thick mud. Hamabe and his 1,000 Mongol warriors successfully held the tidal wave of the 10,000 Russian attackers for two days. That was enough time for Subedei to rush 150 miles to join Jebe; however, Hamabe and his 1,000 men had perished to the last man.

A lizard in ultimate danger cuts off its own tail to save its
  body.
However, it works only when the cut-off tail keeps wiggling.

Jebe and Subedei looked around the Kalka River, and the terrain was already familiar to Subedei. Subedei had trodden this terrain while previously on the way to the west. They discussed the battle plan and tactics, and Subedei expressed his opinion.

"In this battle, I think smoke-screen tactics could work. They are lacking centralized leadership. Each of their groups moves individually. They will join in the battle just as they arrive one by one without any preplanned order. We have to make them confused."

However, they both agreed that they were in Russia not for conquest but mainly for reconnoitering. Their number was too small for that job in such a vast land. They decided to dispatch a team of envoys to tap into any alternative possibilities.

The prince of Kiev, Mstislav III, faced six Mongol envoys in front of his war tent.

CHAPTER 6

Sitting on a portable chair flanked by his generals, he said, "Let them talk!"

One of the Mongol envoys stepped out of his team and said, "We are on our way back to the east, our homeland. We do not have any war plan with Russia. If you allow us to pass through with your God-given generosity and oceanic understanding, you will be praised and rewarded by our lord Genghis Khan and by God himself."

After hearing these words, one of the Russian officers, who was standing next to Mstislav III, bent down and whispered, "I have been told that they gave the exact same words to the Kipchaks. It's a ruse! We'd better not fall for that."

Mstislav III nodded slightly and gestured with his fingers to take them away.

All six envoys were taken away and beheaded; however, two Muslims, who accompanied the Mongol envoys as interpreters, were set free and returned. After this, the Mongols sent another set of envoys with a different approach.

One of the envoys said in front of Mstislav III and the other princes, "We are at war with the Kipchaks. They attacked us first without any reason. We request that the Russians remain neutral in this war. Our advice is not to make an enemy out of us. That will surely bring you calamity on your head and on your people."

Both requests and warnings were ignored; however, at this time, the envoys were returned unharmed. Basically, the Russians were in the light mood that they would never lose the incoming war with the Mongols. Their combined force of Russians and Kipchaks was 80,000 strong, whereas the Mongols had only 25,000. Both of their Russian cavalrymen of 20,000 and their infantrymen of 60,000 were well armored and equipped with a variety of weapons, lances, spears, battle axes, maces, long swords and bows.

The war was inevitable. The Mongols never forgave the groups who killed envoys. All the Mongol's high-ranking warriors and officers gathered under Jebe and Subedei's war council and mapped out a detailed battle plan.

The first group to appear at the scene was the combined army of Mstislav Daring and the Kipchaks, which totaled 30,000. They dashed toward the Mongol vanguard in battle array, who was standing in front of a lowly hill.

Suddenly, the Mongols turned around and began to run away. When the dashing Russian and Kipchak cavalries passed over the hill, flames of naphtha shot into the sky and thick, dark smoke covered the area like a veil. The Mongol vanguard disappeared into this veil. The dark smoke continued to cover the area and the whole world. The Russians and the Kipchaks fell into chaos in the hell of darkness. The disorganized Russian troops tried to turn around and retreat, but they simply ended up putting themselves into more chaos, colliding with their own surging troops.

Several minutes of this uncontrollable chaos were enough time for the Mongol archery unit. At the same time, the Mongols' five army groups began to move forward—especially the two groups, right and left wings—and rapidly encircle the Russians and the Kipchaks. After half-circling the enemies, they showered a hail of arrows onto their heads, destroying half of the combined army. Simultaneously, three groups of the Mongol heavy cavalries pushed and destroyed the rest of them. The rest of the combined army of Russians and Kipchaks began to retreat. They galloped back to the way from which they came.

At this time, two other groups of Russian armies from Kursk and Volynia arrived at the battle scene and dashed to the approaching group of cavalries. They didn't know what had already happened or who was approaching them. They simply thought that the approaching group was their enemy. The thick smoke from the Mongol fire pots drifted across the battlefront, making the area smoky and hard to navigate. They could see only dim images of approaching men and horses. The surrounded Russian army was systematically slaughtered by a hail of arrows and the Mongol's heavy cavalries' spears and battle axes.

Mstislav Daring, who successfully managed to escape under the sacrifice of hundreds of his men, rushed to the rear to join the next approaching group of Russians: Mstislav III's army of 20,000. After that, another group of 10,000 from Chernigov was following them; however, these groups fell into the same fate, were defeated and began to retreat.

By the end of the day, 40,000 Russian dead bodies were strewn across the battlefield, and among them were six princes and almost 70 nobles. The Mongol deathly pursuit continued. The Mongols, without exception, chased the enemy to the end of the world and killed them to the last man.

Mstislav III, with the remnant of his 10,000 soldiers, fled to the area close to the riverbank of the Dnieper. He rapidly built up a fortified camp on the hillside and resisted. They stacked the war wagons, rocks and cut timbers around their camps. The Russians held the position for three days; however, realizing that resistance could not be continued, they began to seek negotiations with the Mongols. They knew that they were surrounded and were running out of water. They built up the fortified camp on top of the hill for easy defense, but it was too far from the water source. They planned to surrender, but they wanted a guarantee of safe passage.

Mstislav III and the Russian commanders met a Mongol envoy, who was about 30 years old, tall and slender.

The envoy said, "My name is Ploskinya. My father is Russian, and my mother is Kipchak. I am with the Mongols with all my people, and it has been quite some time now."

Ploskinya was one of the leaders of the Brodniki groups that had escaped from the Russian serfdom, moved to the southwestern boundary of the Russian border and adapted themselves into a seminomadic lifestyle. They were free men. They fought alongside the Mongols.

At this time in Europe, including Russia, 80 to 90 percent of the population were serfs and unfree laborers, who could be bought, sold or traded with the land. They belonged to landlords and, without the owner's permission, almost nothing was possible—even getting married. They were slaves.

"The Mongol leadership wants to give you an offer guaranteeing safe passage under one condition. You have to leave your banner, your weapons and all of your belongings behind. Only emergency food to your hometown and a canteen for water will be allowed."

At these words, deep silence fell upon the Russian leaders.

Mstislav III asked gravely, "What about horses?"

"Horses will be allowed but only in limited numbers. That will be 200."

"Um …," Mstislav III sighed.

Under his command, there were still 10,000 soldiers and 2,000 horses. Some of the captains and lieutenants insisted on a fight to the end.

After mulling over the offer and the possibilities, Mstislav III asked Ploskinya, "How can I trust their words?"

Ploskinya answered in a convincing tone, "The Mongols are very sincere in their promise. They won't break their own words. I can swear it on the cross. I am a Christian."

Mstislav III squinted his eyes and regarded Ploskinya for a moment. He ordered his soldiers to bring the cross. One Russian soldier was holding the cross in his two hands, and Ploskinya touched his right palm on the cross.

"I, Ploskinya, swear on the cross that I have said only the truth. Otherwise, my body and soul shall be burned in hell forever."

Taking this, Mstislav III ordered his men to disarm and leave the fortified camp; however, when the last Russian man left the camp, from every direction, the fully armed Mongol horse soldiers sprung up. They began to slaughter the unarmed Russian soldiers systematically. It didn't take long to lay down all 10,000 men. The only survivors were the ones who were allowed to ride on the horses, but even they were targets of the Mongol chasing units. They fell from their horses one by one after being hit by deathly accurate Mongol arrows.

The Mongols didn't forget to capture alive Mstislav III and his two sons-in-law—Prince Alexander Glebovich and Prince Andrei—before the massacre started.

THE BATTLE OF THE KALKA RIVER

You can find
What is underneath the water,
Ten feet deep.
You can never find
What is inside of the human mind,
A half inch deep.
You can find
A beauty,
Through your eyes.
You can never find
The truth,
Through your ears.

It was evening, and the sky was covered by man-eating vultures and crows lured by human blood. The western sky was changing into a rich, deep crimson. The air was cool, even in late May.

Prince Mstislav III and his two sons-in-law were taken to the short trial and informed that punishment for murdering the envoys was death with no exception. They were also notified that, in the case of the prince or nobleman, death would be done by asphyxiation.

They tied their hands and feet and dragged them to the feasting place, celebrating the complete victory. They laid them on the ground, face up in all different directions. On top of them, they placed a rectangular-shaped, thick, wooden board made of evenly cut timbers tied together. On it, thick carpets were spread for comfort and, on top of that, a dining table was set up. Due to the heavy weight of the board and dinners, the victims would have labored breathing and would meet a slow death. Since the victims' faces were outside of the board and up, anybody could watch the dying process moment by moment and confirm their final death.

In this Kalka River battle, almost 65,000 Russian soldiers were killed, including 12 princes. Only one out of 10 men survived and returned to their homes.

After this battle, the Mongols were on their home. They went across the Don and Volga Rivers. After crossing the Volga River, they met with the Bulgars. The Bulgars surrendered after losing the battle. The Mongols also faced the Qangli Turks around the Ural Mountains, who were easily defeated. After that, there was nobody in front of them.

They carried an enormous war booty along with 1,000 captives and slaves, composed of Russians, Kipchaks, Bulgars, Alans and Armenians. They were also carrying 1,000 Russian gray-colored horses, which the Mongols favored as good luck. The horses were a gift for Genghis Khan. Their caravan lined up almost 20 miles, including 100,000 slow-moving sheep, which were the main food for the army.

However, the most valuable achievement in this expedition was the spy network, covering all over Europe, which would be crucial for future conquests. They ended up with a fantastic cavalry raid that covered almost 6,000 miles, taking three years. It was the longest cavalry march that was unparalleled before and afterward.

CHAPTER 7

Death of Juchi

It was a time of twilight after the sunset. Inside Juchi's yurt, a couple of Baghdad lamps were burning, emanating dim light and reflecting images of people and furniture. Around his bed, eight or nine people were standing or kneeling, their grim faces imbued with appalling emotion.

In his death bed, Juchi opened his mouth heavily but clearly remarked, "All through my life, I have suffered from illegitimacy. It haunted me and followed me like a silhouette full of demons. I feel sorry to leave this unfortunate legacy to my children."

Juchi paused for a while, controlling his breath. He realized that the last moment had come.

Holding his second son Batu's hand, Juchi let out these final words: "Know who you are. Then …"

Batu, still holding his father's hand, shouted, "Know who you are … yes … but what is next? Let me hear your next line!"

There was no answer.

Inside the yurt, for a moment, deep silence flowed. Suddenly, a high-pitched women's wailing burst out all at once and filled the yurt. All the male attendants knelt on the ground and lowered their heads.

The messengers of death,
They are always outside the door, waiting.
You are afraid,
Because you do not know when they will come in.
You are sad,
Because they are coming in without knocking.

Batu knew his father's life story. Juchi was the first-born son of the Great One, Genghis Khan, which had been acknowledged officially by Genghis Khan himself—however, not by everyone, especially his brothers.

In the past, when Temujin (Genghis Khan) married Borte, the newlywed bride was abducted by the enemy Merkid, and retained for months. When Temujin retrieved her, she was already pregnant. Juchi's real father was a mystery—Temujin or Merkid— even to his mother Borte.

In the past, just before the beginning of the war with the Khwarazm Empire, when Genghis Khan summoned his four sons to decide the official successor of the Mongol Empire, the issue of Juchi's legitimacy was brought up. All the royal family members, senior officials and generals of the empire gathered in one room, and they were witnesses.

"Who should be the next khagan?" Genghis asked Juchi. "You are my first son. You are entitled to speak first. Tell me what you have on your mind."

As Juchi stood up, the eyes of royal family members, noyans, senior officials and generals—about 200 people in total—fell upon him. Just as he opened his mouth and tried to say something, loud shouting came from someone on the other side, loaded with strong disagreement and even hostility.

"He was asked to be the first speaker. Does that mean he will be the successor? No. *Never!* If he becomes the khagan, how can we bow to him and obey the Merkid bastard?"

After this statement, there was a sudden, deep silence, and a feeling of tension filled the air. The speaker was Genghis Khan's second son Chagatai. From an early age, he and Juchi never got along. Why was that? Probably because of mixed emotions of self-protection and jealousy.

The eagle's chick pushes down
Other unhatched eggs from the nest.
The newly born praying mantises
Eating up each other to grow up.

Juchi had achieved many praiseworthy accomplishments following his father, but Chagatai had not.

Upon Chagatai's remark, Borte—Genghis Khan's chief wife, who was sitting next to Genghis—left the room. Two of her maids followed her hurriedly. There was quite a stir in the meeting hall.

Juchi slowly walked up to Chagatai and stared at him, angrily saying, "You rat! How can you *say* that? I have never been discriminated against—even by my father! What can you do better than I can? Are you a better archer or a better wrestler than I am? You are not a match for me!"

The two brothers began to fight by grabbing each other's collars. As they were pushing and pulling, intolerant

CHAPTER 7

Bogorchu and Mukali, who were there on a brief visit from China for the meeting, tried to stop them. Bogorchu and Mukali held Juchi's and Chagatai's arms, respectively, and pulled them apart. Genghis watched the fight without saying anything. The brothers continued to swear at each other, even though they were apart. They were similar in age: At the time, Juchi was 33, and Chagatai was 31. After an awkward moment, Koko Chos, who was Chagatai's personal tutor, got up from his seat and opened his mouth.

In earlier times, when Genghis had assigned Koko Chos to be the personal tutor, he told him, "Chagatai is a very delicate child and pays too much attention to small things. Usually that kind of person fails to see the whole picture of life. One needs two eyes: one for the small things and the other for larger things. Stay with him day and night, and help him develop an eye for the larger things."

Looking at Chagatai, Koko Chos began.

"Chagatai, I always said that your father wanted you to have an eye for the larger world. This means that your father has high expectations of you. This is an occasion for deciding the next generation's leader of the great Mongol Empire—not just for the heir of a family. That's why we are all invited. Your father already confirmed his first son Juchi's legitimacy at the time he was born. In light of that, how can you still talk about it? If you think you are the right person to be the next generation's leader, and all the others in this room agree with you, you will be the one."

Chagatai got on his feet and said, "First of all, I want to give my sincere apologies to Father Khan and to everyone in this room. Moments ago, Juchi said that he could defeat me in every aspect, but I do not accept that. He and I have never had such competition before. I think the best one to be the next leader is Ogodei. He is honest. If he becomes the khan in the future, I promise I will do my best to support him."

At Chagatai's remark, Genghis said to Juchi. "What do you think? Speak up."

Juchi stood up and, with a grim look, said, "I have no objection to Ogodei's succession. I also promise to support him when he becomes khagan."

After his short remark, Juchi sat down right away.

"What do think?" Genghis said to Ogodei, who had been recommended as the successor by his two elder brothers. "Let me know your opinion."

He hesitated for a second and then stood up. "If Father Khan asks me to say something, what else can I say but that I will do my best? I think that whoever becomes the next khagan should sacrifice himself for this nation, which Father Khan has founded, with the plan of eternity and the glory of the Mongols."

Genghis was satisfied with that answer. This time, Tolui was asked to say his words.

"I also agree that my third elder brother Ogodei should become the successor. If he becomes the khagan, I will do long marches and short battles. At the same time, I promise I will be a truthful guardian of my father's decision and my brothers' promises."

CHAPTER 7

After him, Genghis Khan looked over the whole assembly of the attendants from his seat and said in a solemn tone, "You have to keep what you have said. Ogodei is right. Anyone who becomes khagan should sacrifice himself for the eternity of the nation and the glory of the Mongols. In the future, the Mongol Nation might not be able to be ruled by one leader. You and your descendants will have your own land and people to be ruled. This is my will and the will of heaven."

Genghis Khan decided that Ogodei would be his successor.

After the war with the Khwarazm Empire, Juchi did not go back to the Mongol mainland. He headed for the great plain of Kipchak, the appanage (promised land) from his father, with his entire ordu (or ulus, the houses for all the descendants, people, soldiers and properties). He was getting sick and tired of disharmony with his brothers. He really liked the great plain of Kipchak. It was close to the Volga River.

An urgent messenger had been dispatched immediately to inform Genghis Khan of Juchi's death. Genghis had been stationed at the location close to the Gobi Desert and at war with the Shisha Kingdom. Meanwhile, all the official affairs and funeral proceedings were halted until further instructions came from Genghis Khan.

Juchi's body had been embalmed to prevent it from decomposing. He was 41 years old.

Upon receiving the news of Juchi's death, Genghis fell into an intense grief. For three days, he stayed in his war tent. He did not want to show this image of great sadness to his soldiers. Before this, while Genghis was crossing the Gobi

Desert, at the middle point to the battlefield of the Shisha Kingdom, he fell from his horse and was badly injured. His barely recoverable bodily injury and his emotional hardship pushed him to the edge and made it hard to rebound. Genghis sent his younger brother Ochigin Noyan to Juchi's ordu in Kipchak.

One early, summer morning on the eastern horizon, a tiny spot emerged. As time passed, the spot grew and finally formed an image of a man and a horse. It was an urgent messenger from the Genghis war camp near the Gobi Desert to Juchi's ordu in the Volga River basin.

The man on the horse was wearing regular Mongol soldier's armor as well as an almond-shaped helmet. On the back of his right-hand side, a thin, long, wooden post with a rectangular-shaped banner was affixed. This was the typical shape of the Mongol arrow messenger. Nobody could stop an arrow messenger until they arrived at their final destination. Sometimes they carried a small tin bell, which was affixed on the horse's head or neck, especially when they passed through crowded areas. This messenger was carrying Genghis Khan's personal letter to Batu.

The letter was written in the newly created Mongolian script. The letter said that Ochigin Noyan, Genghis Khan's younger brother, was on the way, and he would officially represent Genghis Khan and possess all the power in exactly the same way as Genghis Khan.

Upon receiving this letter, Batu sent his sons, brothers, emirs and high-ranking officials in the ordu to meet Ochigin Noyan and then set out himself.

CHAPTER 7

The following day, after Ochigin Noyan's arrival, Juchi's funeral ceremony commenced. Three days were devoted to mourn Juchi's death. Juchi's body was laid inside a coffin made of fragrant wood from a large log, which had been split in half. The inner side was hollowed out in the form of a human body. When the two pieces were put together, it created a space that could accommodate a human body comfortably.

Juchi was wearing a helmet, armor with a golden belt, and a pair of traditional Mongolian gutuuls (boots). After they covered his body with the other half of the log, the coffin was tied firmly with four golden bands and carried to the burial place on the enormously huge Kipchak plain. They dug a grave about 15 feet under the ground and created a rectangular-shaped chamber with a tiled floor and plastered walls and a ceiling. The grave was large enough for his coffin and for his beloved stallion Tus, with his saddle and rein, ready to ride. They also put in his scimitar, bows and arrows, and a golden bowl for water as well as all of his other luxurious personal belongings.

They placed a thick, stone cover over the chamber opening and covered it with earth, and let out 5,000 horses to freely gallop around the gravesite for three days. The horses leveled the gravesite, making it impossible to trace the exact location of the burial. Then they placed guards, usually from one family, to prevent strangers from approaching the area.

Juchi Khan,
The great hunter.
The conqueror of the Northern Land,
The gate to Siberia.

DEATH OF JUCHI

The conqueror of 16 nations and tribes,
The greatest meritorious prince of the Khwarazm campaign.
Now, his soul soars on wings into the heaven.
Far beyond the horizon.
His soul shall freely roam over the steppe,
Circling around in the sky,
Watching over his children and his children's children,
Over the great plain of Kipchak.
Until the end of time.

CHAPTER 8

The birth of Batu Khan

After three days of mourning, Ochigin Noyan presided over the ceremony for the enthronement of the new khan (prince) of Juchi's ordu, the successor of Juchi. Earlier, Genghis Khan divided Juchi's appanage into two pieces—one from Lake Balkhash to the north of the Aral Sea and another from the northern shore of the Caspian Sea to all the western lands to the Great Ocean (Atlantic Ocean). The eastern side was called the White Ordu and was entrusted to Juchi's first son Orda. The western side was called the Golden (the color of Batu's royal tent) Ordu, which was for his second son Batu; however, the question of who would be the official successor of Juchi, representing the whole ordu, had not been answered until Juchi's death.

One day before the enthronement ceremony, Ochigin Noyan summoned all the sons and family members of the deceased Juchi, and the generals and other high-ranking officials of the ordu, in one place and announced Genghis Khan's decree.

"Juchi's ordu will be succeeded by his second son Batu. All the princes in Juchi's ordu should obey and respect this decision. Anyone who opposes this shall be dealt with by Genghis Khan himself."

The princes and the other attendants at the meeting knelt down while the decree was read. Juchi's first son Orda accepted this declaration without any resistance and happily volunteered to enthrone Batu on behalf of his father Juchi.

No one knew why the Great One, Genghis Khan, chose Batu as the successor while the first son Orda was around and well. Nothing had been explained by the Great One, who was the decision maker.

One thing was clear: The Mongol troops and the society were ruled by the notion that a man should be judged by the question "What can he do?" instead of "Who is he?" One example was Toquchar, Genghis Khan's son-in-law, who failed to show nothing more than just a plain soldier, and he remained a plain soldier all through his life.

Juchi left behind 14 sons and two daughters from his four major wives. While he was alive and active, he was assigned to conquer all the northern and western lands, including Russia and beyond. However, he didn't or couldn't do it, and one of the plausible excuses was his illness.

Why had Batu been chosen as the successor to his father Juchi among all the other sons? Another plausible answer could be traced from the notion that Batu was the one who had been with his grandfather Genghis Khan the most among all the other grandchildren. Genghis had heard many traditional Mongolian stories from his mother Ouluun when he was very young. He told the same stories to his children and, after that, to his children's children. Among all others, he never missed two stories.

The first story was the five-arrow story, which said, "Anybody can break one arrow; however, when five of them are bundled together, nobody can do it."

The second story was about the snake with two heads.

"There was a snake with two heads. It was born that way. One body with two heads was a great convenience. With four eyes, it was easy to find prey and, while one head was sleeping, the other could be on guard. One day, an eagle found this snake. In the blink of an eye, the eagle attacked the snake. The snake tried to find a place to hide. Under a big rock, there was a hole, but the hole was so small, and only one head could fit inside. When the eagle picked up one head, the other head came out together. The snake with two heads was eaten by the eagle."

When his grandchildren grew older and they understood more, he talked about leadership and military tactics.

"To become a conqueror, you should conquer yourself first."

"To defeat the enemy, you should take more risks than the enemy."

"Never leave your enemy behind when you are advancing. Surrender does not mean simply giving up resistance. They should be part of your body and can be maneuvered like your own hands and feet. That is the safe way for the conqueror."

So, when the Mongol army was advancing, two things could happen. Their numbers could increase or they could leave the totally massacred enemy population behind. The surrendered group was always in front of the advancing line, so they had to show their truth, fight to the death for the Mongol army or be killed by the Mongol army. The chances for survival were much higher when they truly surrendered.

Juchi's chief wife was Bektutmish. She was a younger sister to Ibaqa, who was one of Genghis Khan's many wives. At the same time, Bektutmish was the elder sister to Sorqoqtani, who was the chief wife of Tolui. When Genghis Khan conquered the Kerait tribe, he took the policy to amalgamate two groups: the Mongols and the Keraits. Ibaqa, Bektutmish and Sorqoqtani were three sisters from the same womb—the daughters of Jagambu, who was the brother to Wang-Khan, the khan of the Keraits. These three sisters gathered all the time, and so did their children. Juchi's and Tolui's children always got along very well. They were double cousins on both the father's and the mother's side.

From the early ages, Batu showed great possibility from every aspect. He was extremely smart, shrewd and quick-sensed in judgments, showing determination and great leadership. His name Batu signified "firm" or "rock," and this quality was much needed for survival in such a feudal society. He had a little bigger than medium stature, which was covered with nicely balanced and well-developed muscles, and stored great endurance and toughness. In other words, he had a sturdy, muscular physique.

Batu had eagle eyes, and his face was covered with numerous tiny, red spots. When someone looked directly into his eyes for a moment, they often felt as if they were falling into a hypnotic trance and would lose control. With a glance of his face, the viewer might catch inspiration of awesomeness and fear; however, on a second look, they would find peace and friendliness. He was strong in his mind and his body.

Most of all, his belief was in Tengrism, the nomadic people's many-thousand-year-old traditional religion, which believed in the eternal blue sky, as did Genghis Khan.

Early in the morning, when the strong sun's rays poured onto the vast Kipchak plain, the ceremony commenced, designating Batu as the new khan of Juchi's ordu. A huge tent, which could accommodate almost 500 people, had been erected. The tent was a shining gold color—the preference of Batu himself. In front of the main tent, a small, almond-shaped canopy with luxurious decorations was built, which covered the royal seat.

As soon as Batu walked in and sat on the throne, the ceremony began. Batu was in a regular Mongol soldier's helmet, armor, boots and belt. Orda, Batu's elder brother, stepped in along with the program director, who was carrying a round cushion on which a golden baton was placed, symbolizing the ruler of the entire ordu. Orda, after picking up the baton with his two hands, stepped toward Batu and gently placed it in Batu's hand.

Simultaneously, Batu got on his feet, gently bowed to his elder brother and remarked, "Big brother, you are touching my heart, and my soul is full of gratitude, especially this being given by you. We shall work together and accomplish the mission for what our father and grandfather have left on us."

"It shall be done," Orda responded, "and it is within your grasp. My heart is full of joy. I will do my best from the side."

THE BIRTH OF BATU KHAN

After this, Ochigin Noyan, on behalf of the Great One, showed up at the scene and bestowed the new title to Batu.

"From now on, Batu shall be referred to as Sein Khan."

Sein Khan meant "Smart Khan." Batu was 22 years old.

Batu was greeted by his subjects one by one in the order of their ranking. A big celebration event and feast followed. Everybody got their own gifts, small or large. The celebration lasted almost three days.

Before the end, an urgent messenger arrived from Genghis Khan's war camp. The message announced Genghis Khan's death. The Great One, who had ever emerged in the human world, had fallen by the fate that no mortal could avoid.

CHAPTER 9

Ogodei, the new khagan

.

After Genghis Khan's death, Tolui was entrusted with the position of regent for about two years. In the early part of 1229—the year of the oxen in Mongol chronicles—they had a grand-scale kuriltai (a general assembly of all the princes, high-ranking officials and generals) that was designed to make decisions about the direction of the empire and finalize all the important national affairs.

The kuriltai was at the Kerulen riverside—the heart of the Mongol mainland. At this kuriltai, the Mongols elected Ogodei as the khagan (the khan of khans). They carried out the intention of the deceased Genghis Khan.

At this meeting, they discussed many things and exchanged information and ideas. Most importantly, they decided the conquest of the world, from the land of sunrise to sunset, which was the most meaningful decision they ever made and which clearly defined the direction of the nation. They also accepted a new administrative system and decided to build a new capital. The meeting lasted almost a whole month, and they made a detailed plan of world conquest.

Ogodei, the newly elected khagan at age 40, declared, "We will complete the conquest of the Chin at northern China and reconquer Persia and its neighboring kingdoms and people. We will also send troops to Korea at the eastern end. After all these, we will go for the west, which is Europe."

Ogodei reapproved Yelu-chuchai as the chief administrator of the empire. He was originally a Khitan who was a descendant of the royal family of the Liao dynasty. When Genghis Khan conquered northern China, Yelu-chuchai was a captive who later entered into the Mongol administration. Genghis Khan was amazed by his extensive knowledge and sense of loyalty. Yelu-chuchai was almost omniscient in the natural and social sciences and had an accurate sense of the past and the future. He was a chief advisor for Genghis in the government and with administrative affairs. When Genghis Khan conquered northern China, north of the Yellow River, some Mongol generals insisted on extermination or genocide of the total population of 50 million.

Yelu-chuchai was the one who stopped the idea by saying, "Among all the properties, humans are the most valuable. The value of the human source surpasses land or material property. This concept goes equally to individuals or nations. Instead of complete annihilation, if they can be saved and governed by a good and an appropriate system, they will be a source of power to produce enormous riches. Eventually, these riches will come to the Mongol Empire."

Genghis Khan agreed, and the lives of 50 million people were saved.

Yelu-chuchai would say, "The world may be conquered on horseback but cannot be ruled on horseback."

Yelu-chuchai established the administrative system, which included offices for bureaucrats and libraries and schools for the Mongol princes and aristocrats. He was 6 feet 8 inches tall and had a long beard that reached down to his waist. For this magnificent beard, Genghis gave him the nickname Urtu Saqal, which meant "long beard," and everybody called him by that name. His voice was sonorous and persuasive. When Genghis Khan hired him, he was 28 years old; at 39 years old, Ogodei Khan rehired him. As a chancellor, he separated the civil and military powers of the empire.

At the kuriltai, they discussed strategies and tactics based on the collected information and facts, and then established a detailed plan. At the meeting, Subedei gave his report.

"For the conquest of western lands, including Russia and Europe, we might need at least 150,000 warriors and 300,000 horses. It will take three to five years to get everything ready; however, before we go to Europe, we have to reconquer the Persian and Transcaucasian areas. We did not leave a garrison there, so it is in anarchy. This area should be in our control for safety, a route for messengers and a supply line for the European expedition army. Again, this area is important when we advance into Russia and Europe."

"Who is the right person for this job of reconquering the Persian and Transcaucasian areas?" Ogodei asked.

Subedei answered, "I recommend Chormaqan because he has both military leadership and administrative skills. Most of all, he was one of my captains in the expedition troops to those areas and to Russia."

Ogodei appointed Chormaqan as a viceroy of the Persian and Transcaucasian areas and gave him 30,000 royal cavalry to reconquer those areas with their neighboring kingdoms and people. He also gave 6,000 horse soldiers to Saletai, one of his fierce generals, to go to Korea. For the Chin Empire, he decided to go himself with his brother Tolui.

Ogodei was a very intelligent man with characteristics of good judgment, firmness, counsel, fairness and generosity. His name meant "ascend to the top." He invented new weapons and redesigned the catapult for more power and a longer range. On the other hand, he was a pleasure seeker and a wine bibber.

Many anecdotes were told of him, even though they happened at later times. Here are some of the stories:

One hot, summer day on a hunting ground, a man brought Ogodei three melons. Having no gold or silver coins with him, Ogodei told his favorite wife Moge Khatun, who was accompanying him, to give him a pearl earring that she was wearing.

Moge immediately protested and said, "This poor man doesn't know the value of these pearls! This is a gift from the governor of Samarqand. Let him present himself tomorrow and reward him with a gold or silver coin … whatever."

Ogodei replied with smile, "Give him only one instead of both earrings. Believe me. It will surely come back. This poor guy cannot wait until tomorrow."

The poor man took the pearl earring to the downtown jewelry store.

The store owner was amazed with its quality and remarked, "Where did you get this? This pearl fits only the king and queen."

The poor man gave his explanation, and the store owner paid him two silver balish (coins).

The following morning, the store owner went to Ogodei with the pearl earring and was rewarded with silver balish 10 times more than he paid to the poor man.

One day, an Arabic-speaking man, who was believed to be an apostate from the Islamic religion, presented himself to the khagan and said, "I met Genghis Khan in my dream and he said, 'Go to my son and tell him to kill as many Muslims as possible because they are evil people.'"

Ogodei pondered awhile and asked, "Did my father talk to you directly or through the interpreter?"

"He told me directly."

Ogodei asked again, "Do you understand the Mongolian language?"

The man answered, "No."

Ogodei stood up abruptly. "Take this man out and cut off his head! He is lying. My father knew only one language: Mongolian."

Ogodei had a group of merchant visitors from India. They were carrying two huge tusks of ivory, almost 200 pounds each, which they were trying to sell to Ogodei.

He asked, "How much do you want for these tusks?"

"Five hundred balish for both of them."

Without hesitation, Ogodei ordered for the merchants to be paid this amount.

The court official in the treasury stepped forward and remarked, "My lord, they are from India, our enemy nation."

"Commercial activity and politics are separate. It can be done unless it's harmful to us. I am going to make the imperial seals out of ivory. Pay them!"

CHAPTER 10

Jal-al-Addin's dream

In an earlier time, in the year of 1221, Jal-al-Addin—the firstborn son of perished Khwarazmian Sultan Ala-Addin Muhammad II—had escaped to India after losing the final battle at the Indus River. He stayed there for three years under the protection of the sultan of India.

After three years, when the world became rather quiet and temporary peace fell upon his father's original domain— Persia and the nearby area—Jal-al-Addin began to have a dream of the resurrection of his father's empire. He was the only general or prince who gave unbelievable defeat to the invincible Mongol army at the battle of Parwan. He defeated 30,000 soldiers in the Mongol army, led by Shigiqutuqu with his 60,000 soldiers, taking advantage of twice outnumbering the opponent. Jal-al-Addin was 21 at that time; then, at 24 years old, he returned to his father's hometown to have his mission and dream fulfilled. He decided to take advantage of the indifference of the Mongols in those areas who had no garrison there.

Jal-al-Addin arrived at Ray (Teheran) and met his younger brother Ghiyas-Addin, who was 19 and had already started to gather people and plan the reconstruction activities about a year earlier. They were born from different wombs and yet were the only living, direct descendants of the Sultan Muhammad II.

When Jebe and Subedei's Mongol army came into this area, they killed all the male descendants regardless of age, and all the females like wives, daughters and concubines were enslaved and sent to the Mongol mainland.

Ghiyas-Addin was a lucky survivor. When he became 18, he came out from his secret hiding place and began his activity. A large number of men and emirs, who had also been hiding, gathered around him. Among them, Barak Hajib and Oghul Malik were outstanding. They had their own army and united under the name of Ghiyas-Addin. They marched to nearby towns and cities and grew up. Finally, they settled down in Ray. Barak Hajib entered Ghiyas-Addin's service and became one of his chief emirs, receiving the title of Qutlugh-Khan after the corroboration of covenants and an oath. Ghiyas-Addin appointed him the commander of Isfahan.

At this time, Jal-al-Addin arrived. He alighted in his younger brother Ghiyas-Addin's camp and visited his tent.

"Do you recognize me?" Jal-al-Addin asked after not seeing his brother since they were very young.

Ghiyas-Addin was shocked but easily recognized him under the light of the beeswax candle.

"Praise Allah! I open my arms and give my warm welcome to my big brother. This sure is God's will that we got together. I am sure that God is on our side."

CHAPTER 10

They shared greetings by touching each other's cheek with their own, one after another for three times, which was a sign of affection between two completely trusted individuals.

Jal-al-Addin said, "We will put our power together and surely accomplish what we want. You will be my right hand."

Together, they conquered the nearby areas, one by one, and then advanced into Fars, Kirman and Azerbaijan. They took Tabriz, the capital city of Azerbaijan, and made an abode there. From that location, they advanced into the territory of Georgia. All the rulers of that region—the sultan of Rum and the maliks of Syria and Armenia—were alarmed at Jal-al-Addin's power and ascendancy, and they rose up to repel him and gathered in one place.

Jal-al-Addin and his army proceeded to just before Mindor. After he and his army encamped there, he and his staff went onto the hill to check out their enemy power. They were shocked when they saw the size of the enemy and called for a meeting.

His vizier (a high official in a Muslim country) Yulduzchi opined, "Since our enemy outnumbers us possibly by 10 times, I think the best choice is to pass through Mindor and withhold the water source to make them thirsty and their horses grow weak. We'd better wait until we see fit to attack. I know this area well."

Unfortunately for his followers, Jal-al-Addin was not a careful listener. He was just a young man with boiling blood. He didn't know the strategy or have a concept of diplomatic warfare. He was annoyed with the vizier's remarks and hurled a pencase toward him.

"What?" he shouted. "They are just a flock of sheep! Does the lion fear the size of the flock of sheep?"

Jal-al-Addin advanced into the battlefield with his army and sent a messenger to the enemy group.

The messenger delivered his message, which said, "If you have anyone who can beat me in a one-to-one fight with whatever weapon he chooses, come out and get me!"

Jal-al-Addin rode into the field at a canter with one long spear in his right hand and a scimitar hanging on his left side belt. When he stopped at the middle part of the ground, a Georgian captain from the other side rode out, also carrying a long spear in his hand, and faced him at the right spot.

For some moments, deep silence filled the space between them, and thousands of eyes fell upon this unusual dual from both sides.

The two men galloped in full speed toward their respective opponent with spears in hand. When the close fight was done, Jal-al-Addin was still perfect and lively; the opponent wasn't after his stomach was opened, and he fell from his horse. Two other fighters, who were brothers of the fallen Georgian captain, galloped and approached him in great speed. They attacked Jal-al-Addin from two different direction with their swords; however, they were not stronger or faster than their brother's killer. They retreated after one of them was seriously wounded on his back.

Then, an enormous man approached Jal-al-Addin and attacked him with a battle axe. By this time, Jal-al-Addin's horse was already exhausted and moved slowly. When the big man's battle axe was just about to cut Jal-al-Addin's head into two pieces, Jal-al-Addin's jumped down from his horse and hit the big man's horse with his spear. The horse, in surprise, suddenly stood up on its hind legs, and the big man fell down. Almost at the same moment, Jal-al-Addin's scimitar cut off his head.

Seeing their sultan Jal-al-Addin, his soldiers were encouraged and spirited. With a single charge, they pushed their opponent 100 miles away.

CHAPTER 11

The death of Jal-al-Addin

Subedei gave a strong message in front of the war council, which was held by Ogodei Khan, telling the serious nature of what was happening.

"Those areas of Persia and Transcaucasia are important when we advance into Russia and Europe for an alternative supply line and a communication route. We need to reconquer and keep those areas in our firm grip."

After Ogodei became khagan, he heard the bad news of Jal-al-Addin's unexpected restoration of a large part of his father's domain.

Subedei continued, "They are not fully organized yet. They are just a pile of gravel without a strong bond among them. The best way to handle them is to give a surprise attack. We should not give them the time to settle up."

Subedei was well aware of the situation there, thanks to his espionage network—even though he couldn't leave the garrison due to the lack of troops, but surely he built up and left the spy network there.

"What type of man is he?" Ogodei asked.

This time, Subedei said, "He is a gallant-style man, a solo player rather than a commander."

Subedei also described and conveyed a pictured image of a battle scene depicting what happened with Jal-al-Addin and his opponents.

Ogodei thought about this and murmured to himself, "He could be a daredevil or a gambler. If he wins, it would be an excellent strategy for psychological warfare for them; however, if he thinks he will always win, he is stupid. Every battle is different with different enemies and different situations. Strategies and tactics should come out from its own uniqueness."

Ogodei made this decree aloud: "Then, we will send Taimas to handle him if he approaches us with the same tactic."

Taimas was a captain of 1,000 men in numerous battlefields. He was the pinnacle of the advancing unit.

Ogodei appointed Chormaqan as the commander in chief of the expedition Mongol army to the Persian and Transcaucasian areas as well as the viceroy of those regions. His job was to reconquer and then stay there and rule those lands and people. He was one of the former members of Keshik (the imperial guard), which meant Genghis Khan's personal bodyguard as a quiver-bearer. He also joined Jebe and Subedei's long march as one of their captains. He had already trodden those areas. Chormaqan was a member of the Sunit tribe. He was a man of good physics and had a strong voice, a thick beard and a mustache. He was a good commander and was believed to be a good governor and ruler. He was 30 years old.

In the middle of 1230, Chormaqan began his speedy march toward the Persian and Transcaucasian areas. He expected it to be an undetected, surprise attack. Thirty thousand imperial cavalrymen were given to him. Benal Noyan, Mular Noyan and generals like Ghataghan, Toghta, Sunitha, Baiju, Tutu, Khuthtu, Aslan, Okota and Asuta accompanied him. His younger brother Jola, also a distinguished warrior, was with him too.

In early fall, Chormaqan crossed the Amu Darya River. He continued marching and soon arrived at Mazandaran and later Ray (Teheran). This was about the time when the news of the Mongol's arrival was delivered to Jal-al-Addin. Jal-al-Addin was staying in Tabriz, his temporary capital, by that time, but soon moved to the Mughan plain to face the Mongol attack. Without delay, Chormaqan advanced to the Mughan plain, leaving Dayir Noyan in Ray as a temporary garrison commander.

The two armies faced off at the enormously wide Mughan plain. Jal-al-Addin was stationed close to the forest and mountain area, just in case he had to retreat. He was leading about 15,000 soldiers, which was not enough to face the Mongol storm. He failed to make allies with any nearby rulers due to his lack of political sense.

Even though he sent out urgent requests for help to Ala-al-Din, the sultan of Rum, and Ashraf, the sultan of Syria, both of them refused. He knew that he would have to take a gamble when he faced the powerful enemy; otherwise, he had no other choice but to run away. He was a risk taker, and sometimes it worked.

Jal-al-Addin rode his horse into the open ground with a long spear in his right hand and a rectangular-shaped shield in his left. A long scimitar dangled on his left side belt. He was wearing metal armor and an open-faced, cylinder-shaped helmet.

As he approached the Mongol side, he shouted in a loud voice, "I am undefeated so far in one-to-one close fighting or one to two or even one to four. If any Mongol man can defeat me, come out!"

Upon this request, one man on horseback from the Mongol side slowly approached him. He was holding a long spear in his right hand and a round, leather shield in his left. He was wearing lacquered leather armor and an almond-shaped helmet, which was the standard Mongol soldier's protection in the battlefield. His name was Taimas.

Without hesitation, the two men dashed at each other, pointing their spear tip toward each other's heart or neck. At first contact, they couldn't hurt or kill anybody. They passed each other and turned their horses around, trying a second and then a third dash. Still nothing happened. Both were protected with armor and helmets.

At the fourth time, while they were galloping toward each other and neared, Taimas's spear point deeply penetrated Jal-al-Addin's right armpit. When someone was protected by armor and a helmet, the only area open without protection was the armpit. Taimas knew that.

Jal-al-Addin dropped his spear and began to run away the way he came. Blood spurted from his armpit and painted his right-side armor red. Taimas didn't chase him.

This incident was automatically followed by a full-scale attack from the Mongol side. Jal-al-Addin's soldiers began to run away and eventually scattered in all directions. Many ran into the forest and mountain area, but more than half of the

15,000 soldiers were massacred. Soon, the Mughan plain was covered with the dead bodies of Jal-al-Addin's soldiers.

As Jal-al-Addin was running away, he ordered one of his soldiers to carry his banner and let him go in a different direction. The Mongol chasing unit followed the direction of the banner but soon realized they were going the wrong way. They corrected the direction, but it gave Jal-al-Addin enough time to find safe passage.

Jal-al-Addin fled to Quban, soon moved to Qarqaz and then to Gandzak; however, Jal-al-Addin was not welcomed by the people of Gandzak who saw him and his runaway troops as defeated. He moved to Akhlat, but the same thing happened, so he hid himself and his soldiers in the Sufaye mountains through Manzikirt.

His military doctor checked his wounded right armpit, but the result was not very encouraging.

His doctor said, "Sultan, from now on, you need to practice to use your left arm. Your right arm is maimed. That means it has been permanently damaged. The tendon has been severed."

After two months, Jal-al-Addin's whereabouts were not known, and Chormaqan and Taimas decided to employ a fake tactic. The Mongols began to retreat. They moved back to Ray, even emptying Azerbaijan; however, many of the Mongol commandos were hiding in the forests and remote areas, waiting for the signal to attack. They planted spies everywhere and hired the Kurd warriors, who were allies to the Mongols, to hunt for the sultan and receive a reward.

CHAPTER 11

Another two months passed, and Jal-al-Addin was becoming irritable due to the steady arrival of gut-wrenchingly bad news. Before he moved to the Mughan plain to face the Mongols, he entrusted his vizir, Sharif-al-Mulk, to go to Giran with all his treasures and guard his harem and the women there. However, Sharif-al-Mulk changed his mind and revolted. He took all of Jal-al-Addin's treasures and his women.

Jal-al-Addin's tolerance ended, and he sent Bukuqan to locate the Mongol army. Bukuqan and his scouting unit went into Azerbaijan but found no Mongols.

After he returned, he reported, "I couldn't see any Mongols there. They probably retreated to Ray. The residents also mentioned that the last time they saw Mongols was about two months ago."

Jal-al-Addin was delighted with this report and thought that he had time to rebuild his power. On that night, he had a feast with his followers and drank his fill. On the same day at midnight, the Mongol commandos came upon them.

Learning of the Mongol soldiers' arrival, Orkhan, one of Jal-al-Addin's emirs, went to Jal-al-Addin's bedside and tried to wake him up. He was in a deep, drunken sleep, so speaking loudly or even shaking his body couldn't awaken him. Finally, a bucketful of cold water was thrown on his face, and he was roused.

Realizing the situation, Jal-al-Addin fled after giving orders to Orkhan and his followers to resist and hold the line until he was in the lead. Jal-al-Addin, all by himself, moved in great haste toward the opposite direction from which the

Mongols were coming. He galloped day and night until his horse was exhausted and refused to move further.

Jal-al-Addin arrived at the mountain called Hakkar and decided to take a break under a big tree. It was late afternoon, and he fell asleep. He was found by six Kurd warriors, who were hunting around that area for the sultan. They immediately recognized his unusual, luxurious clothing and armor, jewel-embedded scimitar and the gorgeous saddle on his horse. They took off his clothing and jewelry and other decorative items and opened his stomach.

The Kurd warriors were on the way to the Mongol camp for a reward, but they were unlucky. They were captured by Jal-al-Addin's followers—150 of them—and were killed right on the spot.

The fate of the last sultan of Khwarazm

O n the other hand, Ghiyas-Addin, the younger brother of Jal-al-Addin, swiftly retreated, abandoning his left-wing position, when defeat was imminent. He stayed in Alamut for a few days and then moved to Khuzistan.

From there, he summoned one of his retinue Barak Hajib in Kirman and sent an urgent message: "I am on my way to Kirman. If you are still loyal to me, come out to see me and escort me."

Until that moment, Barak Hajib's mind was with him, and he returned this message: "Sultan, my loyalty is engraved in the rock. I shall meet you at the desert near Abarquh. Afterwards, your journey will be an enjoyable one."

Barak Hajib kept his word and welcomed Ghiyas-Addin at the aforementioned place. For two or three days, he gave him a proper treatment with honor; however, he noticed that Ghiyas-Addin was with less than 500 defeated, poorly equipped soldiers while he brought 4,000 well-trained cavalry.

THE FATE OF THE LAST
SULTAN OF KHWARAZM

A devilish, dark intention smeared his brain. He lost interest in supporting his hopeless, soon-to-be collapsed master.

One day, Barak Hajib sat and shared drinks with his master, Sultan Ghiyas-Addin, and stated, "Sultan, I want to marry your mother."

The sultan was dumbfounded and quickly looked around inside the tent. All 10 armed guard soldiers had been replaced with Barak Hajib's men. Ghiyas-Addin quickly sensed that he was a prisoner of Barak Hajib.

Sultan Ghiyas-Addin was 20 years old, and his beautiful mother was still in her 30s and there with her son.

Ghiyas-Addin, not knowing how to answer, said, "Ask my mother."

Barak Hajib sent a messenger to the sultan's mother, asking for her hand.

The messenger came back with this answer: "No."

Barak Hajib sent the messenger again, but the answer was still "no."

He sent the messenger for the third time and whispered to him to convey this message word for word: "If you keep refusing, your son's life will not be guaranteed."

The sultan's mother quickly sensed that something very undesirable was happening. Without resistance, she gave her consent. On that night, the sultan's mother entered Barak Hajib's house with a few servants, and the marriage was consummated. From then on, Barak Hajib openly addressed the sultan as "my son."

Days after they arrived at Kirman, two of Barak Hajib's kinsmen came to the sultan secretly and said, "Barak Hajib should not be trusted. He is treacherous and deceitful. We found an opportunity. If we get rid of him, you will be sultan again, and we will be your truthful servants."

However, the fortune was not with the sultan.

Talks in the daytime,
Could be heard by birds.
Talks in the nighttime,
Could be heard by rats.

One of Barak Hajib's intimates heard these words and informed him. Barak Hajib immediately arrested the two kinsmen and Sultan Ghiyas-Addin. He examined them, and they all admitted what they had planned. Barak Hajib ordered his soldiers to cut the kinsmen's limbs in front of the sultan. The soldiers cut their arms and legs into pieces with a battle axe, and soon the smell of blood filled the tent. The sultan was temporarily detained in the prison. Soon afterwards, an executioner was sent, and he placed a bow string around his neck and strangled Ghiyas-Addin.

The sultan cried out, "Didn't you make a covenant to become one of my loyal retinue? Why did you break it without cause and betray me?"

The sultan's mother, hearing her son crying, screamed and wailed loudly. Both of them were strangled, and all the remaining sultan's followers were massacred.

Where no lofty poplars exist,
Bushes and shrubs could be the tallest.

THE FATE OF THE LAST
SULTAN OF KHWARAZM

Where no lion roams,
Old fox could be the king of beasts.

The head of Ghiyas-Addin, the last sultan of Khwarazm, was put into a wooden box filled with salt and sent to Chormaqan with this message: "You have two enemies: Jal-al-Addin and Ghiyas-Addin. I am sending you one of them."

After receiving Ghiyas-Addin's head, Chormaqan gave an order to Taimas.

"Advance to Kirman and destroy Barak Hajib and his troops. Bring Barak Hajib, dead or alive."

Taimas advanced to Kirman with 5,000 warriors and subdued Barak Hajib and his 4,000 troops easily. Barak Hajib was brought to Chormaqan, who regarded him for a while.

Chormaqan said, "Your merit for the Mongol Empire has been approved by bringing the head of Ghiyas-Addin; however, we don't accept someone who betrayed their master. You will be punished just like an enemy, but your two sons might be accepted once the khagan approves. I will send your two sons to the khagan in Karakorum with Ghiyas-Addin's head. It will depend on your children how they will attribute to the Mongol Empire."

Barak Hajib was strangled by the soldiers in front of Chormaqan in the same manner that he used for Ghiyas-Addin.

Chormaqan also subdued Armenians and Georgians and continued his conquest in the nearby area. His territory was bounded by the Amudarya River at the east, the Persian Gulf at the south, the Zagros Mountains at the southwest and the Arexis River at the northwest. He ruled those areas for 10 years.

CHAPTER 13

Over the Appalachian Mountains

Gog and Megog,
The two foul giants,
They are the gatekeepers of hell.
Over the Appalachian Mountains,
There lies the hell,
Tartarus.
The domain of the devil,
The hometown for monsters, freaks and evil creatures.
Their horror is beyond imagination.
Cyclops—the one-eyed, man-eating, monster giant,
Cynocephali—the man with the head of a dog,
Acephali—the human-like creature with its face on its chest,
Minotaur—the man-eating, half-man, half-bull creature,
Argus—a 100-eyed creature,
Echidna—the man-eating, half-woman, half-serpent
    creature,
Centaur—the half-man, half-horse creature,
Chimaera—the fire-breathing monster with a lion's head and
    a serpent's tail,

Hydra—the snake-like monster with nine heads,
Manticore—the creature with a human head, a lion's body
    and a bat's wing,
Orthrus—the two-headed dog,
Chuvash—the fire-breathing dragon,
Azuzu—the foul pigmy,
Lotan—the demonic dragon,
Lebini—the demonic woman eating only man.
When the time comes,
On the doomsday,
The gate will be opened,
By the order of the devil,
Releasing the monsters,
To destroy the world.

In the year 1235, the year of the sheep in the Mongolian zodiac, in early spring, a grand-scale kuriltai was held in the heart of the Mongol mainland in the basin of the Kerulen River. This meeting occurred one year after they completed the conquest of the mighty Chin, the nation with 50 million people, in the northern Chinese continent north of the Yellow River. During this campaign, Ogodei lost his younger brother Tolui due to diarrhea and an unknown fever.

The meeting was planned to continue for one month. They began to discuss and were going to make decisions on many current issues and future plans. In a huge tent, which could accommodate more than 200 people, all the princes, generals and high-ranking officials were gathered.

CHAPTER 13

The royal seat was arranged on the northernmost part of the tent for the khagan. Alongside the wall, east and west, wooden benches for the attendants were lined up. The entrance was covered with a thick, flap door located at the southern end of the tent. Outside, nobody was allowed to come near the tent inside the half-mile radius, which was guarded by Ogodei's personal unit, 1,000 of them, who were the most loyal and fearless in the Mongol army. They were discussing the plan of a Russian and European invasion.

Subedei, who was called "Subedei the valiant," had already conquered several scores of kingdoms and nations and won hundreds of battles and military campaigns. He was undefeated and had achieved the position of orlok, which meant "supreme general of the Mongol army." He was now 60 years old.

When Subedei was young, he was wounded in his right hand, which made it a little crooked, but he didn't have any limitations when using his arm. The second blow struck his face, very close to his right eye, which gave him a scar, but he was lucky to keep his eyesight undamaged.

"We have already reconquered the Persian and Transcaucasian areas. Those areas are now secure. Before we advance into Russia, the first step we have to take is to conquer the Bulgars and subdue the Kipchaks around the Volga River for safety measures. Once it's done, we can safely move into the Russian mainland."

While the praying mantis
Focuses on its prey,
Grasshopper,

Lizard will wait for the best moment
For its prey,
Praying mantis.

The Bulgars were originally nomadic in nature, but they gave up their nomadic lifestyle once they got involved in fur trading, where they became rich and eventually built houses and settled down; however, their inborn nature of nomadic blood came out when they were agitated.

Subedei said, "It will take about two to three years to get everything ready. We need at least 150,000 warriors and a minimum of 300,000 horses."

Up to this point, the khagan, Ogodei, who was just listening in the royal seat, asked, "My revered general, what is your idea of strategy and tactics to conquer the Oruss people and their lands?"

Subedei answered without hesitation. "Russia has big land with a population of around eight to nine million, I guess. Eight princes share the land, and they have their own territory. They are separated so far among them that a connection of their kinship or friendship is very thin. They are not helping each other. They are, rather, just a rival or an enemy to each other."

At this remark, Ogodei slapped his knee and let out guffaw. "That's *perfect* for us!"

"We had better advance in wintertime," Subedei continued. "Many parts of their land are covered with mud and swamps. Our horses might not be able to move freely in that condition, so it would be better on the frozen land."

Ogodei asked, "What about their protective system and facilities?"

"They have already experienced our superior power, so they might be more on the defensive side rather than coming out to face us on the field. The wounded boar tends to hide from their predators in a den or a ground hole. Their city wall is mainly made of wood, so our catapult can easily handle them; however, they usually build their city on a location with a geographical advantage for defense from attack, like at a riverside or on high hills."

Thanks to Subedei's extensive espionage network, he saw the enemy area like his own palm.

Ogodei asked, "What about the European side?"

"Our main target in Europe will be Hungary. Hungary has the most powerful cavalry in Europe. Originally, they were horsemen, like us, but now they are sedentary."

After this, Ogodei murmured, "I have been told that our Mongol ancestors went into that area a long time ago."

"You are quite right," Subedei added, "but that was 700 to 800 years ago. They are different people now."

After this comment, most of the attendees nodded at Subedei's explanation, and he continued. "Most of the European city walls or protective walls are made of stone with a deep moat around them ..."

Ogodei responded with a short "Um!" and spat out, "Like Chinese!"

"... but they are good at defense but just a baby in offense. Their scale is smaller than the Chinese. We, however, should prepare for a large number of seize engines. In the European campaign, we might be able to take advantage of black powder, which can exert more destructive power and bring enormous psychological impact upon the enemy soldiers' morale, which they have never seen or experienced before."

When the Mongols conquered Chin in northern China, they had captured about 200 black-powder manufacturing technicians and seize-engine specialists. Chormaqan had also sent about 80 Persian captives who specialized in seize-engine design and production. They discussed and decided to have the technicians create and invent various forms of weaponry utilizing black powder.

"What about the Crusaders?" Ogodei asked. "Who created them, and what is their reason for being? What are they doing?"

"The Crusaders are a group of soldiers that emerged from the European Christian kingdoms or the Christian world to protect their pilgrims to their holy city of Jerusalem," Subedei explained. "They believed that, at least once in a lifetime, they should visit Jerusalem; however, it was frequently blocked by Islamic Seljuk Turks, who had more power in these areas. They formed a large body of military force to take over the holy city. Basically, it was created by their religious leaders, including the pope; however, their kings of every region and the ruling class support it."

"Was it truly from a religious motivation?"

"Yes," Subedei added. "At least at the beginning; however, soon the real truth or motivation began to show up. The pope wanted more religious power, and their kings and aristocrats wanted more land to rule."

Up to this point, Ogodei was just listening but then asked, "Who joins them?"

CHAPTER 13

"Nine out of 10 people in Europe are slaves in a serfdom. They enslave their own people. Their kings and the ruling class hold the land along with the enslaved people. They sell and buy their land along with the enslaved serfs. If they join the Crusaders, the pope promised that they will get freedom. Every Crusader has a variety of motivations. Some want guaranteed heaven after life, some want to get rich quick, some want adventure—even for plundering and looting."

At these comments, Ogodei clicked his tongue and loudly remarked, "They enslave their own *people*?"

At the time, in Mongol society, there was no slavery system among them or even for the foreign-born who joined them, though the war captives or population from the conquered land who refused to surrender were considered slaves.

Subedei added, "Europe is the region ruled by religion—Christendom. The pope is the most powerful, and the bishops have the right to collect taxes and even draft and gather the army."

"What about their kings?"

"Even the kings have to bow to the pope and obey; however, some of them refuse and acknowledge the pope's power."

"Who is it?"

"The Holy Roman Emperor Frederick II, by their pronunciation."

Ogodei thought for a while and then asked, "To which side are their soldiers leaning?"

"Some of them pledged allegiance to the pope and some to the emperor."

Inside the tent, a deep silence continued as all the attendees listened carefully to the two men's dialogue: the khagan
Ogodei and supreme general Subedei.

Ogodei asked, "The crusaders are religious-based soldiers.
What about their doctrine or belief for going to war and killing people?"

"At the beginning, the pope declared that killing people of
other religions was not murder."

Ogodei jumped up and shouted with a clenched fist,
"That's too selfish! Let's destroy and conquer the world without soul! This will be the will of the true god!"

At the time, the Mongol society practiced religious freedom so that, even among the Mongols, there were Christians
and Muslims as well as Tengrists from their own ancestral
belief of Tengrism.

Ogodei declared, "We will conquer them! We are the
bravest, the smartest and the strongest. We are destined to
rule the world. Let's go!"

At this, all attendees stood up, punching their fists into
space, and chanted in one, loud voice, "GO! GO! GO!"

CHAPTER 14

Yelu-chuchai's theory

Yelu-chuchai opened his mouth and said, "If we conquer both—the Chinese and Persian civilizations—we can declare that we conquered the world."

About 200 attendees in the royal tent carefully listened to this 6-foot, 8-inch tall man. His silver, sparkling beard was so long that it reached almost to his navel. His voice was so sonorous that it was like music to the listeners.

He was wearing a white, long-sleeved, Khitan-style garment, which covered his whole body, falling down to his ankle with a loosely tied string belt on his waist. This ancestral garment didn't waste his image or dignity as a high-ranking officer in the Mongol Empire. He was first recognized by the great one, Genghis Khan, and served in the Mongol administration as a high-ranking officer. Now, he was the chancellor of the Mongol Nation and the chief advisor for the khagan.

He separated military leadership from the governing body of the empire, making them independent of each other. The khagan held the supreme power on both sides, yet Yelu-chuchai was the head of the administrative side.

He also said, "Military power that is not backed by intelligence and reasoning power can be dangerous and even self-destructive."

Yelu-chuchai built schools and libraries for the children of the royal families, aristocrats and ruling classes.

"We are on the way to conquer the lands from sunrise to sunset or great ocean to great ocean; however, the real meaning of world conquest will be conquering the two civilizations I already mentioned."

At this moment, a deep silence remained in the tent. Then, a question came from one side of the corner. It was Boroldai Noyan, one of the great generals in the Mongol army.

"What about Russia and Europe? We have already decided to go there, and we are all here to discuss the plans. You sound like Europe is not important."

Yelu-chuchai replied, "That's true. They are lagging. They are quite behind. They have been closed themselves by their own will or forced by others for almost a thousand years, and it is still going on."

Another question came from Toqolqu Cherbi, who was in charge of the imperial guard Keshik.

"If Europe is not an important area, why should we go there with a great army of 150,000 horsemen and 300,000 horses?"

"Our sacred leader—the great one—mentioned many times before that our Mongol Empire should be on the land from sunrise to sunset, and it should be on the foundation of 1,000 years long. Usually, the great empires in human history have lasted about 300 to 400 years. To put the foundation of 1,000 years, we should conquer not only the past and the present but also the future."

Yelu-chuchai looked around to make sure that his audience fully understood and was following his story.

"They are sleeping now," he continued. "However, someday they will wake up. At one time, they had a splendid civilization, which was Greek and Roman. Flowers bloom when they are in the right condition. We have to conquer not only the past and the present but also the future. That is the real meaning of conquest."

After these words, Yelu-chuchai walked back to his seat and sat down. This time, the khagan, Ogodei, got on his feet and opened his mouth.

"That's a great story! Conquering the past and present but also the future. Let's talk about who will lead this great expedition. It came to my mind that, based on the size of the group and the size of the land we are going to deal with, I think that I am the only one who can lead this group."

Yelu-chuchai stood up again. "My lord, our Mongol Nation is a big empire now. The head of the empire cannot be far away from the western front for too long. There should be someone who can handle all the affairs that will come from every corner of the empire and, after all, from all over the world. We just started construction of the new capital Karakorum, the job that needs constant, close supervision all the time. I believe that all these jobs can be handled only by the khagan himself, my lord."

Nobody said anything against this comment; in fact, the atmosphere was heavy with the feeling that it was quite agreeable, natural and reasonable.

Finally, Ogodei got on his feet and remarked, "Fine! I believe the chancellor made it quite right. I will stay. Now, we must decide who will lead this expedition group."

Again, Yelu-chuchai stood up and said, "For the western land conquest, the leader should come from Juchi's ulus. As long as we agree to this, the rest of the job will be on the kha-gan's hand to decide who will be the leader of this army."

When Yelu-chuchai said "ulus," it was the same meaning as "ordus." When Genghis Khan was around, he realized that the world was too big to be ruled by one man or one family. So, he began to think of the concept of ulus. Genghis meant four different ulus for his four sons—one for each of them and their descendants—to rule their own appanages. Based on this concept, the western land west of Lake Balkhash, the Aral Sea and the Caspian Sea to the Great Ocean (Atlantic Ocean) belonged to Juchi's ulus.

"My revered chancellor," Ogodei said, "you are right once again. All the western land beyond Lake Balkhash belongs to Juchi's ulus. So, the leader of this expedition should come from Juchi's family."

After this remark from the khagan, they exchanged ideas, talked about many things and finally confirmed that Batu was the right person to lead this army group. Batu's leadership and valor was recognized by many in the Chinese and other campaigns. Most of all, he was Juchi's official, primary successor. His declared appanage was from the Volga River as well as the Caspian Sea to all the western lands, many of them not conquered yet. The area between the Volga River and Lake Balkhash was Batu's elder brother Orda's appanage.

CHAPTER 14

The khagan, Ogodei, was about to declare that Batu was the supreme leader of this group; however, from one corner, a loud yell burst out.

"Objection!"

All the attendees' attention fell upon one man, who was sitting with his brothers and other princes in the middle of the right-hand side from the khagan's royal seat.

Kuyuk, the firstborn son of Ogodei, got to his feet and said, "The lands we are planning to conquer—Russia and Europe—are big. We are all going … men from Juchi's ulus and men from all the other three ulus. We should consider this."

Kuyuk was unhappy with the idea that all the conquered land would belong to Juchi's ulus, making them the largest ulus among the others. Kuyuk had a long-cherished desire to be the next khagan, even though his father Ogodei made it clear that his successor would be his grandson Shiremun.

Kuyuk was not comfortable if Batu's territory and power grew. From an early age, Kuyuk thought of Batu as his rival. They were in same age group, with Batu being one year older. Batu was the official primary heir of Genghis Khan's firstborn son Juchi, and Kuyuk was the firstborn son of the current khagan Ogodei.

Yelu-chuchai stood again and asked, "Prince Kuyuk, what is your lofty idea, and what is your suggestion to the empire? What do you think could be the best way?"

"We can go there with our old-fashioned, traditional way. Each ulu will have their own leader and make their own campaign plan and will get what they have acquired, respectively. We should share what we get but not for only one ulu."

Before Genghis Khan's time, when the group of clans or tribes made alliances together and attacked other clans, they used to elect a khan as a campaign leader; however, each clan still had their own individual leaders. The soldiers were loyal to their own clan leader rather than to the elected khan. War booty was the main thing they pursued, so they were competitive and kept what they had taken; however, Genghis Khan put an end to this system, and the Mongol society was reborn as a centralized unit. He initiated an equitable system of dividing up the loot. A jarqu, which was a special committee, administered the payout.

Yelu-chuchai said, "Why do we have to go back to an old system that we gave up a long time ago? It is also against the spirit that the sacred Great One built up—the Mongol unity."

After these words, Ogodei stood up abruptly and said, "Unity is the utmost importance for our nation! Whoever goes there, wherever your horse treads and whichever nation you conquer, it will be still under the name of the Mongol Empire. You will have only one commander for this army group! Batu will be the supreme commander."

He made it very clear in front of all the attendees that Batu was the commander in chief and no one else. At the time, the Mongol commandership was extremely strict, and disobedience to the khan's order was considered treason, and the punishment was death.

The following day, they had a short ceremony to appoint Batu as the commander of the Russian and European expeditions army group.

CHAPTER 14

The khagan gave this decree: "From this moment on, Batu shall lead the western land expedition group, and he shall have the freedom to make decisions related to this whole group and expedition from beginning to end."

After this decree, Batu was given a golden baton, which was a symbol of the supreme commander; however, Ogodei didn't forget to put a condition to Batu's commandership: As long as military operations were concerned, Batu needed consent and agreement from Subedei. Making a plan and carrying out the military operation could be possible only when they both agreed. That was the consideration of Batu's relatively young age and Subedei's unlimited power of military genius. Batu was 30 years old.

CHAPTER 15

The dawn of the new era: the Golden Ordu

In early spring of 1236, a great number of Mongol armies began to gather at Sighnaq, the capital city of White Ordu, which was the domain of Batu's elder brother Orda. One time, this city was well known as the hometown for rich merchants with its elegant buildings, clean streets, stores with luxurious goods and rose gardens everywhere.

However, at the time of the war with the Mongol Nation and the Khwarazm Empire, much of the city had been destroyed, so Orda had to repair and reconstruct after he took over the city. Like other Mongol leaders, he didn't like to live in the city and preferred to live in a tent town on the steppe, yet he still kept the city in the best condition for his sedentary people under his rule. At the eastern side, the Karatau Mountains were lined up as if they protected the city from afar, and the city itself was located on the bank of the Mutkan River, which was a tributary of the Syr Darya River.

By that time, the number of Mongol soldiers gathered was 120,000. The majority was from the elite imperial army, and the rest were conscripts and recruits. There were several additional units of Chinese and Persian engineering corps, whose main function was to attack the walled city by using their specially designed weaponry, like catapults.

However, the most formidable weapons were cannons and rockets that used black powder, which was being carried under the protection of a top military secret. Nobody knew what it was like except for the black-powder firing unit. The number of Mongol soldiers was growing each day, though there were some delays due to a strict screening procedure.

Each Mongol soldier had to pass the screening, and anyone who was unsuitable for the long journey and far-away expedition was eliminated. Each of the soldiers' family members had to pass the screening also; otherwise, they had to return to the spot where they started. This meant keeping the soldiers and their family members separate until the expedition's end was considered inappropriate. Even with the strict screening, most of the family members passed, mainly because they prescreened themselves voluntarily. This policy or tradition, which allowed each married Mongol warrior to move with their family members, provided a tremendous emotional edge to their souls and contributed to their mental stability and psychological power.

Batu was accompanied by his first wife, Boraqchin Khatun, and four other wives. He was also accompanied by two concubines whom he loved the most: a Persian girl named Zohreh (meaning "Venus") and a Kipchak girl named Kedi (meaning "cat"). Batu used to pick up his concubines mainly for practical reasons and not out of curiosity. By that time, the Mongol society was an open and multicultural society.

THE DAWN OF THE NEW ERA:
THE GOLDEN ORDU

Out of Batu's 40 wives and concubines, the concubines were selected by Batu's mother, Ukhaa Ujin, who said, "They should be loyal and capable of comforting my son at night from the day's hardships of battlefield."

Among the Mongol soldiers, they were known as the seven yildiz (stars). Batu himself was referred to as Sein Khan by his soldiers, which meant "Smart Khan," or they simply called him Smart One. It was taboo to mention his name directly among the soldiers.

Batu was also accompanied by two chroniclers: one was a Chinese man named Chun Lee, and the other was an Arab named Faqih Ashraf Aziz. They accompanied Batu on many occasions and followed him like shadows. They recorded what they saw and experienced, independently, and even Batu could not ask to see what they had written.

Before the beginning of summer, also in 1236, 11 khans (princes) from all four ulus gathered: Batu from Juchi's ulu; Batu's elder brother Orda; Batu's younger brothers Seiban, Tangut and Sinkur; Ogodei's sons Kuyuk and Kadan; Chagatai's son Baidar; Chagatai's grandson Buri; and Tolui's sons Manku and Bujek.

Besides these people, Kulqan Khan, Ogodei's half-brother, joined the group, which meant that he was the son of Genghis Khan from his fourth wife Qulan. In Mongol culture, only sons from the first wife can inherit their father's position and property, so he didn't have any of his own ulus. He was much younger than his half-brothers; rather, he was in almost the same age group with his nieces.

CHAPTER 15

The basin at the Mutkan River was covered with hundreds of thousands of war tents, making a huge tent city. From the end of the left wing to the end of the right wing, it spread out over 20 miles. At the center of the tent city, a large, open space was created that was designed for massive gatherings, and all the tents and yurts were lined up in a very organized way in a radial pattern.

Between all the lines of tents, there was a road with the width that four horsemen could trot through side by side without trouble. Batu's official and private tents were in the northernmost part, above the open space, along with his seven wives' and concubines' yurts. Encircling these, numerous military tents were built for Batu's guard unit of 1,000 elites, whose main function was to protect their commander.

Outside the boundary of this city limit were quarters for livestock like cattle, sheep and camels, which were mainly resources for food and transportation for the army; however, the horses were different. They were kept in closer proximity to their dwelling places because the Mongols considered horses as weapons.

Their first plan was to conquer the Volga Bulgars, which was the Bulgar Kingdom and Cumania, whose people were living on a wider area alongside the Volga River, before they moved into Russia. The Bulgar Kingdom was well known for its riches, which came from fur trading and gold and silver craftmanship. They were the commanders of the Volga River.

Their capital city of Bilar was a thriving, rich city, and Bolghar was the trading center between the east and the west. Their trading partners were Vikings, Bjarmaland, Yugra, Nenets at the north and Baghdad and Constantinople in the south as well as east to China. Their city was well built and protected by natural surroundings like mountains, rivers and woods.

At one time, they were nomadic; however, once they became rich, they changed their lifestyle and became sedentary city dwellers. Because of their riches, neighboring strong nations were always running their eyes over them to pick up a chance to take advantage. Their king Puresh knew about this and tried to build up an effective protective system from invaders; however, on numerous occasions, Russians from Vladimir and Novgorod sacked and looted his domain, weakening his power.

Cumania was a semideveloped nation built by Cumans whose residents were nomadic in nature and spread out in a wider area alongside the lower Volga. Russians called them Polovits, Hungarians called them Cumans and Mongols called them Kipchaks; however, they were the same people, only with different names, and their original blood was of Turkish origin.

About 10 days before advancement, they held a war council and mapped out the plan of their campaign. At the council meeting, Batu appointed his cousin Monku, who belonged to the left-wing group, as the commander of the Cumania campaign division. Three tumens, about 30,000 horse soldiers, were given to Monku. Batu would move into the Bulgar Kingdom with Subedei, leading the main body. Under his arm, numerous top-ranking Mongol generals were with him, including Boroldai Noyan, Mengguser of the Saljuut tribe, Gegetai of the Kuman tribe, Hushitai of the Hushin tribe, Barku Noyan and more. All of these generals were noy-ans, which meant "the head of 10,000 men."

Three days before departure, early in the morning, all the Mongol soldiers gathered at an open space at the center of the tent city. The morning air was cool at the river basin, even in the middle of summer. They were clad with armor and helmets and mounted on horses. Their spears shone under the morning sunlight.

Batu shouted on the mounted podium in the open space, in front of 100,000 warriors, "Brothers! We are destined to rule! The land from the sunrise to the sunset has been bestowed upon us from God! We will be the ruler of all the living creatures and master of the past, present and future! The one who accepts and follows God's ordainment will survive and thrive; otherwise, they shall perish from Earth! We will crush the enemy into pieces, and the resistant powers will be put under our horses' hoof steps! We are invincible! No one will dare to stand against us! We will dash to the end of the world and build up the nation bigger than ever before, and it will never be built so big again! We will enjoy the never-ending victories and will wake up every morning in the sweetness of glory. We will all enjoy this together! May the eternal blue sky bless the Mongols! May all mighty God protect our soldiers."

The soldiers chanted in one voice, "Batu Khan! Batu Khan! Batu Khan!"

This chanting lasted for a while and echoed into the unfathomable deep blue sky.

THE DAWN OF THE NEW ERA:
THE GOLDEN ORDU

After the chanting subsided, the state shaman Buge Eechu stepped onto the mount and blessed the army. He was clad in a traditional shamanistic costume—a long, white, one-piece dress covering his whole body—and on his head a cone-shaped, white cap with flaps covering his shoulder was donned. The color white was believed to be sacred and reserved only for shamans. He was holding a big fan, about 5 feet long, made with a willow branch and decorated with birds' white feathers. The willow branch was believed to chase off evil spirits, and the birds' white feathers symbolized nature's spiritual blessing. All those beliefs came from steppe people's thousand-year-old traditions.

Buge Eechu swung his fan over the heads of the soldiers three times and shouted this poem:

Heaven and Earth,
The sun and the moon,
The spirits of mountains, rivers and forests,
And all other spirits in nature,
The 99 deities ruling human fate,
Tengri, the supreme ruler of everything, seen or unseen,
Bless the Mongol soldiers!
Let them be unbreakable!
Protect them with unseen, impenetrable shields!
Let them crush their enemies!
All the spirits of the great steppe,
Save the Mongol blood!
Bring the victory for the brave!
Allow us glory!
So, be it!

After these words, he swung his fan three more times.

After Buge Eechu's poem, each soldier, by their military ranking, dismounted their horses and walked through the two columns of flames that were built for the purification of their soul and for protection from evil spirits. There were about 20 sets of these two columns of flame, all about 7 feet high and erected in the open space, with about 50 yards between each set.

The shaman, still on the mounted podium, said the magic words:

Mother of fire!
The deity of fire!
The noble spirit of fire!
And the king of fire Maraja!
We pray by proffering grease!
May we stay in boundless ecstasy,
By having victories over victories,
By achieving countless war booties,
By having unaccountable livestock.
The magnanimous mother fires!
Let our life be long,
Let us live in incomparable rapture,
Let our offspring prosper,
The propitious fires!
Let the fortune never cease to come to us,
Let the arrows of destruction bypass us,
Let the evil spirit never fall upon us.
The holy fire from the heaven!
Let our heart be an iron,

THE DAWN OF THE NEW ERA:
THE GOLDEN ORDU

Let our body never get rotten,
Let us have the geyser of energy,
Let us have a never-ending fountain of youth!
Reincarnate our valiant souls,
Over and over again!
So that death can never come,
Upon the braves!

It took almost half a day for all the soldiers to complete their customary ritual. It was optional, but most of the soldiers went through it. Among the Mongol soldiers who were of Keraiti ancestral origin, most of them were Nestorian Christians. For those who were Turkic or Uighur, many of them were Muslims.

In earlier times, even in Genghis Khan's time, the Mongol society had freedom of religion; however, most Mongols were believers of Tengrism—the traditional steppe people's shamanism—that worshipped the eternal blue sky.

CHAPTER 16

The conquest of the Volga Bulgars

Batu and his army began to move to the west. They were moving in three columns: the west wing, the main body and the right wing. The distance between each column was 20 to 40 miles. Between the columns, messengers were coming and going every day, sometimes several times a day. Batu was well informed about the movement of the other wings, like seeing it on his own palms.

The chronicler Faqih Ashraf Aziz wrote:

It was a majestic scenery. The whole army was moving—soldiers and war horses—in a very organized way. Each Mongol soldier wore an almond-shaped helmet and lacquered, leather armor; a long spear with a curved hook in their right hand; two bows, one for long range and the other for short; a quiver with about 30 arrows on their shoulders; a scimitar on their left side waist belt and a battle axe on the other; a rope and a noose on the horse's rump. All of these things seemed to be the basic armament for each individual soldier.

In front of them, a banner carrier held the tuk—the Mongol army's banner—made from the tail of nine horses. Anyone watching this army's organized movement and magnificent, dignified and grand appearance would become awestruck before they got the feeling of fear. Who will beat this army on this earth?

The other chronicler Chun Lee wrote:

They commenced advancement. They seemed to already have a concrete plan. The Mongol army never made any movement until they had a detailed plan for victory. I read, from their vibe, that even the lowest ranking soldier was full of the confidence of victory. This army never knew defeat. Even God might not be able to change their belief—unless they did by themselves!

Mongols had made a plan long ago.

At the time, in the war council, Subedei explained, "For the Volga Bulgars, our first target will be their biggest city Bilar, and then next one will be Bolghar and Suvar. After these, we will take Cukataw and all of the other cities."

At this, General Boroldai Noyan asked, "What could be their population and the size of their army?"

"We don't know yet; however, we presume that the population of each city is around 100,000, and the total combined size of their army could be 40,000 to 50,000. We presume that their main forces are stationed in the big cities like Bilar, Bolghar and Suvar. After these, we have to deal with Puresh.

He has his own kingdom named Murunza with his Moksha people."

The Volga Bulgar was at the middle part of east and west. This trading center covered a large area, which meant that many different people from many different areas gathered and claimed that it was their land. It was like a multiethnic world; however, their majority were indigenous people who lived there from generation to generation.

Even though they were categorized as the Volga Bulgars, they were subdivided into many different tribes, and sometimes each tribe had their own king. Unfortunately, they had suffered at the hands of their neighbor—the Russians—and were looted and sacked frequently. Their economy and military power became much weaker ever since.

Batu said, "We need the Bulgars as a guide during Russian expeditions, and we need their craftsmen and leatherworkers as well. They might be cooperative once they surrender to us because they might not like the Oruss people," he concluded with a guffaw.

After they crossed the Ural and approached the Volga, the Mongol army began to divide. The left-wing group, 30,000 of them, was led by Monku, and Bujek headed for the south to conquer the Kipchaks around the lower Volga area. The other main group spread out to cover the area around Bilar.

The city of Bilar was built by the indigenous people of the Bilyar tribe and protected by a stone wall. Inside this wall was another layer of a wooden wall. The city was located at the bank of a small river, a tributary of the Volga, and nestled on a large hillside with a cliff at the backside around which the river snaked. It was built with the concept of maximum security and natural protection.

The Mongols began to encircle this city from afar. As the Mongols approached, the people inside the city began to panic. Their usual population inside the city was around 100,000; now, it was slightly increased to more than 120,000 due to refugees from a nearby area.

Batu sent out three envoys to persuade their leaders to surrender. The Mongols always gave a chance to surrender before they attacked. Three envoys—two Muslims and one interpreter—reached their leader Mir-Ghazi and handed over Batu's letter, which was written in Uighur script.

The letter read, "You people were at one time dwellers of the steppe in the most purified, honest form of life. You have chosen a sedentary life form, which we are going to destroy by God's ordainment. However, if you choose to join us and voluntarily help us to accomplish God's will, that is the sure way to please God."

Mir-Ghazi's answer was cold. He knew that, in the city, they had enough provisions for at least six months for the whole population and 20,000 in the garrison. Their protective city wall was made of stone and enhanced by another layer of strong wood. He thought that, if they kept their city for some time, other cities might come and give a helping hand.

Mir-Ghazi responded, "We have made a choice to remain fully sovereign and to be the master of our own destiny."

After receiving Mir-Ghazi's answer, Batu opened a war council and discussed their next step.

CHAPTER 16

Batu asked Subedei, "Orlok, let me know your lofty idea."

Batu called Subedei "orlok," a title that went to only one man who held the supreme commandership alongside Batu.

Subedei answered, "Since they are protected by a stone wall, it will remain a mystery until we take action. We have to assemble the catapults, the stone-throwers, the siege engines and possibly the ladder carrier."

The ladder carrier was a wooden structure designed to safely carry the commandoes over the fortified city wall when they attacked a city with a high protective wall. The front and side views were rectangular and covered with wooden plates for protection from arrows. It moved with four to six wheels and was installed with a large ladder, which could pour the number of commandoes over the wall in a very short time. The commandoes were safe as long as they were behind the huge frontal wood plate.

The more developed and sophisticated form of ladder carrier was called a siege tower. Its effectiveness and usage were limited, especially if there was a large, wide moat around the city wall, which prevented a close approach, or another inappropriate geometrical condition. When the Mongols were moving, they disassembled them for an easy carry.

Subedei added, "Maybe we should attack the nearby small cities and towns at the same time and get some necessary levies for additional support."

"Levies" meant selected captives among the enemy population—even soldiers—who were qualified for hard labor and pledged loyalty to the Mongols.

"We should choose the way to minimize our loss, Smart Lord."

Subedei usually called Batu Smart Lord or Smart One and occasionally Sein Khan. Batu was always a good listener to Subedei. Batu learned many things from Subedei on many different occasions in their campaign. One time, the Great One—Genghis Khan—told Subedei to be a tutor for Batu to let him learn about the art of war. Batu had a chance to accompany Subedei on the way to the Chin expedition.

The Mongol artillery unit assembled the catapults, and the other group collected and gathered the rocks for their catapults. However, it wasn't easy to find rocks on the steppe land, and it took many days. After 10 days, they began to attack the city. At the same time, the right-wing group led by Kuyuk Khan made their move to sweep the nearby towns and small cities that did not have fortified, strong defense systems.

For seven days, the Mongols attacked Bilar with their catapults to no avail. The Mongols couldn't find enough rocks, so they had to cut the trees to make the projectiles. The artillery unit carefully calculated the target distance and adjusted the lever for accuracy. Well-designed catapults, mainly by Persian specialists, threw away the rocks of 45 to 120 pounds with 80 percent accuracy; however, the stone wall was as tough as their resistance. Batu and Subedei got together and shared their opinions.

Subedei said, "Maybe we should employ the tactic of a frontal head-on attack as well as filling up the moat. To do that, we need levies. So, we should wait until the right-wing group brings the levies."

The city was protected by a stone wall as well as a wide and deep moat around the wall. The frontal main gate was big and thick, also made with hard wood. The gate was designed to be raised or lowered. In defense mode, the gate would be raised, so they could completely block egress or ingress of the traffic. In peace time, they lowered the gate to make a bridge over the moat, making an opening.

In about 15 days, Kuyuk Khan's right-wing group came back with about 8,000 levies. With these levies, they resumed the attack. The levies began to fill out the moat. From the city wall, defense soldiers attacked the levies with a showering of arrows. They had to kill their own people. The Mongol archery unit counterattacked from afar. The levies completed the job five days later with the loss of 2,000 lives.

The next step was to break the main gate, and a huge battering ram was employed. The battering ram was brought in front of the gate on the six-wheel carrier. The battering ram was made of a huge beam with numerous U-shaped metal handles affixed on it. A total of 40 levies lifted the battering ram—20 for the left-hand side and another 20 for the other side—and they began to hit the gate. The front side of the beam, which was covered with a ram's head made of strong metal, continuously rammed the gate with a loud noise. The defending Volga Bulgars poured boiling oil over the levies, but it was only a matter of time and eventually the gate gave out.

Through the open main gate, the Mongol cavalry unit poured into the city. At the same time, the Mongol commandoes climbed over the city wall from numerous spots using ladder carriers. For half a day, the street fighting continued. Eventually, the streets were covered with dead bodies, and the city drainage system was blocked due to clogged human blood.

High in the sky, groups of condors and flesh-eating crows circled over the city, making a lot of unpleasant noise. Many of the citizens hid inside their houses, and many more went into public buildings or mosques. Most of their population was Muslim. It was 45 days after the Mongols commenced the attack.

The chronicler Faqih Ashraf Aziz wrote:

After the collapse of the city defense system, the Mongols systemically sacked the city. For three days, they were allowed to plunder. During this period, many Bilar citizens perished. They resisted, and instant death fell upon them. After three days, they set the entire city on fire, including Islamic mosques where a lot of people fled, believing that it was their haven. They rushed out of their hiding places due to the heat and smoke, and then met their death. The Mongol soldiers shot them down with arrows or cut off their heads with scimitars. The whole population was massacred, including women and babies. The Mongols seemed to try to make an example for other cities as a warning.

The chronicler Chun Lee wrote:

It took 45 days for the Mongols to take over this city. The people of Bilar refused to surrender and tried to fight till the last moment. It seemed that the Mongols tried to show what would happen and what tragedy would fall upon them if they resisted.

CHAPTER 16

It was horror itself with unimaginable atrocities. All the girls and young women were raped in front of their family members before they were cut in half. Anybody who resisted or made trouble for this unbearable scene was impaled.

When they did this horrible punishment, they took off the victims' clothes. Then, they hammered a sharp-pointed, thick, long, wooden pole into their anus, or vagina in the case of women. The bodies gradually fell due to their own body weight. They set the pole securely on the ground. The tip of the pole traveled through the victim's internal organs, and finally the tip would appear through the victim's neck or mouth. If the victim wriggled in pain, it moved their body down the pole faster. Among them was their leader Mir-Ghazi.

Then, they set the fire. The entire city was quickly enveloped in flames, which lasted for three days. The city was completely annihilated; however, they didn't forget to set free about 200 survivors on purpose. They were the truthful witnesses and messengers to their own people who lived in other cities.

CHAPTER 17

Surrender of Puresh

The Mongols moved to their target city: Bolghar. It was situated on the bank of the Volga River, not far from the confluence with the Kama River. Bolghar was the intermittent capital city of the Volga Bulgar along with Bilar and Suvar.

The reason they had to move their capital city from one place to another was due to Russian incursions. The Russian pirates invaded and sacked Bulgar whenever they had a chance. In a normal situation, the city of Bolghar was the most populated and prominent one. It had a lot of good points as a trading center being located near the confluence of the Volga and Kama Rivers, north to south, which was an easy transportation route through the water and an easy land course through the east and west.

The city was already in a panic. The survivors from the city of Bilar truthfully completed the task that the Mongols wanted: passing the words of terror. They witnessed and described the horror of scenes that they never could have imagined.

Unfortunately, the city of Bolghar was not fortified as strongly as Bilar. Actually, it was a harbor city. The city of

CHAPTER 17

Bilar was built under the concept of protection whereas the city of Bolghar was built for the best commercial success and the convenience of trading.

The leaders of the city convened a meeting and said, "We'd better surrender. We already know what has fallen onto the people of Bilar ... no survivors! Survival is the utmost choice that we have to consider."

However, another voice was much stronger.

"If we surrender, we will end up becoming their slaves! Our boys will become their instruments on the battlefield or human shields for enemy arrows. And our girls will be nothing more than their toys for entertainment and pleasure. Which way do you want to go?"

They refused to surrender, which was another beginning of tragedy and horror. Their resistance lasted for three days. The Mongol bombardment from the catapults breached the stone wall and made an opening. Through the opening, the Mongol heavy cavalry unit poured in. Inside the city, street fighting lasted for half a day.

After three days of killing and plundering, the city was set on fire. The city had two main gates—one on the southern front and the other facing north, which was connected to the harbor. Many of the citizens and residents jumped into the river; however, unfortunately for them, the river at that point was enormously wide and choppy. It was extremely challenging, and most of them perished. On the field, outside of the city, another 2,000 impalements were displayed.

The chronicler Faqih Ashraf Aziz wrote:

SURRENDER OF PURESH

When you walk through the forest of impaled human bodies, you feel like you are walking through the death valley or the gate of hell. Their wailing, screaming, sighing and lamenting makes your heart stop. The already dead faces with their unfocused eyes make you chilly—even in the summertime. The unbearable decaying odor invites numerous flies. From the bottom of the ground, the ants come out and cover the posts with the still-alive human bodies. When they set fire to the entire city, the flames and smoke reached the zenith and lasted for three days. I saw the jahannam [hell].

The chronicler Chun Lee wrote:

Many citizens and residents refused to leave their homes and remained inside. As the flames and smoke enveloped their homes, horrible screaming burst out like a chorus. Some came out with their children in their hands but soon perished under the Mongol swords and spears. About seven days later, the city changed into an endless pile of soot. The city had been leveled.

The Mongols continued their conquest. Like a tempest, they destroyed every city, town and village in their path. Nobody knew how many lives had perished.

At about this time, the horrible news reached Puresh's ear. Puresh was the kanazor (ruler) of the Murunza Kingdom in the middle of the Volga region. He was worried about the whole Volga Bulgar race's annihilation from Earth. Based on the report from his men, almost all the population had perished where the Mongol soldiers stepped, with very few survivors.

Puresh held a meeting and discussed this situation with his son Narchat and other important officials.

After he looked around all the attendants, he said, "Now the Mongols are here—only a half-day's marching distance. We all heard about their atrocities and mercilessness. At this time, we are in an important moment to decide which way we have to go: living or dying."

There was a deep silence because they all knew they could not stop the Mongol tidal wave.

Suddenly, Narchat shouted, "Let's fight to the last man! I would prefer glorious death than disgraceful survival!"

Puresh said in a peaceful but strong tone, "My son, I understand your mood; however, in life, there's always a moment when you have to consider choosing reality over pride. That's the way you can win in the long run. We need the next generation of our own."

No one dared to comment on Puresh's remark. They decided to make an unconditional surrender. They sent a messenger to Batu's headquarters, which was about 5 miles away from the city. Two translators worked on the letter, which was written in Latin to translate into the Mongol script. After careful review, Batu handed the letter to Subedei.

Early the following morning, the Mongol main body marched toward Bolghar and arrived at the point about a half mile from the city's main gate. Puresh, his son Narchat and all the important people in the kingdom opened the gate and came out to see Batu, their conqueror. They had already unarmed their soldiers, about 10,000 of them, and piled up all the weapons and armors in the front of the gate.

Batu set up the temporary war camp and received Puresh and his group. Two Moksha girls in their traditional costumes stepped out from their group and presented silver plates stacked with salts and bread, which were the symbol of welcome. Then, they presented two white horses, which was the symbol of surrender. Puresh stepped out, knelt on one leg and bowed, which meant complete submission. Puresh also brought a group of Mordvin-Moksha beauties, 20 of them, as a gift to Batu.

Batu remarked loudly, "Our meaning of surrender is not simply giving up resistance. You and your people should be a part of us. We should pursue the same goal. Are you ready for that?"

After receiving these words through the interpreter, Puresh bowed again, giving the sign of consent.

After Puresh and his group left, Batu dispatched Boroldai Noyan to take over the city.

Batu shared the conversation with Subedei and asked, "Can we trust him?"

Subedei answered, "For now, maybe. We need them for our Russian expedition as a guide, and they should be our vanguard."

Batu nodded.

When Batu was very young, he had heard many things from the Great One, Genghis Khan, including this: "You should develop your intuition. All people have five senses. You need more than these to lead others and make it in the world. From the early ages, I tried to understand nature. I learned many things from nature. All living creatures on this earth are constantly struggling to survive, and the conflict goes on every day and in every moment. Many creatures have their extraordinary instinct for survival. You might be able to develop this talent that the others don't have. For example, many living creatures fake death to fool their predators. On the battlefield, you need the sense to differentiate the real dead body or enemy soldiers faking death.

"When you are marching, you should sense if there's any danger lurking over the hill, in the forests, across the river and more. You should sense that the enemy captive is telling a lie or the truth—even among your own men. When you are talking to someone, you should sense what is on their mind and what they want. You should understand the mosaic of the human mind and the power balance and the flow of nature. For all these, you should find it yourself. That's the only and meaningful way to achieve this very valuable, much-needed talent for your survival."

The chronicler Faqih Ashraf Aziz wrote:

By surrendering, Puresh saved his Mordvin-Moksha people, 200,000 of them. Those were the only group of people that escaped the Mongol tidal wave among one million Volga Bulgar population. Did he do the right thing?

The chronicler Chun Lee wrote:

After the completion of the conquest of the Volga Bulgar, the Mongols began to categorize the population. First, they picked up leather workers and gold and silver artisans to send them to Sighnaq, the capital city of White Ordu, along with mountains of war booties. Sighnaq was the temporary warehouse for Batu. They were allowed to accompany their family members. Secondly, they picked up levies and, among them, if they were qualified and pledged loyalty to the Mongols, they could be put into the Mongol vanguards. From that moment on, they must fight for the Mongols.

CHAPTER 18

Conquest of Cumania

Cumans and Kipchaks are basically the same nomadic people of Turkic origin. Hungarians called them Cuman, Russians called them Polovit and Mongols called them Kipchak. In reality, they were subdivided into two large tribes: one that lived in the lower Volga area and the other that lived in the area between the Volga River and the Don River.

Batu divided the left-wing group, 30,000 of them, into two groups of 15,000 each, and gave one group to his cousin Monku and the other to his younger brother Berke. Monku headed to the south to deal with one group of Kipchaks, which was led by Batchman, and Berke headed to the west of the Volga to meet the other group, which was led by Koten. Monku, with his younger brother Bujek, pursued Batchman. Since they were nomadic, like Mongols, they didn't build houses but instead spread out over the large area.

Before they left, Subedei gave them a piece of advice.

"Since they are spread out in a large area, you must use the tactic like we do in hunting. Cover a large area and gradually close it. They will be like hunting games in the encirclement."

They moved to the south along the Volga River. They advanced in a semicircular form. Once they found a large group of Kipchaks in their encirclement, they began to close it. A great number of Kipchaks fell into this encirclement. They slaughtered all the Kipchaks who showed resistance. Pillaging and plundering were common in the conquered area. They picked up the levies among the captives and continued their march. They marched for seven days and still couldn't find a trace of Batchman and his main Kipchak army.

Monku and Bujek moved slowly, side by side, on horseback along the riverbank. They moved further south. It was late afternoon, and the river water was choppy but shiny. It reflected the afternoon sun's ray, and it looked peaceful.

Suddenly, Bujek raised his arm and pointed to something on the water's surface. It looked like dead human bodies. There were so many of them that it looked like the whole river was covered with them.

Monku stopped his horse and ordered his men to pick up one of them. The soldiers fished one out with a hooked spear. Monku dismounted his horse, neared the body and carefully examined it. The dead body looked like a Bulgar man.

Monku murmured, "Batu took the city of Bolghar!"

Monku routinely dispatched scout units ahead of him as he advanced to get information on the whereabouts of the enemy's main body, but it was to no avail.

When they passed one area, Monku noticed a very old woman sitting on the side of the road. She looked frail and vulnerable, and even small movements weren't comfortable for her. Monku stopped the horse at this curious and unusual scene and sent a soldier to ask her why she was there.

Through an interpreter, she answered, "I was with my family, but when I got tired and could not keep pace with them, they abandoned me. They didn't even leave any food."

Monku took pity on her. He ordered his soldiers to leave some food and something to drink. The soldiers left her a dried flat cake, some dried mutton and a bagful of sheep's milk. When Monku was ready to leave the spot, the old woman raised her hand and pointed somewhere. Monku sent the same soldier to find out what she was trying to tell him.

The soldier came back and said, "About a half day's walking distance to the south, there is a large island covered with a thick forest. All the Kipchak soldiers and people went there to hide."

Monku was stunned to get this valuable piece of information unexpectedly. He immediately dispatched a scouting unit. Before dark, the scouting unit came back with the report that what the old woman said was true.

Based on this report, Monku discussed his battle plan with his brother and generals and announced, "They think they are well protected by the river and forest, but it's opposite! They entrapped themselves. We will attack them with fire!"

The following day, the Mongols assembled the catapults and got ready for the barges. Monku brought about 100 barges in case they crossed the river or needed a landing operation. One barge was large enough to carry up to 100 soldiers and 100 horses. Both the Mongol soldiers and the horses were well trained in the water. When they were ready, they left very early in the morning to get to the island before dawn.

At daybreak, the Mongols commenced their attack. The catapults that were stationed at the riverbank shot big balls of naphtha flame and tar into the island forest. Flames and smoke enveloped the forest where Batchman and his 20,000 soldiers were hiding. It didn't take long to put them into ultimate chaos.

On the southern side of the island, there was a wide beach. All the astonished and shocked Kipchak horses and soldiers showed up on the beach, escaping the fire and smoke. This was the time that the Mongol landing operation began. A big massacre started. The beach sand was stained with Kipchak blood, and so was the river. It didn't take long before the Mongol landing unit dominated their opponents in this battle.

Finally, after more than half of the Kipchak soldiers were massacred, they gave up. Batchman was brought in front of Monku.

Monku asked him, "Do you want to live or die?"

Batchman, with his hands tied back and kneeling, answered clearly and with a loud voice, "I want to die. I refuse shameful living!"

Monku slowly pulled out his scimitar and, with one breath, cut off his head. For some moments, blood spurted out from his severed neck and stained the sands.

What's in there, deep inside the human mind?
Selfishness.

CHAPTER 18

*What are they craving most, deep inside in the human
    mind?*
Respect.
What are they angry at most, deep inside the human mind?
Ignorance.
*What gives the most powerful motivation to the human
    mind?*
Compassion.

While Monku was subjugating the Kipchaks, Berke marched westward, chasing Koten and his people; however, Koten was a wounded deer. He already experienced Mongol ferocity at the Kalka River and already heard what had fallen upon the Volga Bulgars. He heard that Batu's great army had arrived and was nearby. He decided to give up a meaningless, head-on confrontation and seek refuge at this moment.

With his 40,000 huts (households), Koten moved to Hungary; however, many Cumans remained on their own land, trying to defend their territory, but Berke easily subjugated them. Berke amassed about 20,000 levies among the Cumans.

CHAPTER 19

The Arab merchants

B atu decided to stay near the city of Bolghar for some
time to consolidate the conquered land and get himself ready for the expedition to the Russian mainland.
He knew that the soldiers needed some rest, so he waited for
reinforcement from the Mongol mainland. He was expecting
30,000 more imperial cavalry units before he stepped into the
Russian soil; however, the most important consideration in
the Russian campaign was timing and weather.

Subedei mentioned strongly, "We should go there in the
winter when the river and the earth are frozen. Our horses
might not be able to move freely on the wet, marshy and
muddy land."

In the summertime, most of the Russian land was covered
with marsh and mire and, in some areas, many spots were
deep enough to swallow men and their horses.

One day, a group of Arab merchants made an honest
request for an audience to Batu Khan. Bilguun Cherbi, the
captain of Batu's 1,000 day guards, approached Batu and
reported their request.

Batu asked, "What is the purpose of their visit?"

CHAPTER 19

Bilguun answered, "I don't know in detail, but they seem to have some request for their business."

Batu allowed two of them to meet him in his war tent. Both men wore cream-colored, long tunics that covered their whole body. On their heads, similarly colored scarves and black ropes were gently donned. They both had thick beards and mustaches.

One of them said, "Great Khan and the great conqueror, the ruler of a million men and owner of the land from ocean to ocean, God's right hand to fulfill God's ordainment on this earth. It is a great pleasure and honor to see you. We are giving you the heartiest appreciation for the generous granting of your attention."

Batu nodded and said, "I admire your silvery tongue and flowery words. Go on!"

"My name is Ahmed, and his name is Qadir. We are from the desert land close to Jerusalem. We are traveling merchants. We buy and sell merchandise for profit. During earlier times, we worked with the Mongol army—even back to the times of the sacred Great One whose name is so great that I cannot even put his name on my tongue." He put his right hand on his forehead and bowed.

Batu nodded again. "Go on!"

The Arab merchant tried to explain that some Mongol captains didn't allow them to contact the soldiers, so they could not do smooth business. They were seeking Batu's permission for free business for mutual benefit. Batu knew that where the Mongol army went, the Arab merchants always followed. It was like when big fishing boats went to the sea or the ocean, flocks of sea birds like seagulls followed. Batu also knew that it was of mutual benefit, and his soldiers needed them too.

Batu called Dawa, who oversaw Batu's army supply unit, and asked, "How many groups of caravans are out there who try to deal with our soldiers?"

"I believe there are almost 60 of them. Each group consists of 40 to 200 men, and they deal with a variety of items."

Batu learned that the most popular items for the Mongol soldiers were all kinds of nuts (almonds, walnuts, pistachios, ginko nuts and betel nuts), dried fruit, dates, dried rice cakes, sorghum flour, wheat flour, small hand instruments, clothing, furs and even chain mail (a protective, tiny, metal ring mesh in the form of a shirt), which was not supplied by their military unit. On the other hand, the Arab merchants bought everything from soldiers who had looted, like jewelry, gold and silver utensils, decorative items from palaces and churches and any kind of valuables.

At the time, the property concept for the Mongols included humans. The captives from the battleground or enemy citizens could be slaves, so they could be sold; however, citizens of surrendered cities were treated differently and not as slaves. When the Mongols attacked a city or a region, for three days the soldiers were allowed to plunder and loot. Once the battles were over, they had to report what they had gotten.

Army officials divided the newly acquired properties for each soldier and, until the officials' judgments came out, it was not the soldiers' property. Usually, one fifth of the acquired property went to the khagan in the Mongol mainland, another fifth went to Batu Khan and the remaining three fifths were for the soldiers.

Batu ordered Dawa to make a list of the items that each Mongol soldier could buy or sell. For the merchants, they had to register the name of their group and pay taxes based on their profit. When all these conditions were satisfied, a paiza (a guarantee for safety and supplies) was issued to them. Only the merchant group with a paiza could do business and was protected.

Individual soldiers were not allowed to possess any slaves. All the slaves were the property of the Mongol Empire. The price for the slaves was cheaper than the price for horses. For the Arab merchants, slave trading was the important part of their business, and some of their groups were specialized exclusively in the slave business. Throughout the campaign, enormous numbers of Kipchaks were sold or exchanged for gold, and many of them were exported to lands as far as Egypt.

Batu issued these decrees:

Decree 1: From now on, each Mongol soldier can have commercial activity of buying and selling only through the merchant group with a paiza.

Decree 2: Each soldier can buy and sell the items only on the list.

Decree 3: Any soldier who violates the above two decrees shall be punished with the same degree as theft.

THE ARAB MERCHANTS

At that time, Mongol army law punished theft. If it was intentional and above a certain level, the punishment was death.

Batu met the two Arab merchants again and granted the paiza.

The two merchants bowed deeply and said, "Your wisdom and generosity will remain in people's mouths for 1,000 years!"

In return, they left one Arabic dagger with a golden handle, which was decorated with a precious stone fit for a king or an emperor, as well as seven high-quality pearl necklaces for his seven wives and concubines.

CHAPTER 20

A man called Ivan Vladimirovits

The year had changed. In the year of 1237, Batu was in the middle part of the Volga River for a few months. It was late summer, and there was a big rainstorm and deluge in the area. Due to the swelling of the river, Batu's whole ordu had to move to a higher location. According to the natives, this was the rainy season; nonetheless, it was an exceptionally longer one. Luckily, the Mongol soldiers were ready for the hay and fodder before this unusually strong hit from nature.

Batu was having dinner with his usual group in his usual dinner tent, which could accommodate up to 60 people. They put carpets on the ground, and numerous cushions were available. The diners could use one or two cushions to make themselves sit comfortably. Batu's seat was always arranged on the northernmost spot. Princes and generals usually sat on his right, and his wives and concubines were on his left, making a half circle. Sometimes his brothers sat immediately to his right, and other times it was Subedei or someone whom Batu designated.

On that day, Subedei was sitting next to Batu. There were about 30 diners and about 20 cooks and servers. In wartime on the field, they rarely set up the dinner table and chairs, so the servers would walk around and pick up the wasted material or used utensils.

The first course was boiled sheep's head. The server held a big, silver plate with the head on it and stood in front of Batu. Batu picked up the small serving knife and cut off his favorite part of the sheep's head: the lip. Then the server moved to Subedei. For the women's side, a different group of servers was doing the same job but with a different plate.

The next course was boiled mutton. The two servers held an even larger plate with a whole cooked sheep, which was precut and repositioned in its original shape. The diners could tell which part of the sheep they were choosing.

Traditionally, the next course would be vegetable soup or stew mixed with mutton, wild onions, garlic and a local vegetable. The Mongols ate vegetables and fruit, even in small amounts, to avoid getting scurvy.

The typical final course was dessert—usually fresh fruit, dried fruit or yogurt. Their usual drink was cow's milk, sheep's milk or kumiss, which was a fermented mare's milk. On that day, the dessert was local watermelon.

After dinner, they would occasionally see guests or visitors. They also had entertainment, which was usually women dancing or singing. People from the conquered lands would also tell stories or play musical instruments.

Bilguun Cherbi, the captain of Batu's 1,000 day guards, came into the tent and reported that Batu had a visitor. Before dinner, Batu had gotten a report that he had a visitor and decided to give him an audience after dinner.

A man stepped into the tent and bowed to Batu, bending one knee, and Batu gave him a gesture to stand up. The man was over 6 feet tall and had shoulder-length hair and a thick beard and mustache. He had a prominent nose and a steep chin. His deep-set eyes showed that he was a Slavic Russian rather than a Kipchak Turk. He was wearing a worn-out, dirty fur coat, which looked wet from the weather.

He said, "Great Khan, my name is Ivan Vladimirovits, and my father's name was Gleb Vladimirovits. At one time, my father was the ruler of the city of Ryazan, a rightful one. The city of Ryazan was founded about 150 years ago and, ever since then, numerous princes had to be killed through internal strife. It was like a dog-eat-dog fight, and the people of Ryazan never enjoyed peace. When my father became the rightful ruler, he made a plan to put an end to the rivalry and the never-ending strife once and for all. He invited all the troublesome princes in one place and sent them to hell."

At this point, Batu gestured for the storytelling to stop.

Batu turned to Subedei, who was sitting next to him, and asked, "Do you believe his story?"

After a moment, Subedei replied, "Maybe half of it. Gleb Vladimirovits invited a total of eight princes, but only six showed up. He killed all six with the help of Cuman mercenaries. The other two princes who didn't show up survived, and one of them was Yuri Igorevich, the current ruler of Ryazan."

Batu nodded. He understood most of the Russian's words, even though there was an interpreter. He knew some languages besides Mongolian, thanks to his schooling at

Yelu-chuchai's school. He was also surrounded by servants from many different backgrounds, cultures and languages from an early age.

Batu turned to the visitor and told him to continue.

"My father had to face the revenge from one of the survived princes, Yuri Igorevich, who instigated a public revolt, and then finally made my father leave. Ever since then, my father could never step back onto Russian soil until he died, so he stayed on the Polovits' land."

At this point, Batu stopped his story. "So, what do you want from us?"

"Great Khan, I still believe that my father was the rightful heir to the city of Ryazan. I believe that the current ruler, Yuri Igorevich, is not the rightful one and is my father's enemy. I want to be a guide when you move into this city."

After a brief silence, Batu asked, "Is there any way you can prove that you are the son of Gleb Vladimirovits?"

The Russian took off a ring from the middle finger of his left hand, handed it to Bilguun Cherbi and Bilguun brought it to Batu. It was a gold ring with a sapphire. On the inside of the ring, the Latin inscription said, "Gleb Vladimirovits."

Batu returned the ring and gave him permission to stay in the Mongol army, putting him in the guiding and pacifying unit.

If you don't know the history of a man,
You will misunderstand him.
If you don't know the history of the people,
You will misunderstand them.
If you don't know the history of the world,
You will misunderstand the world.

CHAPTER 21

Batu's advance into Russia

On the northern land, winter arrived early. In early December, the Volga River was frozen. It was the time that Batu and his Mongol army had been waiting for. Batu had already received the reinforcement of 30,000 cavalry from the mainland, making a total of 150,000 under his commandership. It took three days to cross the river. The front liners consisted of the surrendered Bulgars and Moksha warriors, who were guides as well as vanguards.

The Mongol army was divided into three groups, and each group crossed the river in a different location as a safety measure. In Batu's main group, five khans joined him: Orda, Berke, Kadan, Bury and Kulqan. After regrouping, they marched toward the west. On their way to Ryazan, they swept the small cities and towns like a tempest. They devastated Bilogorod, Isteslawetz and Pronsk.

The Mongol strategy for attacking big cities was to ruin the surroundings for isolation, which would cut the supply line and create emotional pressure for the enemies, who would lose their fighting spirit and eventually surrender.

On December 7, 1237, the Mongol army approached a point that was 5 miles from the gate to Ryazan.

The garrison soldier of Ryazan saw something very unusual on the faraway eastern horizon, which he could never have imagined. He called out to other garrison member on duty, and both men carefully examined the unusual images. Due to the snowfall on the previous day, the whole world was covered with snow. The dark images, which covered the horizon from one corner to the other, were subtle yet moving and growing.

Soon, they discovered that the images were of numerous men and horses. The Mongols had arrived! They had never before seen such a humongous number of men and horses. Soon they heard the clattering of horses' hoofs, rumbling like huge rocks rolling on a gravel field. The sights and sounds, which were like standing in front of a tidal wave, scared them.

The garrison captain and other citizens wondered, "Who are they, and why they are here?"

The Mongols stopped approaching when they were a safe distance from the city.

Early the following morning, from the Mongol side, three horses galloped and neared the gate to the city of Ryazan.

When they arrived in front of the gate, a woman shouted loudly, "Open the gate! We are the messengers from the great khan Batu. We have a message for you!"

The people on the wall whispered to each other, "She seems to be a sorceress! She will curse and bring the evil spirits upon us!"

The woman shouted again to no avail. The gate never opened, and eventually the riders of the three horses returned. The woman, who had been chosen, could speak colloquial language, the same language—Russian—as the people inside the city used.

Later, a man from the Mongol side approached the gate.

He shouted to the people on the wall, "Open up! My name is Ivan Vladimirovits, the son of Gleb Vladimirovits. Everybody in this city knows my father. Now I am with the Mongols. God is on the Mongol side! Don't put yourself in the whirlpool of destruction. Save yourself! Save your children and your children's children!"

This time, Yuri Igorevich showed up with his son Feodor.

Yuri shouted to the man on the horse, "Your father was the enemy of the people of Ryazan! That's why he was kicked out! Now you are working for the Mongols. You are a betrayer of the whole Russian people. Tell your new master that I will send my own messenger to talk to him directly."

On the same day, Yuri Igorevich summoned his retinue to figure out the best possible option and asked, "What do they want? Why are they here?"

Nobody dared to give a quick answer.

After a brief silence, Boyar Nicolas reluctantly opened his mouth. "Probably, they are here for looting. Nomads are not independent people. They cannot produce everything they need. They constantly have to attack other people to satisfy their needs. So, in my opinion, the best bet is to give them what they are asking."

Many of the 20 people at the meeting nodded in agreement.

However, one young man in the back seat showed a sign of disagreement and said, "No! There are too many for that cause. Their numbers are more than the stars in the sky. The best way is to talk to them directly and find out what they want."

The following morning, a group from the city headed for Batu's camp. The heads of the group were Prince Feodor and Boyar Nicolas, and with them were about 30 guards and porters. They were carrying a big chest of gold and silver coins, and another chest was full of precious stones and pearls. On their gift list were about 15 of the finest Russian stallions, five big pots of old mead and 10 horse loads of luxurious furs, including ermines.

The group arrived at Batu's camp in the afternoon; however, the audience had not been allowed immediately and had to wait until dinnertime. Finally, when they were allowed to step into Batu's tent, almost 40 people were dining there, making a half circle. Only Prince Feodor, Boyar Nicolas and the voivode (general) Andrey were allowed to enter; however, there were no seats or tables arranged for them. They didn't know what to do, so they were just standing there.

Ivan Vladimirovits stood up and shouted in a loud voice, "Kowtow! Bow! Touch your forehead on the ground! You are uninvited guests. That's why you don't have seats. You are facing the great conqueror and future tsar of Russia! Bow!"

Still standing, Feodor lowered his head lightly and said, "Greetings, tsar of the Mongols! I came here for peace. I have already heard the great name of Genghis Khan, and I also know that you are his grandson. We can build up a great relationship based on mutual respect and cooperation. We can expect common prosperity by supplying what we need from each other as good neighbors and as equal partners. That's what we want, and that's why we are here!"

Batu gestured to his nearby servants to make seats for them and serve the food. The servants brought cushions and put the wooden plates on the ground in front of each of them. The usual Mongol food was designed to be picked up with fingers and eaten without utensils—even with soup, porridge or stew was in a bowl.

Sadly, the regular dinner among the attendants was almost finished, and the food that the servants brought looked like leftovers.

Feodor and the others whispered, "We are not welcome here! We might be lucky if we can get out of here with our lives. Let's not make them upset."

After dinner, Batu said to the visitors, "I know that you have brought some gifts. We always have entertainment after dinner, such as singing, dancing or storytelling. What did you bring in that regard?"

Ivan Vladimirovits, who was sitting below Batu, turned and whispered to Batu, "His wife is a Greek princess, and her beauty is well known throughout Europe. You should see her."

Batu added, "I just heard that your wife has extreme beauty. Why don't you bring her here to amuse us with her beauty?"

Feodor replied, "It is not our culture to boast of the beauty of married woman to other men. If you have a second choice, let me know."

A dark cloud passed over Batu's face as he spat out, "This man continues to be equal to me!"

Batu's wives and concubines whispered to each other and giggled, "He is a real man!"

Batu jumped up abruptly and said in a loud voice, "Listen up! I am here as your conqueror—not as a friend! I am here to fulfill God's ordainment to conquer all of the western lands, all the way to the other side of the Great Ocean. You and your people have only two choices: surrender or die! Which one you want?"

Feodor stood up as well. "Over our dead bodies! You can have what you want after all of us have died!"

Feodor and his entourage kicked out the flap door. Subedei glanced at Batu and tried to imagine what Batu's reaction would be.

Batu shouted, "Yukel!" (Yukel meant "death" in Mongolian.)

Batu declared his sentence and Subedei and Bilguun Cherbi immediately stepped out.

Sometime later, Subedei came back with a report.

"They are all dead; however, I allowed the second man, Boyar Nicolas, to go back to their place and tell them what has happened today."

Batu nodded without comment.

CHAPTER 22

Sorrow of Princess Euphrasia

The Mongols threw away the dead bodies of Prince Feodor and his accompanied guards and other members, about 30 of them, into the nearby forest. The prince's neck was almost severed, so his head was still connected to the body but only with some skin. In this kind of situation, dead bodies were taken within a few days by forest scavengers, like wolves, wild dogs, bears and foxes.

The four Mongol horse soldiers escorted Boyar Nicolas, the lone survivor, to the farthest Mongol post. He was on his own horseback. Yet, with his two hands tied behind him, one of the Mongol soldiers had to guide his horse and hold the reins. When they arrived at the last Mongol post, they could see the faraway image of the city of Ryazan. They untied Boyar Nicolas and handed the reins to him.

One of the Mongol soldiers raised his hand and pointed. "Gerti kari! Gerti kari!" meaning "Go home!"

Boyar Nicolas hesitated and then acknowledged the meaning and galloped toward the city.

As he approached the main gate, he shouted, "Open the gate! Urgent news! Terrible!"

The garrison soldiers recognized Boyar Nicolas and opened the gate immediately. In no time, he rushed to the palace to report the sad news, and the guard soldier ushered him into the prince's living chamber. Prince Yuri was astonished at the news and an image of sadness was imbued on his face.

"They gave us two options: surrender or death," Boyar Nicolas explained. "When Prince Feodor refused surrender, they killed him—all of us—but they didn't kill me so they could use me to make a report."

Prince Yuri stared into space, and then spat out, "I wouldn't have surrendered either!"

He immediately dispatched urgent messengers to Roman Igorevich of Kolomna, Grand Prince Yuri Vsevolodovich of Vladimir and Prince Mikhail of Chernigov, warning them of the approaching danger and requesting help.

Yet, time wasn't on his side, and it was too late. The messengers galloped their horses for hundreds of miles without pause and arrived at the city of Kolumna and then at Vladimir. Kolumna, a fortressed city, was in the middle part of Ryazan and Vladimir. Roman Igorevich was in charge of Kolumna and Yuri Igorevich's brother; however, Yuri wasn't ready or couldn't realize the seriousness of the situation at Ryazan. Upon receiving the urgent message, he couldn't make a quick decision. Deep inside his mind, he was lacking the strong motivation to give a helping hand to the neighboring princedom.

He said to the messengers, "Sorry, we have to protect this city," so there was no immediate help.

CHAPTER 22

On the other hand, Princess Euphrasia couldn't sleep very well after she bid farewell to her husband Prince Feodor. She was a Greek princess who was married to a Russian prince, according to the European monarchical tradition in which a princess was married only to a prince. It had been about a year and a half since she stepped onto Russian soil and, in her arms, she was holding a four-month-old baby named Ivan Feodorovich, who was the firstborn and only son of Feodor. When she came from the Greek land, she had almost 30 personal retainers and servants, including a dresser, a hairstylist, cooks and storytellers. One of them was Konstantina, her wet nurse when she was a baby, who always stayed with her and never left her for even a single day.

Princess Euphrasia had noticed unusual movements and noises around the palace, which added more uneasiness to her already sad mind.

"I am going to make a deal with the toughest people on Earth. Everything will be fine. It will take a day or two. Take good care of the baby." Prince Yuri left with these words behind.

At this moment, Konstantina hurriedly stepped into her room. Princess Euphrasia's heart sank when she looked at Konstantina's face because it was very unusual to see it full of frustration, deep sorrow and despair.

"Princess! Princess! I cannot tell you this story myself. You had better see Boyar Nicolas and listen to him directly."

After handing over the baby to Konstantina, Euphrasia stepped down to see Boyar Nicolas. Boyar Nicolas knelt in front of the princess and couldn't raise his head for a while.

After hearing the full story, Euphrasia went into her bed-room and didn't come out. All through the night, she wept in deep sorrow and pondered her destiny and future. When she heard that her beauty had been the topic of unhappy conversation between the Mongol khan and the prince and that it became an accelerating factor for a wrongful outcome, she despaired. She felt like falling into an abyss from which she could never crawl back.

"I might had been cursed by something, but what could it be?"

Before daybreak, she made up her mind. She went into the top room in the palace and opened the window. It was a five-story building, and the ground level of the palace was covered with hard, flat stones. She jumped from the window with the baby in her arms. Her dead body was found by the garrison guards. She died with her eyes open. From her mouth, nose and ears, blood flowed. She was holding the baby tightly, but it was dead too.

CHAPTER 23

The fall of Ryazan

Batu and Subedei, side by side on horseback, looked around the city of Ryazan from afar. The city was protected by the natural defense of a deep river named Oka on the west side and artificial earthwork on the east. It was a big city, positioned on a flat, high hill, occupying a large area and surrounded by a wooden wall and towers.

Batu said, "Orlok, what is their defensive power and population?"

Subedei gave his answer without pausing. "They have 10,000 of defensive power that is garrison, and their peacetime population could be around 20,000; however, the number could be doubled because of the refugees."

When the Mongols attacked a big or main city, they usually did preemptive strikes first where they swept away the surrounding small towns and villages to let the surviving population move into the city. They did all good things for the attacking Mongols, making the defense more difficult. The swelled population emptied the reserved food and water faster and told their neighbors about the horror of the Mongols, escalating the panic. It was psychological warfare. In case the city dwellers refused to accept the refugees, the Mongols used them as human shields, making them attack the city. They had to kill each other for their own lives.

Later that day at a war council, Batu declared, "Ryazan is the first city in my Russian campaign, and they refused to surrender. I presumed that their resistance would be fierce. What could be our choice?"

Subedei responded in a high tone, "I think we have to make this city an example. We have to show them what could happen to them when they ignore us."

It seemed that all the participants in this war council agreed.

Batu remarked, "My revered war counsel is quite right. We must show them our power. We must destroy their spirit of resistance completely! We have a long way to go, and we must show them our determination from the beginning!"

After this declaration, they discussed all the detailed tactics and strategies.

The Mongol attack commenced on December 16, 1237. First, they used catapults for the bombardment of rocks and flaming naphtha. The city had dark smoke everywhere, and soon many buildings were enveloped with flames. Continuously hammering the wall with rocks produced gradual damage and eventually tore it down or made holes.

The Mongol commandoes, with ladders, climbed the steep earth hill to the broken wall. The defenders threw large logs and rocks toward the climbing attackers, and the battle continued. The huge battering ram, designed to be handled by more than 100 people, was used to break down the main city gate. The workers for the battering ram were mostly captives of the Russians and levies from previous campaigns.

It took two days for the Mongols to break down the walls and the gate. Once they stepped into the city, the street fighting began, but soon the defending power collapsed. The streets were covered with dead bodies of defending soldiers as well as citizens. Blood from the dying bodies blocked the street drainage system, making it flow everywhere.

Prince Yuri Igorevich tried to reorganize his garrison troops at the northern end of the city but failed. The last man standing on the Russian side collapsed. The resistance ended. The city became quiet; however, it was like a stillness just before the tempest. An indescribable atrocity and a grand-scale massacre had begun.

The chronicler Faqih Ashraf Aziz wrote:

I saw the hell! The city of Ryazan fell to the Mongols on December 21, 1237. I am the eyewitness. I am writing this for future historians and people in general. I believe that future generations should know about this, and it is my duty and obligation given from God. All mighty God, forgive me.

The horrible thing began from inside the church. Many people were inside the church praying and singing the hymn. The Mongol soldiers broke into the church and pushed all of the worshipers into one corner. They selectively picked up all the young girls and women, including nuns. They took off their clothing forcefully and began to rape. It was being done while their parents, husbands and brothers watched. Any resistant one lost his or her life instantaneously by losing their head or had their chest pierced by a spear. Same thing happened in all four churches in the city and in the palace. It lasted quite a while.

After this, they locked the gates and all the doors and lit the fire. Soon the church was enveloped with fire and thick smoke. The people inside screamed, and some of them tried to break down the door. If they were successful and came out, they would only end up with Mongol arrows. The Mongols picked up royal and aristocratic members, men and women, took off their clothes, tied their hands back with rope and put them on the board, face down in a prone position.

Then they began to impale. For this purpose, they used a sharp, pointed, wooden pole at one side, about 7-8 feet long. Then, two Mongol soldiers held the victim from both sides, and a third man hammered the pole into the victim's anus or vagina. When the tip reached halfway through the body, they erected the pole and secured it into the prepared ground hole. The victim's body weight did the rest of the job. The sharp, pointed tip of the wooden post traveled through the body and eventually came out through the chest or neck. They made human skewers, all 400 of them, and displayed them in the nontraffic area of the city. Among these victims was the Ryazan ruler, Prince Yuri Igorevich.

After this, the Mongol soldiers, three to five of them in a group, began individual looting and plundering. They searched each house, almost all of them half burnt, took all the valuables if there were any, and continued to kill and rape.

The chronicler, Chun Lee, wrote:

They even killed children and babies. It seemed that they tried to eliminate all the life forms in this city. They burned the priests to death, tied them on the posts with a pile of wood under their feet and lit the fire. Almost 20 priests and some old nuns were among the victims. Amazingly, they rarely screamed, and even some of them were praying and singing a hymn while they were in flames. I am sure that I am the condemned one to be born in this world at this time.

Batu conducted a funeral ceremony for the fallen Mongol soldiers. They found about 400 dead bodies of their comrade soldiers and put them on a wooden structure designed for a funeral process with a huge pile of wood underneath it. They lit the fire. It was evening, and mountainous flames enveloped the structure in no time, making the large surrounding area look like daytime.

Batu shouted:

Brothers! Farewell!
I thank thee!
A man should die with the scimitar in his hand!
A man should die on his horseback!
A man should die in the battlefield!
You died like God!
You will live forever,
In the name of the great warrior,
In the name of the great conqueror,
In the glory of the Mongols,
Until the human race remains on this earth!
Until the end of the time!

THE FALL OF RYAZAN

The Mongols systematically leveled the whole city of Ryazan, and it disappeared from Earth forever.

Greek mythology (night one)

There were about 200 survivors in the city of Ryazan. The Mongols spared them to serve as eyewitnesses and messengers for other Russians. They were set free and allowed to go to neighboring places to warn others about the Mongol ferocity that was near them. That's what the Mongols wanted them to do.

Among the survivors was Konstantina, a middle-aged woman, and an old female cook named Acacia. They were both from Greece and used to be the retainers of Princess Euphrasia. When Batu heard about them, he decided to spare them because he had been told that both were talented: one was good for storytelling about Greek mythology and the other for cooking. Konstantina also used to be the wet nurse for Princess Euphrasia. Wherever Batu went, he didn't hesitate to try local or foreign food but only used the food that his own cooks prepared. He encouraged his cooks to learn how to prepare the local cuisine.

At the dinner table one night, Batu was served a dark-colored soup and asked, "What is this?"

The chief chef answered. "This is Greek-style black soup made from boar's feet and blood. I learned it from the Greek cook today. All the food I am serving today is in the Greek style. Let me know if you like it, my lord."

Batu picked up the bowl, sipped a little bit and then put it aside. The next course was a barley flat cake soaked with honey, and Batu finished it. The following course included baked ducks and geese followed by smoked young goats. The last serving was a dessert of Greek-style yogurt.

After dinner, it was the entertainment hour. All eyes fell on Konstantina, who was standing in front of Batu's dinner group, including khans, generals, Batu's wives, concubines and other women. Konstantina was supposed to tell the story about Greek mythology, which she used to deliver to the late Princess Euphrasia when she was young and recently to the ruling families of Ryazan. For her storytelling, an interpreter was employed—Russian to Mongol—because she could speak Russian. She was wearing a Greek costume, and her hair was decorated with ornaments that she had brought from her hometown.

She started a long, long story about Greek gods, goddesses and related men and women that they created:

In the beginning, there was nothingness—empty, dark and completely silent. From there, something was born and began to fill up the universe. It was Eros, and it was the first god. From Eros, the god of earth, ocean and forest was born, which was Gaia as well as Uranus, god of the sky. These two gods, Gaia and Uranus, got married and bore many children, including three cyclops, three hecatoncheires and 12 titans. The cyclops were one-eyed giants, and the hecatoncheires were 100-handed giants; however, the father Uranus wasn't happy with these monstrous children. He imprisoned them in the darkest part of Earth: Tartarus.

The mother Gaia, who was enraged about this decision, made a plot.

"Even though they are ugly, they are still my children. How can he do this without my consent?"

She created a giant flint sickle and gathered her 12 titan children.

"Your father is sleeping now. I want to get rid of his genitals. Who can do this job for me?"

Nobody dared to volunteer for that job, saying, "How can we castrate our own father?"

However, one volunteer showed up. He was the youngest son, Cronus. He approached the sleeping father with a giant sickle and cut off his genitals in one swing. From the cut wound, the blood spurted out like a fountain, and the father woke up.

Cronus picked up the cut genitals and threw them into the sea so as not to be re-put by his father.

Uranus cursed his son Cronus and cried, "How can you do this to your own father? You will be punished for your deed! Since you harmed your own father, you will be harmed by your own children!"

Cronus became the ruler of the universe. He married his sister titan Rhea, and they began to have children; however, he was paranoid of his father's curse that he would be harmed by his own children, so he swallowed each of them when they were born.

After Cronus swallowed all five children, his wife Rhea couldn't tolerate it anymore. When the sixth child was born, Rhea hid the baby in a cave in a mountain on the Crete Island. Then she wrapped a rock with a swaddling cloth and gave it to Cronus, who immediately swallowed it.

When Zeus, the sixth child of Cronus, grew up, he plotted to avenge his father. He approached his father masqueraded as his cup bearer. Cronus, who did not recognize him, had a drink given to him, which could make him vomit. Cronus vomited all the five children whom he had swallowed. They all came out unharmed because they were gods. They appreciated Zeus and elected him as their leader. Knowing this, Cronus was enraged and began a war with his own children.

All the titans were with Cronus except Prometheus, Epimetheus and Oceanus. The commander on the titan side was Atlas. Zeus felt that he would be a predicted loss in this battle, so he looked for an ally. He went down to Tartarus and unchained the three cyclops and the three hecatoncheires, who fought for Zeus. Their power was enormous—especially the 100-handed hecatoncheires.

The war between them lasted for 10 years. Zeus subdued many of the titans with his main weapons: lightning bolts and thunder. The victory was with Zeus's side. Zeus put all his defeated enemies into the tartans and became the ruler of the universe. He made Mount Olympus his hometown and lived there with his siblings.

CHAPTER 24

Konstantina was a talented storyteller and an actor. Sometimes her voice was persuading and sweet like music, and other times it was heavy and authoritative. She used her whole body and facial expressions to attract her audiences.

"A great story!" Batu exclaimed. "How long will it take to complete your story?"

"Maybe a whole year or two at this pace."

Batu was surprised and said, "I have one question. You said that Zeus's main weapons were lightning bolts and thunder. Where did he get them?"

"His ally, the cyclops, made them for him."

Batu shouted, "Zeus was an imaginary figure or god, but I am the real one. I have the lightning bolts and the thunder! I have the black powder and the canon!"

CHAPTER 25

Greek mythology (night two)

Konstantina continued her story on the second night:
The mother god of all gods, Gaia, was very unhappy with what was happening in the cosmos, so she decided to create her last son to wipe out everything. The worst monstrous creature, named Typhon, came into being in the cosmos.

Typhon was a winged and serpentine creature and immensely powerful. From his shoulders grew 100 snake heads with dark, flickering tongues. From the thighs downward, he had huge coils of vipers, which could be reached to his head and emitted a loud hissing. Fire flashed from his eyes, and all the snakes on his shoulder spat out showers of poison.

Typhon challenged Zeus for the rule of the cosmos. They fought for seven days and nights. During this time, the earth was shaking, the ocean was boiling and all the trees in the forests burned down.

At last, the powerful Zeus's thunderbolts subdued Typhon, making the worst monstrous creature his prisoner. Zeus imprisoned Typhon under the mountain of Etna, which was impossible to escape.

Konstantina felt very comfortable to see that her audience was fascinated by her story. She continued:

Zeus set a punishment for the enemy commander Atlas, who was the commanding leader of the enemy titans: Atlas had to hold the earth on his shoulder for eternity.

However, Prometheus, which meant "fore thinker," was a smart god as his name implied. Prometheus was a titan and didn't fight against Zeus, so he was spared imprisonment. He remained a free god and could roam the universe, developing himself into a craft master.

Zeus saw admirable talent in him, so he gave Prometheus a task to create a man. Prometheus shaped a man out of mud, and the goddess of war, Athena, gave him a life and eventually made him breathe. Prometheus designed a man to look like God, in an upright position on his two feet, with two free hands and a head on his shoulders.

Prometheus loved his creature; however, he took pity on him because he was weak and had no weapon for survival. He decided to give him the fire. The fire was limited only to God, but Prometheus violated this rule.

When Zeus found that Prometheus had broken God's rule, Zeus was enraged and put a harsh punishment on him. He nailed Prometheus to the rock in the Caucasus Mountains and let a giant eagle eat his liver every day, which was replenished every night, over and over again. This was an endless, never-ending, horrible torture.

At this point, Batu stopped the storyteller and asked, "Why did Zeus decide to create a man? What was his motivation?"

Konstantina showed an image of uncertainty and answered, "I don't know that part. I am just a storyteller."

"Where did you learn this story? Who taught you?"

"I learned it from my mother, who was also a storyteller. I heard that my mother learned it from her mother."

Subedei, who was sitting next to Batu, commented, "Maybe they were bored. They needed pets, like dogs and cats," and ended with a loud guffaw.

Konstantina continued:

Zeus was afraid that the man with fire would become powerful like God. So, he decided to put a limitation to the man. He created a woman with stunning beauty, a deceptive heart and a lying tongue. Her name was Pandora, and she was the first human woman. Pandora was given a box and told never to open it. Eventually she was sent to Earth to the man and stayed there.

Curiosity is a powerful emotion, and Pandora could never resist it. Finally, she opened the box. Out flew all manner of evils: unhappiness, fear, sorrow, injustice, plaque and misfortune. Surprised, she hastened to close the box, only to lock up the desirable qualities of hope and expectation.

Pandora,
The beginning of a race of women,
An uninvited guest to the world of man-only,
Unblessed of God,

CHAPTER 25

Harbinger of misfortune,
Will follow the man like a shadow,
With Pandora's box in her hand.
All through his life.
Only a lucky man will evade this.

At this point, Batu stood up, turned his head toward the women's side, and said in a loud voice, "You have all heard this story. It defines a woman as a condemned being and a misfortune to the man. Do you all agree with this?"

All the women in the dinner group exclaimed in one voice, "No!"

In Mongol mythology, a man and a woman were created out of clay at the same time after heaven and earth. In reality, a woman was viewed as a copartner, and she had complete and equal rights of a man. The man was for battle and war, and all the rest of the jobs was for the woman. In a family, if the father died, the mother would be the head of the family—not the firstborn son. If the khan died, his wife became the regent and ruled his domain until the next khan was elected.

It seemed that Pandora's story didn't have much appeal to the women at the dinner group.

Greek mythology (night three)

Konstantina continued her story:

One day, in the gods' town of Mount Olympus, there was a wedding ceremony for Peleus and the nymph Thetis. At the wedding banquet, when they were all in a good mood, one goddess showed up with a very unhappy face, threw away an apple in the middle of the crowd and disappeared without saying anything.

It was a golden apple written with these words: "For the most beautiful, immortal woman in the universe."

The unhappy woman was Eris. She wasn't favored by many because she was the goddess of discord.

When the message on the apple was announced, three goddesses—Hera, Zeus's wife; Athena, the goddess of war; and Aphrodite, the goddess of love—hastened to pick it up. Each of them wanted to get the title of the most beautiful goddess. They quarreled, wrangled and brawled with no end.

Eventually, they took their case to Zeus, the king of gods and goddesses; however, Zeus couldn't take a side.

He abruptly said to the three goddesses, "I think the best judge for this case would be the fairest man in the mortal world: Paris, the prince of Troy. What do you think?"

All three goddesses agreed and brought Paris to Mount Olympus.

First, Hera approached him. "If you give that apple to me, I will make you the most powerful man in the world."

Next, Athena said, "If you choose me for that apple, I will make you the richest man in the world."

Lastly, Aphrodite told him, "Let me have the apple, and then you will have the most beautiful woman in the mortal world."

The Troy prince gave it some thought and finally handed the apple to Aphrodite.

Aphrodite was exhilarated, but the other two goddesses were disappointed and angry at Paris.

Aphrodite then told Paris how he could get the most beautiful woman in the mortal world.

"While you're on the way back home on the Aegean Sea, stop by the city of Sparta. Helen, the queen of Sparta, is the most beautiful woman you will ever have; however, she is already married to Menelaus, the Spartan king."

Paris asked, "If she is already married, how can I get her without trouble?"

Aphrodite answered, "Just follow my directions. Go and see Menelaus and tell him that you just stopped by for a greeting. He will welcome you as a Trojan prince and open a banquet for you. When you meet Helen, I will ask Cupid to shoot an arrow into Helen's heart. She will desperately fall in love with you and will never resist you. In the night, you will take her and run away from there."

Everything was done as the goddess Aphrodite planned, and Paris triumphantly returned home. Menelaus, upon finding out that his wife Helen disappeared with the Trojan prince Paris, was enraged. He immediately sought help from his brother Agamemnon, the king of Mycenae. Agamemnon immediately sent messengers to 29 allied Greek cities and gathered a great army. They set sail with more than 1,000 ships and 100,000 men toward the city of Trojan.

Trojan was a magnificent city and an impregnable fortress on the Aegean coast with great riches and a large population. Their king was Priam, and Paris was his second son. They also had a great army, so when the Greek army arrived and asked for the return of the queen Helen, they didn't move at all.

Thus, a nine-year war between the Greeks and the Trojans began. It was a war between two powers in the mortal world as well as among many gods and goddesses. The goddesses Hera and Athena were on the Greek side, and Aphrodite supported the Trojans. Since Athena was the goddess of war, Aphrodite worried about the unbalance of power. She decided to invite another war god named Ares. During the nine-year war, numerous war heroes emerged and perished. Even after nine years, nobody could see the end of the tunnel of misery.

Athena postulated a scheme that couldn't fail. She sent a divine message to Menelaus, the king of Sparta, through his dream.

"Make a fake retreat, leaving a huge wooden horse hollowed inside. Put the most courageous 30 warriors inside the wooden *horse and wait for the right time. Wait for the moment that the Trojans pull the horse into their city."*

That strategy worked. In the Trojan court, before they made the final decision, they had a long debate. Cassandra, who was the Trojan king Priam's daughter, strongly resisted the idea.

"Burn it!" she said. "It will bring disaster to the Trojans!"

However, the majority of the group said, "It will be our souvenir. It will give us a fresh memory of our victory over the Greeks for our children and our children's children and into many future generations."

Eventually, they decided to keep the wooden horse and pulled it into the city with two lines of rope and 1,000 men on each side.

That night, they had a big feast. All the citizens of Troy celebrated their victory and made merry. They danced and drank deep into the night. When they were drunk and exhausted, the streets of the city sank into deep silence.

At this time, the secret door opened at the bottom of the belly of the horse. Thirty Greek commandoes landed on the ground through the rope and immediately opened the city gate, approaching the Greek fleet of ships. They were waiting on the sea and taking advantage of the darkness of the night. The leader of the 30 commandoes was Odysseus, the Greek hero.

Thus, the war between the two great cities—Troy and Sparta—ended.

At this point, Batu stopped Konstantina. "You told us that the war god Ares was on the Troy side, and yet they still lost?"

"That is right. However, another war goddess—Athena—sided with the Greeks. It was a war between two war gods."

Batu thought and then asked, "What is the difference between the two gods?"

"Ares was more powerful and destructive. On the other hand, Athena was more strategic and intelligent because she was also the goddess of intelligence."

Batu thought about this again. He stood up and looked around the audience.

Then, in a loud voice, he said, "These are just stories, but we have a god of war in the real world! So far, he has won hundreds of battles and wars, and he has never lost any of them. He will never lose any incoming battles or wars. He is sitting next to me—my revered orlok, Subedei Bagatur!"

Suddenly, big roars of applause and deafening cheers filled the large, royal dining tent.

"Subedei! Subedei! Subedei!"

When things cooled down, Zohreh—Batu's concubine—asked Konstantina, "What happened to Queen Helen and Prince Paris?"

Konstantina continued:

Prince Paris was killed in the battle; however, he was successful in killing Achilles, one of the Greek warriors. In return, he was killed by an arrow from one of the Greek soldiers. After Helen was captured, she was handed over to her husband, King Menelaus.

When he saw her, he raised his sword to cut his unfaithful wife.

CHAPTER 26

At that moment, she dropped her robe from her shoulder. The site of her beauty caused Menelaus to let the sword drop from his hand.

There was a moment of silence inside the tent.

Zohreh asked, "After that, did Helen live happily ever after?"

In response, Konstantina finished the story:

Helen lived for some time; however, in her widowhood, she was driven out by her stepsons and fled to Rhodes. It was a wrong move, and she wasn't welcomed there. Rather, Polyxo, the Rhodian queen, put a rope around Helen's neck and hanged her in revenge for the death of her husband Tlepolemus, who died in the Trojan war that Helen caused.

CHAPTER 27

Kolomna, the city of death

Georgy Vsevolodvich, the grand prince of Vladimir, addressed three of his sons, his nephews, the voivodes and the generals.

"The Mongols are coming to us. What is the best way to stop them?"

Vsevolodvich didn't move while Ryazan was burning; however, enormous numbers of refugees were pouring into his city, destroying its natural balanced habitat. Vladimir was big, with a regular population of 20,000; now it swelled to between 40,000 and 50,000 people. It was a fortified city, nestled on a high hill with a deep moat around it.

At the time, Vladimir and Georgy were holding the grand princedom of Russia. In this urgent situation, nobody dared to open his mouth when they realized that there was no known cure for this calamity. Andreyev, an old voivode, was believed to have battle experience with the Mongols at the Kalka River battle about 15 years ago.

"I think the best option we have now is to send some troops to defend Kolomna to delay their advance and others to Moskov [Moscow] to distract their attention," Andreyev offered. "Our city of Vladimir is well built with a defense system, so it is expected to last quite a while. In the meantime, we can send messengers to every corner of our domain—especially Kiev and Novgorod—to send their supportive troops to reinforce us."

Grand Prince Georgy couldn't think of another option. At the time, Kiev was the biggest city in Russia, with a 50,000 regular population, and his brother-in-law Prince Mikhail was ruling the city. Among Georgy's war council, some of them already knew they were doomed. They knew what had happened to Ryazan and their people. Yet, the younger generation—especially the princes—were full of vigor and eager to fight.

Georgy Vsevolodvich asked, "Who is at Kolomna now?"

"Roman Igorevich—Yuri Igorevich's brother—is there. I don't know if he was there from the beginning or if he escaped from Ryazan."

"How many troops are there for defense?"

"Maybe 3,000 or 4,000."

After hearing this information from Andreyev, Grand Prince Georgy made this decree: "I will send my son Vsevolod with 700 knights and 7,000 foot soldiers to Kolomna. The voivode Ermei Glebovich will assist him as the commander in chief to hold the Mongols there if possible. For Moskov, my other son Vladimir will be there with 3,000 troops. In case the Mongols ignore Moskov, hit them from behind. Moskov is a small garrison town with a strong fortress. I will leave for the Sit River basin to muster the new troops. During my absence, my other son Mstislav shall be in charge of the city of Vladimir. You shall do your best. God will be with us."

The grand prince left for the Sit River basin with 3,000 troops, leaving all of his family members and princes in the city of Vladmir with 10,000 garrison troops. He had already dispatched hundreds of messengers to every part of his domain, including the cities of Kiev and Novgorod. He truly believed that his city of Vladimir could provide enough time for him to muster the new army from all parts of his domain.

The Great One, Genghis Khan, used to say, "Sometimes the outcome of a pivotal battle or the whole war relies on a piece of information."

All of the Russian movements were reported to Subedei through an espionage network, which was enormously accurate and prompt. Subedei always collected information first through his superb espionage network before he made any movements.

In a discussion with Batu, other khans and generals, Subedei said, "They divided their defending troops. The total defending manpower under Grand Prince Georgy is estimated at about 23,000 men. They sent 7,000 of them to Kolomna and 3,000 to Moskov. The grand prince took another 3,000 to the Sit River basin. In the city of Vladimir, only 10,000 were left. They believe that the city of Vladimir is impregnable. They built it up on the elevated hill with a thick defense wall with battlements. There's also a deep moat around the city. There are four main gates into the city, and all of them are strongly fortified."

Batu asked, "What about Kolomna?"

Subedei continued, "The usual normal population of that city is about 4,000, and they have about 2,000 or 3,000 garrison troops. Prince Roman Igorevich is in charge. Georgy's son Prince Vsevolod and his general, Ermei Glebovich, joined them with their 7,000 troops, so their total defending power is 10,000 now. They are in charge along with Roman Igorevich, side by side. In this war, speed matters. We should not give them time to reinforce, recruit or get aid from other cities. After we destroy Kolomna, we should go to Moskov before we go to Vladimir. Otherwise, we will be attacked from behind. After that, we have to advance in two sides: one for Suzdal and one for Vladimir. We will destroy Suzdal first, and then attack Vladimir with combined force."

Batu looked at the khans and the generals and asked, "Who wants to be the vanguard for the battle of Kolomna?"

As soon as he heard Batu's question, one man got on his feet and shouted, "Leave that to me! I want to get the number one merit in this battle!"

The man was Kulqan Khan, the son of Genghis Khan and his fourth wife Qulan. The Mongol rule only recognized sons from first wives as legitimate to inherit their father's position and property. Because of this rule, Kulqan Khan couldn't inherit anything from his father and couldn't be recognized as a legitimate child even in the records; however, he was popular among the Mongol soldiers and had charismatic power. He was Batu Khan's uncle, but he was 27 years old while Batu was 32 at this time.

The Mongols moved and encircled half of the city of Kolomna. They sent a team of five envoys and, when the

Mongols arrived in front of the main gate, one of them shouted to open the gate and surrender. In return, they received showers of arrows. One of the Mongols was struck by the arrows, fell from his horse and met instant death. The rest of the envoys retreated.

After hearing this news, Batu gave the signal for a full-scale attack. After a half-day bombardment of rocks and naphtha flames, the Kolomna defense system began to collapse. Many parts of the city wall had broken down, letting attackers swarm the city.

Kulqan Khan, at the front of the vanguard unit, shouted, "Attack!"

He and his 2,000-man vanguard unit galloped toward the city wall of Kolomna. Showers of arrows greeted them from the battlements of the city wall. The Mongol attackers covered themselves with shields on their left hands and continued to gallop to the wall.

One of the arrows lodged deeply into Kulqan's neck, and he screamed, "Auck!" and fell from his horse.

About 20 soldiers gathered around him. One soldier carefully pulled out the arrow and immediately pressed silk cloth on the wounded area. They called for the military doctor; however, heavy spurts of bleeding continued—even through the fingers of caring soldiers. For some moments, Kulqan Khan's eyes were open, but he slowly lost focus, and they eventually closed. He was dead.

The attack on Kolomna continued without interruption. Within another half day, the city was in the Mongols' hands. The sad news of Khan Kulqan's death was immediately reported to Batu and Subedei.

Subedei clicked his tongue and uttered, "The commander is like a brain, and the soldiers are like his hands. Each part has its own function. He was probably too young to control his hot blood. His hot blood went into his brain."

Batu was worried about the morale of his soldiers because, by that time, no prince or khan had been killed on the battlefield. He ordered the complete death of this city, which meant that all living creatures would perish. They were scapegoats.

However, there were survivors. Despite the sacrifice of hundreds of their soldiers, Russian Prince Vsevolod and his voivode Ermei Glebovich escaped to the city of Vladimir.

On the other hand, Prince Roman Igorevich was captured and flayed by the Mongol soldiers. They made him naked and hung him on a tree trunk while two skilled butchers carefully skinned him from top to bottom, like they did to horses. His body, with red flesh and no skin, wriggled for a while.

It took three full days for the Mongols to completely eradicate the entire population of Kolomna. During these three days, the sky above the city was full of man-eating birds, like crows and vultures. Their croaking and cawing were deafening.

The Mongols leveled all of the standing structures, so they could not be used as shelter or a bulwark for future enemies.

CHAPTER 28

Into Moskov (Moscow)

The Mongols advanced to Moskov, which was a small garrison town on the western border of the Suzdal-Vladimir principality. Though it was small, it was protected by a thick, high, wooden wall with a moat around the town.

Batu and Subedei arrived at a hill where they could see the faraway image of Moskov. It looked peaceful. Batu was impressed with the scenery, which gave an image of vastness of the land with unlimited possibilities, stretching out to every direction.

"What's the name of the river?" Batu asked, pointing to the river that wound up near the town.

Subedei, who was next to him on his horse, answered, "Its name is Moskov."

Batu nodded and murmured, "*Aha!* They picked up the name of the town after the river. Where is the final destination of this river?"

"It originates from the Oka River and merges into the Volga River. Then the Volga flows into the Caspian Sea."

Batu pondered this information and, a moment later, said to Subedei, "Orlok, I think I will make the town of Moskov the trade and cultural center of all of Russia after I complete the conquest of Russia, if my judgment is right."

"I believe you have the third eye like your own grandfather, the Great One," Subedei noticed. "Even with my eye, this location is wonderful with unlimited possibilities. So be it!"

The Mongols encircled the town of Moskov. Batu sent out three messengers, demanding surrender as usual. At the time, the customary rule among the nations was not to kill the messengers. Usually, they were unarmed, and their function was communication, sending and receiving messages; however, the Russians frequently violated this rule, so Batu allowed two shields for the messengers: one was secured on their back and the other was on their left hand. They also were allowed to shout in front of the main gate but not physically enter the city.

One of the three messengers shouted in Russian, in front of the gate, "You are surrounded! Batu Khan wants you to surrender! Open the gate, drop your weapons and surrender! Save your life and your family!"

The messengers shouted for a while, but the gate never opened. In return, they got a shower of arrows like they did at Kolomna. This time, all three messengers returned safely.

Batu ordered a full-scale attack. Regardless of the thick, strong, wooden city wall and moat, within a half day the Mongol commandoes were already in the town of Moskov and through the broken wall. It had been torn down by the Mongols' accurate and powerful catapults, and the moat had been filled with dirt by levies.

INTO MOSKOV (MOSCOW)

The street fighting continued until dusk and was followed by a massacre. All the town's buildings and houses collapsed with flames and smoke. Agonizing cries and screaming continued deep into the night.

About noon the following day, it became rather quiet. Russian Prince Vladimir had been captured alive and was brought in front of Batu. Batu sat on the folding leather chair in the open field, and Prince Vladimir knelt in front of him with his two hands tied back.

Batu regarded Vladimir for a while before he said, "Surrender! Then you will keep your princedom."

Vladimir raised his head and shook it to the left and the right, meaning "No!"

At this point, the collaborating defector intervened.

"Surrender! I am the prince, Ivan Vladimirovits. God is with the Mongols. Don't put yourself into a whirlpool of destruction. Save yourself for the future of your princedom! You should be grateful to Tsar Batu for giving you a second chance!"

Vladimir raised his head, stared at Ivan and spat out one word: "Traitor!"

"Keep him alive," Batu told his soldiers.

The Mongols didn't stay in Moskov for too long. After leveling the town, they proceeded to the next target: the city of Vladimir, which held the title of princedom for all of Russia.

The fall of the Suzdal-Vladimir principality

The Mongols surrounded the city of Vladimir. It was a big city with a regular population of 20,000; now it was between 30,000 and 40,000 due to the added refugees. Though only 10,000 troops were defending the city, they were the best among the Suzdal-Vladimir principality.

The protecting wall was on the earthwork (a manmade flat, high hill) and made with millions of giant logs that were 40 inches thick and 10 feet high. There were four main gates into the city, and the city itself was protected by a deep moat around it. In some areas, its protection was reinforced with an earthen rampart.

After Batu destroyed and sacked the city of Suzdal, he brought about 3,000 prisoners to be turned into levies. Suzdal was about 5 leagues (16 miles) from the city of Vladimir from the northwest direction and was the old capital of the principality. As planned, Batu attacked and destroyed Suzdal ahead of Vladimir, while Subedei waited at Vladimir, encircling the city. The Mongol vanguard unit proceeded to the front of the city's main gate, which they called the Golden Gate.

THE FALL OF THE SUZDAL-VLADIMIR PRINCIPALITY

The captain of the vanguard unit, Kuchi, who was also the captain of 1,000 men, shouted, "Who oversees this city now? We know that your ruler, Prince Georgy, is not here!"

There was no response from the city.

The Mongol captain continued, "Surrender! Put down your weapons and open the gate! Save your city!"

There was still no response. Instead, a shower of arrows greeted them. The Mongol vanguard unit retreated but came back with one prisoner: Prince Vladimir. His hands were tied back, and his neck was lassoed by a Mongol soldier.

Kuchi shouted, "Here is Prince Vladimir! Surrender! Otherwise, we will cut his neck!"

Hearing these words, the images of two men emerged on top of the wall: Princes Mstislav and Vsevolod Vsevolodvich. They confirmed that their brother Vladimir was in the Mongols' hand; however, they knew they could do nothing, and the two images simply disappeared.

Captain Kuchi pulled out his scimitar and cut off Vladimir's head. The human head rolled over a few times and stopped. Blood spurted from the neck, and the body without the head fell to the ground, making a dull sound.

The Mongols started a full-scale attack. The 20,000 levies were mobilized to fill up the moat, and the battering rams were engaged to destroy all four gates at the same time. After the moat work, the Mongol catapults bombarded the city wall and rampart with rocks. All day and all night, the attack continued.

On the following day at dawn—February 8, 1238—the Mongol commandoes stormed all four gates at once. Despite the large garrison, the chaos created by the panicked residents and citizens made it impossible to resist and build up an effective defense. By noon, the city was covered with mountains of dead bodies, and the blood flowed like a stream.

The princes, Mstislav and Vsevolod, were killed during the battle. The bishop took the grand princess, her daughters and her granddaughters to Our Lady of Peace, which was already crowded with sheltering people. They barricaded the doors of this cathedral and made a space in the choir loft for the royal family. The Mongols set fire to the building. Soon, swirls of dark smoke swept across the floor of cathedral. Mothers covered their children in their arms, couples embraced each other, and the bishop prayed with his folded hands. The cathedral was quickly enveloped with flames and horrible, heart-piercing screaming burst out. They all burned to death, and the whole building collapsed.

The other four churches in the city, the palace and the monastery of St. Dmitry were in a similar situation, and sheltering themselves in those places didn't guarantee any safety but only extended their lives a few more hours.

The Mongols rushed to chase Grand Prince Georgy Vsevolodvich at the Sit River basin. He was with his nephews, who were the sons of his brother, Prince Constantin, and Vasilko, the prince of Rostov. Georgy was with 3,000 troops, but the main reason he was there was to wait for reinforcement or rescue troops from Novgorod and Kiev. He was waiting for something that would never happen.

Within a half day after their departure from the city of Vladmir, the Mongols caught up with the grand prince and his troops, surrounded them and began their slaughter. It was a one-sided game, and there were just a few survivors. Until the last moment, Georgy never took his eyes off the north-western horizon where the rescue army might have shown up. The sky above the Sit River basin was crowded with circulating, man-eating birds, and their croaking and cawing were deafening.

One of the survivors—Vasilko, the prince of Rostov—was brought in front of Batu.

Batu regarded him for a while and then told him, "Surrender! Come under the Mongol banner. Keep yourself and your people safe!"

An unknown Russian chronicler described and recorded their exchange:

You are the enemy of my people,
You are the enemy of my country,
You are the enemy of Christ.
You shall never be my friend.
You are doomed to perdition.
There is God,
Who will never accept you,
For what you have done,
You shall be destroyed,
When your cup is full.

The same unknown chronicler also wrote this:

CHAPTER 29

War is not a sentimental game,
But a terrible struggle for existence.
With the enemy's sword at your throat,
Every treacherous word deemed honest,
Every cruel expedient justifiable.
Resistance will bring only destruction,
While submission purchases safety,
When it is not compromising in any way to
The victors.

Batu gave a signal to Kuchi, the captain of 1,000 men, and left.

Prince Vasilko was surrounded by 10 Mongol soldiers and was kicked until he looked like a rump of meat wrapped with rags. He was kicked to death.

CHAPTER 30

Vast land, harsh winter

The Mongols divided their next expedition army into three groups. The Russian land was huge, and numerous small- and medium-sized towns and cities were spread across the nation like stars in the sky. During the springtime, many parts of the Russian land became like a swamp or a marsh due to thawing, which made it hard for horses to run around. It was an inevitable strategy to sweep out as many towns and cities as possible in the limited time of winter.

The eastern division of 30,000 warriors was entrusted to Boroldai Noyan. Boroldai attacked the cities of Rostov and Yaroslavl. These two cities were burned and leveled, and all the residents and garrison soldiers were wiped out, which meant that it was a massacre with no survivors.

Batu's middle group of 60,000 men moved to Yuryev, Pereslavl, Dmitrov and Tver. After conquering these cities, one by one, he headed for the city of Novgorod, which was on the northern side, with a usual population of 35,000. Subedei's 60,000 troops conquered cities, including Myshkin, Uglich, Semyonov, Ignatovka, Stanilovo and Voskresensk. Within a two- to three-month period, they conquered more than 14 medium-sized cities.

CHAPTER 30

The chronicler Faqih Ashraf Aziz wrote:

Why can't Russian people unite themselves to resist the Mongols and the conquerors? I don't understand. They were simply giving out, one by one, making it easy for them to swallow. Probably their land is too big and wide to keep intimate relations among them. The Mongols are not the ones who were overwhelmed or sank into the vastness of the Russian land and were not intimidated by the harshness of the Russian winter. Rather, those conditions were favorable for them, and they were taking advantage of them fully.

The chronicler Chun Lee wrote:

The Mongols won every battle they engaged in and very likely will do the same in the near and far distant futures. Why? How could this happen? Probably they have a very organized army, a strong military discipline, superior tactics and strategies and superiority of individual soldiers as warriors. Disobeying orders is regarded as treason and punished with the death penalty.

The various qualities of Mongol soldiers are:
They have the courage of lions,
Endurance of dogs,
Prudence of cranes,
Cunning of foxes,
Far-sightedness of ravens,
Rapacity of wolves,
Keenness of fighting cocks,

Wiliness of cats,
Impetuosity of boars.

Batu headed for Novgorod. He was moving at a regular pace. Next to him was Zorik, the captain of 1,000 men as well as the chief of the espionage unit that was accompanying him. They were riding their horses side by side.

Batu asked Zorik, "Who is in charge of Novgorod now?"

"Alexander Nevsky. He has been there for two years, and he is 17 years old now."

Batu turned his head toward Zorik and regarded him with astoundment. At the time, the Mongol society was accustomed to deciding their leaders by election; however, the candidates came from blood lines. Even though the predecessor picked up his successor, the succeeding leader still needed approval or consent from Aka (the elder prince) and Inis (the younger prince). While Genghis Khan decided that Ogodei, his third son, would be his successor, Ogodei still needed approval and consent from all his uncles, brothers and sisters.

Batu murmured to himself, "Is a seventeen-year-old boy the head of the second largest city in Russia?"

Batu tried to understand the European feudal society, where only the nobility owned all the land and the enslaved people, and murmured again, "If the boy is smart and courageous, he will find a way. Only if they are lucky. I will wait and see."

The messengers came and went among the three columns of the army, usually twice a day. Batu was always fully aware of the exact point of the other two columns. Batu and his Mongol army arrived at the small city of Torzhok, which was near the small Tvertsa River and the gateway to Novgorod. They had to pass through Torzhok before they got to Novgorod. At first, Batu thought about bypassing this city to save time for Novgorod. He dispatched the messengers for surrender, but the answer was "no." It took two weeks for Batu to annihilate this city.

Batu continued to march. When the Mongols arrived at a point 60 miles from Novgorod, an unexpected, horrible report came up. One of the captains of 100 men at the front line galloped to Batu. At the time, Batu's middle column of 60,000 cavalry stretched out almost 15 miles long. Batu was at the middle part. The captain of 100 men gave a detailed description of the incident. He slowed down his breath and made a report in a loud voice.

"My lord, the Russian prince Ivan has drowned!"

"What is it? Go on!"

"He was at the very front of the line, saying that he would be a first stepper. At a certain spot, when he stepped on it, suddenly the earth collapsed, and he disappeared into the mud with his horse. The next soldier behind him tried to save him but failed. He and his horse were also swallowed by the mud. He simply followed him. It was like a quagmire. It happened in the blink of a moment, so nobody could give a helping hand. After him and another one disappeared into the mud, it looked like nothing happened on the ground."

Batu rushed to the spot. The soldiers around the spot opened a way for Batu, and he carefully examined it. It was very difficult to differentiate the area of the quagmire with solid ground. He thought that the quagmire had probably

swallowed two men and two horses connected to an unfathomable underground chamber filled with mud. It was already
late March and thawing. Batu told the captain of 100 men to
put pickets around the accident area along with a rope for a
danger warning.

Batu murmured, "It must be God's will."

At that moment, Batu decided to turn back 60 miles from
his main target of Novgorod and shouted to his followers:

Though he spoke Russian,
His merit surpasses many,
Remember his name,
He was one of us.

CHAPTER 31

Kozelsk, the city of woe

Batu continued to march toward the west. His next target was Kozelsk, which was one of the main cities of principality of Chernigov and the troops' gathering place. The city was on the bank of the Zhizdra River.

Batu opened a council with the other princes and generals, and Zorik, the captain of the spying unit, made the opening remark.

"Kozelsk is a well-fortified city. It is on the bank of the Zhizdra River and protected by a strongly built wall and ramparts. The population could be, I presume, about 15,000, and about 9,000 garrisons are there. The city is under the rule of Prince Vasily, who is the grandson of Mstislav Vsevolodvich, who is the grand prince of Chernigov that was killed in the Kalka River battle years ago. Prince Vasily is 12 years old now."

Zorik went back to his seat at the council meeting inside the tent. Suddenly, a deep silence fell upon the attendees.

Moments later, Batu carefully asked Zorik, "Did you say that the city was under the rule of a 12-year-old boy?"

Zorik stood up again and answered, "That is right, my lord."

They discussed many things until late in the day.

Prince Vasily of Kozelsk learned that the Mongols were nearby. He made a visit to his mother, Princess Natasha, and asked for advice.

"The Mongols are here. I need your wisdom to protect the city and all of us. What should I do?"

The princess embraced her son and said, "My son and my lord, your grandfather and your father were both killed by the Mongols, and you should not be killed by them again. Before they came here, they went to Novgorod, but they had to give up because of thawing. Their horses could not move freely in the mud. The frozen Zhizdra River that is covering our city is not strong enough for the Mongol horses to cross over. It is already half melted. It will protect us. In the daytime, you'd better concentrate on defense. In the nighttime, attack them. Never go out onto the field to face them. Make a long war. Make them get tired and make them give up, and then they will bypass this place."

The Mongol army half surrounded the city of Kozelsk from a distance, making a large, half-moon encirclement. Batu looked around the city from afar. Kozelsk looked like an island in the middle of the Zhizdra River. It was late afternoon, and the picturesque scenery of the island city and the river was peaceful and stunning. The river wasn't wide, but slush would surely make it an impassible valley.

Batu sent out a sentry unit to uncover more detailed information. After two days, the sentry unit came back with a rough sketch of the city and the surrounding Zhizdra River. The two bridges that were connected to the city had been destroyed by the defending side—the citizens of Kozelsk—for protection.

Batu said to Zorik, "Do they have enough provisions in the city?"

"We don't know."

"We don't know! But we should assume they have. How many horses do they have in the city?"

Zorik answered, "I presume about a thousand."

"They can use them as food in an urgent situation."

Batu immediately dispatched an arrow messenger to Subedei, who was at that time attacking the city of Boshonka. The urgent messenger was holding rough sketches of Kozelsk, the direction of the river and near and far-away hills and mountains.

Three days later, the answer arrived. It would be better to wait until the water became a little warmer because the soldiers could not stay too long in the icy water in order to construct interim bridges. To deliver Mongol commandoes into the city, a bridge was needed. But how? Who could stay in the icy water for half a day to construct the bridge?

Batu decided to wait.

Seven days passed. Batu woke up one night due to an urgent report from the guard. Batu's tent and his seven wives' and concubines' tents were protected by a unit of 1,000 night guards.

The captain shouted from outside of the tent, "My lord, I have an urgent report! We are being attacked—a surprise attack!"

Batu got on his feet and asked, "Where?"

"At the northern flank, my lord!"

Batu rushed to the site. When he arrived, it was already subdued.

The captain of 1,000 men reported, "We killed them all. There were about 400. They were the Russians from Kozelsk."

"What about our losses?"

The captain of 1,000 men lowered his head. "I presume almost the same numbers. It was a surprise attack."

Batu murmured, "They must be on a suicide mission."

The next day, Batu held a war council, and Mangguser Noyan spoke.

"Looks like they are avoiding a frontal attack. They might continue surprise attacks as well as hit-and-run warfare to lower our soldiers' morale. We should get ready for that."

Zorik gave his opinion by saying, "We should find out where the Russian surprise attackers are coming from. They surely came from the city, but where and how did they cross the river?"

A moment later, Batu spoke.

"My question to myself is, 'Where did this 12-year-old boy get all these ideas? There is probably someone behind him. Who could it be?'"

They decided to reinforce the nighttime guard and put a regular patrol squad all along the front line.

Another two weeks passed, and the same thing happened. This time, the number was doubled: about 800 suicide attackers fell upon the Mongol war camps. The attack could have been subdued, but the Mongol casualties didn't improve; however, this time, the Mongols detained two captives.

Zorik began his interrogation.

"We all know that you are from the city. We need to know how you got here from the city. Tell us!"

Zorik knew that they wouldn't talk easily. When they had volunteered for the suicide mission, they probably gave up their lives.

Zorik ordered his soldiers, "Bring the dogs!"

Soon, the Mongol soldiers brought 50 to 60 large-sized, fierce dogs, making the area quite noisy with barking. At the time of Genghis Khan, the Mongols didn't keep dogs in the army unit because Genghis Khan didn't like dogs. Yet, from the third generation, things had changed, and it became routine to keep military dogs in their camp.

The trained dogs could do many things that humans couldn't accomplish. The Mongols took good advantage of them in the battlefields. They even had a position titled Nokhoi Avarga for those who specialized in dog breeding. They usually fed the dogs with leftovers from the soldiers; however, sometimes they fed them with human flesh, which was abundantly and intentionally available in the battlefield. The Mongol army kept about 800 dogs at that time.

Pursuant to Zorik's order, the soldiers stripped off one of the captive's clothing and tied him to the arm of a tree by his hands, about two feet off the ground. They brought out hungry dogs that hadn't eaten for two full days. The dogs growled and snarled with bare teeth at the hanging man. Suddenly, the area became intolerably noisy due to the barking dogs, which were forcefully and roughly jumping around for their food. With a signal from Zorik, the soldiers let the dogs go.

The dogs began to eat up the feet, the legs and the thigh of the hanging man. The continuous, horrible screaming burst from the man's mouth, a painful outcry that many people had never heard in their lives. The dogs ate the captive's genitals— their delicacy—and then opened the abdomen. Amazingly, the man was still alive until half of his internal organs were gone. When the dogs began to eat his liver and stomach, he became quiet. The Mongol soldiers cut the rope that held him to the tree, making the body thud on the ground. Scores of dogs feasted on the remaining body. Within no time, there was nothing left, and no human trace whatsoever.

The dogs looked still hungry. The other captive was forced to watch every moment, giving him intolerable horror and enormous psychological pain.

When the soldiers approached him and began to strip off his clothing, he dropped his head and shouted, "Stop it! Please! I will talk!"

The Mongols found an area of the river at the northern side, which was so shallow that even a horseman could cross it. At nighttime, the attackers crossed the river on horseback, and the other group retrieved the horses back to the city. Based on this information, Batu made a plan, but he didn't put it into action immediately; rather, he decided to wait. Instead, he reinforced the guard units in that area.

In early May, Subedei rejoined Batu, and they looked around the city of Kozelsk.

CHAPTER 31

Subedei said, "My lord, Sein Khan, you did the right thing. For this kind of a big city, a two-sided, simultaneous attack is the way to go. The water is rather warm now, so we should build the bridge."

The Mongols did bridgework mainly at night to minimize the casualties. It took about 10 days to complete the two interim bridges at the north and the south. The bridge was so strong that two horsemen could cross the river side by side.

Batu sent out the messenger for surrender, and the reply was cold.

"We will fight to the last man!"

The unknown Russian chronicler wrote:

Though our prince is young,
We, as true believers,
Should die to the world,
Of martyrdom
To leave a good name,
And behind the coffin,
To receive the crown,
Of immortality.

Early in the morning on the following day, the Mongols began to hurl rocks and naphtha flames into the city. The houses and residential buildings, which were mainly made of wood, quickly caught fire. The dark smoke from the burning buildings covered the sky, which was seen from 10 leagues (35 miles) away.

The Mongol commandoes climbed up the wall despite the showering of arrows, rocks and logs. In the afternoon, the image of the victors was looming. The horses in the city were horrified by the flames, the smoke and the human screaming, and they jumped around, putting the city into uncontrollable chaos.

In the late afternoon, the resistance ended. Batu's order was to not leave any living souls—no survivors.

In the nighttime, the Mongol soldiers, in groups of four and five men with torches, patrolled the street and confirmed the killings. The dead body of the boy prince, Prince Vasily, was found in the palace with his mother, and they were both beheaded.

The city of Kozelsk burned for three days. The Mongols saved as many valuables as possible, including horses. After that, the city was leveled with no standing structures.

Batu asked Zorik, "What is our damage?"

"Almost 2,000."

It was the highest number of Mongol mortalities that they had experienced in a single battle. Batu held a funeral ceremony for the fallen Mongols and left the city. They couldn't stay there too long because of bad smells and toxic gas from the decomposing dead bodies.

As he began to move further west on horseback, Batu looked back at the leveled city and told his followers, "Kozelsk is the city of woe."

CHAPTER 32

Into Crimea

The Mongol army headed south to the Don River basin. They needed a long rest. They had to refill military necessities like weapons and armor and, most of all, new soldiers and horses.

Before they took a break, however, they needed to conquer, reconquer or pacify the southern Russian area mainly for safety measures, so they divided into five groups. For these divided, small, individual expeditions, many of Batu's brothers and cousin princes joined in: Berke, Seiban, Bujek and Buri. They conquered the Circassians, Alans, Kipchaks, Maris and Votyaks. Batu and Subedei went further south, chasing down Cumans and Russians. They subdued Mordovia and moved into the Crimean Peninsula.

Batu asked, "What place is Crimea like?"

Subedei answered, "Some of the area is covered with mountains, especially in the eastern and southern sides. Other than that, it is grassland. We have information that a large number of Kipchaks and Kievan-Russians are sheltered in the mountain area. Along the southern shore, the Venetians, one of our allies, have their own port cities."

Batu murmured, "We will root them out."

Batu arrived at the spot where he could see the vast Black Sea. He stood on the hill, on horseback, with Subedei next to him.

Batu saw an image of the beautiful, peaceful and enormously large, blue sea and asked Subedei, "What is the name of this sea?"

"I don't know, my lord. I heard some local people calling it the 'Inhospitable Sea' or the 'Black Sea.'"

"Why?"

Subedei responded, "I had been told that when the stormy season comes, it is hard to navigate, and the sea looks black with high waves."

Batu thought for a while and said, "We will call it the Black Sea and change all the records and maps accordingly."

The Mongols used this same tactic in group hunting to remove remnants of Russians and Kipchaks who hid in the mountain area. They devastated each town, one by one, eliminating all the resistant forces in the peninsula.

Batu returned to the Don River basin where he planned to stay for some time—probably for at least a year. All the other groups arrived, one by one, bringing enormous amounts of war booty and many prisoners and captives. A huge number of horses, cattle and sheep was added to the Mongol inventory.

Suddenly, a big tent city emerged at the Don River basin. The news had spread to the Arab merchants and to others who were closely following the Mongol army for their businesses. Only the merchant group with a permission tablet could do business with each Mongol soldier. Each Mongol soldier was allowed to plunder for three days and had to report whatever they got. Then, Jarqu would do his job and divide the booty fairly among the soldiers. In the case of the captives or prisoners, they were the property of the khagan or the Mongol Empire; however, like Batu's independent expedition army, the commander of the army, Batu, owned all the official properties, including captives and prisoners.

The chronicler Faqih Ashraf Aziz wrote:

I saw many captives and prisoners sold to slave traders. Sometimes they bought them by numbers, or sometimes they would check each captive and prisoner for their body condition and then decide the price. Mostly they were young boys of nomadic origin, which they valued highly. I saw almost 2,000 sold and paid for with four chests full of gold. I heard that they will be sold again to an Egyptian sultan.

The chronicler Chun Lee wrote:

There were slave traders who specialized in girls. When they picked up the girls, first they made them naked. Then, they checked every part of their body. If they found any scar tissue or deformity, the price went down. They favored girls with golden hair and blue eyes. They said that they could be sold at a higher price to wealthy Arabs and tribal chieftains. I heard that those girls could be found only among the people of northern European origin or from cold weather lands, like Finnish and Swedes. I was also told that their ancestors moved to the south about 100 years ago, or they were brought down by Vikings.

CHAPTER 33

Disharmony among the princes

It was early autumn when the seasonal changes began. The sky was clean, reflecting only oceanic blue, and the air was pure and arid. The Mongols were busier at this time of the year to reap the hay for their livestock and smooth the leathers and felt. They were thousands of miles away from their home; however, wherever they went, it was their homeland as long as the blue sky and Mother Earth were there.

The royal, golden tent—gold was Batu's favorite color—had been erected for the special occasion of celebrating the successful campaign so far: 55 battles with 55 wins. The inside of this tent, which could accommodate a maximum of 200 people, was arranged with military folding chairs and tables based on the number of anticipated attendants. On the northern side, Batu's seat was arranged; to his left, his wives, concubines and all the other women sat. Subedei sat to his right, and Batu's cousin Monku was next.

As the banquet started, a team of seven or eight musicians began to play their musical instruments, bringing smooth music into the tent. After making sure that everybody was there, Batu gave the signal to the banquet director. Slave boys and girls from different backgrounds, in their own traditional costumes, began to serve appetizers from a huge, silver plate. In front of every participant, a silver dish and goblet were arranged, and they could choose their favorite drink from many different varieties. The Mongol's kumiss, Samarqand wine, Russian old mead and fermented barley drink were served.

The Mongols had very specific traditional and cultural drinking rules. The most prestigious, powerful, high-ranking person in the meeting drank first, and the second drinker was the second in rank. They didn't know who made that rule, but it was perhaps a thousand-year-old social and cultural tradition. Because of this unique culture, peaceful and friendly gatherings sometimes ended up with unexpected relational soreness or even tragedy.

At this special celebrational banquet, the worst-case scenario turned into reality. After confirming that everybody had their own goblet, Batu got to his feet with his golden goblet in his right hand.

"To the glory of the Mongols!" he shouted, and then emptied the goblet in one breath and sat down.

As Subedei was about to pick up his goblet and say something, a man in the corner stood up abruptly and said, "Wait! I have something to say. We are all here to fight for the Mongol Empire—not for one particular person. When we are sharing same hardships and destinies, we deserve to be equal."

The man was Kuyuk Khan, the firstborn son of the current khagan Ogodei. Among the soldiers, Kuyuk's name was frequently mentioned as the next khagan. He had a retinue of 2,000 soldiers, which belonged to Ogodei's family, and he tended to move independently. He had an interwoven emotional complex with jealousy and fear toward Batu.

In reality, all the Russian and European campaigns were for Batu because the conquered land would be in Batu's domain. At the same time, if Batu became too powerful, he could not be sure that his ambition of the next khagan would be smooth. At the same time, he had bitter feelings because all the important campaigns were entrusted to Monku, Batu's double cousin as well as his best friend. The disharmony among the princes started from the second generation with Batu's father Juchi, who could never get along with his brothers Chagatai and Ogotai due to illegitimacy. This disharmony continued to the third generation.

Batu said to Kuyuk, "What is the way that you suggest?"

"We should drink at the same time, all together!"

Batu paused and then remarked, "I just followed our tradition. I am the commander in chief for this army group. I deserve to be the first drinker. The tradition cannot be changed overnight or by one person. I cannot accept such a suggestion."

Another man stood up and shouted, "You are stubborn like an old woman. You are just an old woman with a beard!"

This other man was Buri Khan, the grandson of Chagatai, who was the elder brother of the current khagan Ogodei.

Kuyuk and Buri jumped to their feet and walked out of the golden tent, refusing to continue the banquet. Inside the tent, deep silence flowed for a moment, but Subedei picked up his goblet.

"To our fallen soldiers!" he shouted.

The banquet continued without interruption, and the musicians continued to play their musical instruments and make smooth music.

Kuyuk and Buri returned to Karakorum, the new capital of the Mongol Empire, after spending almost a month to travel back. They were accompanying their retinue of 2,000 soldiers; however, Batu sent out an arrow messenger who held a letter to Ogodei, which arrived at Karakorum 10 days before Kuyuk and Buri arrived.

Batu's letter described all the incidents in detail. Upon reading Batu's letter, Ogodei was greatly disappointed in his son Kuyuk's behavior and felt great despair. When he heard that Kuyuk had arrived, he avoided seeing him for 15 days.

When Ogodei finally saw Kuyuk, he said, "You are a deserter! The punishment for deserters is death! Batu is the commander in the field. He is out of my hands, and he is the final decision maker. Go back to him and wait for his judgment."

At the same time, Chagatai furiously reprimanded his grandson Buri and said, "The only way you can save your life is to go back to Batu and beg for his mercy. He is the only one who can handle this incident. All is in Yassa, the Great One's decree."

When Batu saw these two men again in his tent, he pondered awhile. Ever since Batu became the legitimate successor of Juchi's ulus, he was always trying to find out the answer to this question: "Why did the Great One make me the successor?"

DISHARMONY AMONG THE PRINCES

The answer came to Batu, he believed. It was the Mongol unity. Genghis Khan feared that the empire he built would be split into many smaller fractions after his death.

Batu faced them with a smiling face and said, "Brothers! I have already forgotten! Welcome back to our expedition!"

The fall of Kiev:
The carnival of death

In autumn of the year 1239, the Mongol army began to move again. They received fresh horses and reinforcements of newly trained royal cavalry from the Mongol mainland.

Batu's main target was the city of Kiev; however, before he got there, he had to cross two big barriers: the city of Chernigov and the city of Pereyaslav. Both cities were located along the Dnieper River, and Pereyaslav was just 50 miles from Kiev. It wasn't an easy job to take over these two cities because the population of Chernigov alone was about 30,000.

At the council meeting, Subedei mentioned, "If we take over the city of Kiev, it will conclude the conquest of all of Russia. Kiev is the Russians' political, cultural and religious center. Their population is more than 50,000—the biggest number that we have ever met in a Russian campaign."

Batu asked, "Who is their ruler now?"

"Their inner conflicts for hegemony among their princes are still going on—even at war time. At this moment, Prince Michael Vsevolodovich is in power."

Batu continued by asking, "What about the city of Chernigov?"

Subedei said, "Prince Mstislav Glebovich is in charge."

Batu's cousin Monku was entrusted with conquering the city of Kiev. Batu moved to the Cuman land (Donbas) and, from there, dispatched two groups of armies to attack the city of Chernigov and Pereyaslav, respectively. The Mongol army destroyed the small cities or towns of Hlukhiv, Kursk, Rylsk and Putivl, one by one, which were on the way to Chernigov and Pereyaslav.

One group finally arrived at Chernigov. Upon the news that the Mongols had arrived, Prince Mstislav came out from the city to confront the Mongol army with his regular troops and a militia of 7,000; however, he soon found that to confront the Mongols outside of the city was suicidal and an unwise tactic.

The Mongols destroyed Mstislav's army just like farmers cut grass with their scythes. Mstislav retreated to the city after losing almost half of his troops and closed the gate. Chernigov could last just a few more days. As the city's protective wall was breached by the Mongol catapults, there was no more resistance—just a huge massacre. Prince Mstislav managed to escape under the sacrifice of many of his soldiers, ending up losing everything but a few of his druzhinas (members of his personal retinue).

It was October 18, 1239—the end of the principality of Chernigov. The end of the city of Pereyaslav came almost at the same time by the other group in the Mongol army. Pereyaslav met the same fate as Chernigov. The church of St. Michael in

Pereyaslav was destroyed and Bishop Simon was killed; on the other hand, Bishop Porfyriv of Chernigov was spared.

Porfyriv shouted to his people, "The power is coming from God! Obey! That's God's will!"

When Batu heard these words, he said to his followers, "He is the true priest. Politics and religion should be separate. Save him and let him continue his priestship."

The Mongols relocated Bishop Porfyriv to Hlukhiv and allowed him to continue his priestship.

In the autumn of 1240, Batu's cousin Monku arrived in Horodok Pisochny while he was scouting in the vicinity of Kiev. He was on the banks of the Dnieper River and could see the image of Kiev across the river. He was taken with and fascinated by the splendor of the city.

The magnificent city,
On the high bank of Dnieper,
Ancient Byzantine treasure,
White wall, beautiful gardens,
The metropolitan city of Russian princes,
The seat of the chief patriarch of all Russia,
Thirty churches with gilded cupolas,
The grand church of Tithe,
A chef d'oeuvre of Greek architect,
The monastery of Petchersky,
With its golden cross,
It is sure of,
the city of God.

Monku wanted to take over the city undamaged and sent out the envoys for surrender. The seven envoy members—three of them being Russians—were captured just after they entered the city and held in custody.

On that day, Prince Michael Vsevolodovich of Kiev summoned his voivode Dmitry and said, "Listen! I am going to get out of the city with my family. I am heading for Hungary, and then to Silesia. I will try to get help from there. While I am out, you will oversee the city and the people. Can you do that?"

It was very clear that the ruler of Kiev was trying to run away, abandoning his city and its people for his own safety.

Dmitry, one of his loyal retinue, asked, "When are you leaving, my lord?"

Prince Michael replied, "Tonight, at midnight. Keep this to yourself. Don't even tell the guard soldiers at the gate."

"I will not breathe a word. But what shall I do with envoys?"

"Kill them!"

Dmitry bowed to Prince Michael and said, "As you wish, my lord."

That night, around midnight, 10 wagons and carriages passed through the gate. Due to their luxuriousness, the guard soldiers quickly noticed that they were a train of the royal family. The news, which was supposed to be kept secret, spread like wildfire. Some of enraged citizens chased the train and caught up with them at Sroda. They attacked, plundered and killed the prince's granddaughter. Nevertheless, the prince and his family escaped into Hungary.

Dmitry, who was now in charge of the city, immediately cut off the heads of all the seven Mongol envoy members who were held in custody. He ordered his soldiers to show off their heads by hanging them on the main gate.

Monku marched toward Kiev, and his Mongol army surrounded the city. He commanded 20,000 levies to close off the moat around the city. When it was done, the Mongol catapults hurled stones to breach the wall and one of the three main gates. With endless bombardment of large stones and naphtha flames, Kiev was forced into uncontrollable chaos and enveloped in flames.

On December 6, 1240, the protective wall and the gate had been breached, allowing the Mongol commandoes to get into the city. The street combat began and allowed the main body of the Mongol army to pour into the city. A horrible massacre and destruction followed, gradually changing the city into a living hell. It was the carnival of death.

Many people escaped to balconies and flat roofs of churches, but they soon collapsed under the weight of people who were standing on them, crushing many. The killings, plundering and destruction lasted for about seven days. Most of the city had been burned, and only six out of 40 major buildings remained standing. The death toll was 48,000 out of 50,000, leaving only 2,000 survivors. This completed the conquest of the city of Kiev and opened the gate for the Mongols to step into mainland Europe.

Oh! Kiev,
The mother of all Russian cities,
Grandeur of the cathedral of St. Sophia,
The great spirits of the Russian soul,

THE FALL OF KIEV: THE CARNIVAL OF DEATH

Splendid city with architectural monuments,
Reduced to ashes and rubble.
The bones of the holy men,
The tomb of Olga,
Trampled under horses' hoofs.
Oh! Holy Mary,
Where art thou?

The chronicler Faqih Ashraf Aziz wrote:

The Mongol soldiers captured voivode Dmitry in front of Batu and Monku. Dmitry's hands were tied back, and he was badly injured. Looked like he got two shots of arrows: one in his left-side eye and the other on his waist. Even though he survived, he will suffer from being disabled. Batu and Monku talked to each other for a moment, and then they left. Dmitry had been shown mercy. They set him free, probably for his loyalty.

The chronicler Chun Lee wrote:

The Mongols said that about 50,000 Russians were killed in this campaign, but I think it was more than that. I've never seen such a big pile of dead bodies before. It was on every corner of the city. When I saw the dead men's and women's faces, it was horrible and goose-bumping. Their last images were imbued with enormous physical and emotional pain. All their eyes were wide open with a fierce glare of something. They said that there are about 2,000 survivors, but most of them were girls and small children. I presume that the girls were saved for their own pleasure and the small children were saved to sell as slaves.

The fate of the Cuman king Koten

Koten, the Cuman (Kipchak) king, escaped to Hungary, thus averting the tidal wave of the Mongol onslaught, and 40,000 huts (households) followed him. Based on a prior agreement with Hungarian King Bela IV, Koten would convert to Christianity and become his loyal follower. Koten was supposed to be baptized once he stepped onto Hungarian soil. King Bela IV was a zealot of the Catholic church and a crucial opportunist. He knew that the Mongols were coming and wanted to reinforce his defensive power, so he accepted about 40,000 war-experienced Cuman horsemen.

When Koten, the Cuman chieftain and king, and his 40,000 huts crossed the border, King Bela was waiting for them.

"Welcome friends! My Hungarian pasture is wide enough for you and your people. We will build a flourishing and prosperous future on this land together. This is God's will."

Bela baptized the Cuman chieftain Koten on the spot. In return, Koten alleged his loyalty to King Bela, and the king guaranteed Koten's safety by oath. Bela allowed the huge group of Cuman people to move into a sparsely populated area in his territory and stay there; however, King Bela's decision turned out to be a poorly calculated and an unwise one.

When one makes a decision, he always consider the pros and cons and weighs which side is heavier. What motivated King Bela's decision to accept Koten's request for permission to move into his territory? Perhaps he could save 40,000 souls and make them Christians. Perhaps he could use the Cuman horsemen as human shields when the Mongols came. Who knows?

Not everybody in King Bela's kingdom agreed with his decision. The first group to reject his decision were the bishops. At that time in Europe, two powers were tussling for hegemony all the time: the church and the monarch. In many cases, the church was more powerful.

Bishops were the leaders of churches, had the power to collect taxes and, most importantly, had military power. They could recruit soldiers and organize and lead the army. They lived in the palace next to the kings and had a luxurious life. Bishops primarily belonged to the pope. When the king needed military power, he needed agreement from the bishops and nobles. When it came to the agreement, the bishops and nobles recruited the soldiers. In this case, the adopted Cumans and their chieftain Koten would be loyal to King Bela only—nobody else—like a personal army.

The Cumans (Kipchaks) were widely unpopular and unwelcome among the Hungarian people. The basic problem was that the Hungarians were sedentary while the Cumans were nomadic. When the Cumans came into the Hungarian territory, they came with huge numbers of cattle, causing severe damage to pastures, crops, gardens, orchards, vineyards and other goods of the Hungarian people. The worst part was that the Cumans were wild people, so they committed many petty and serious crimes, yet they were rarely brought to justice. They frequently raped poor peasant girls and stole valuables from their Hungarian neighbors.

For these reasons, enmity grew between King Bela and his people—especially when it became known to the people of Hungary that King Bela received a letter from Batu. They began to believe that their king invited calamity by accepting the Cumans.

When Batu received a report that Hungarian King Bela IV accepted 40,000 Cumans, the news annoyed him.

He immediately dispatched a messenger with this letter:

I am Batu, the messenger and captain of the all-powerful God, to whom he has given on Earth to exalt those who submit to him and cast down his adversaries. I have sent you, the king of Hungary, messengers many times. You have sent me back none of them nor did you send me messengers of your own or letters. I know that you are a rich and powerful king, that you have many soldiers under you and that you govern a great kingdom alone. Therefore, it is difficult for you to submit to me voluntarily.

Further, I have learned that you keep the Kipchaks, my slaves, under your protection. Whence I charge you henceforward that you do not keep them with you, and do not make me your enemy on their account. For it is easier for them to escape than for you since they, having no house, are continually on the move with their tents and may possibly escape. But you, living in a house and possessing fortresses and cities, how can you flee from my grasp?

One day, a big crowd gathered in front of the palace where King Bela and Koten were staying.

The crowd began to clamor in a loud voice, "Kill Koten! Kill Koten! Koten must die!"

King Bela heard this, but he just sat on his throne with his eyes and ears closed. What was in his mind? He probably knew that he needed a scapegoat to lead his people. He already forgot the promise of safety, which was fastened by oath.

The throng broke into the palace and found Koten in one room. He was with several of his guards, who tried to protect him with bows and arrows, but they were simply outnumbered. The throng of Hungarians and Germans rushed into the room, captured Koten and cut off his head. They threw away the head through the window of the palace to the crowd outside.

Upon receiving the news that their chieftain had been murdered, the Cumans retaliated. They began to kill the Hungarians and plundered, burned and destroyed the houses. They took valuables, cattle and horses, and got out of the Hungarian territory.

They returned to the steppes through Bulgaria, and many of them surrendered to Batu.

Into the center of Europe

Subedei, orlok (field marshal) of the Mongol army, remarked, "The war with Hungary will be the pivotal battle in the conquest of all of Europe."

He said this at the war council in Batu's tent, which could accommodate a maximum of 200 people. All the princes, noyans, generals and captains of 1,000 men attended.

Subedei added, "Hungary has the most powerful army in Europe, and King Bela claims himself as the protector of Europe. His soldiers are good horse riders, and they could have up to 100,000 troops—maybe more."

Baidar, a prince and Chagatai's son, who was sitting in the corner, asked, "What could be the whole population of Hungary?"

"We don't know," Subedei responded, "but we presume four to five million. Before we face Hungary, we have to deal with the northern and southern sides of Hungary first, which means Poland and Silecia at the north and Transylvania and Wallachia at the south. Otherwise, we could be surrounded by them in case their cooperation among them goes smooth. If we hit them successfully first at both the north and the south, then we can concentrate on their center, which is Hungary."

Zorik, the spy chief, said, "In the north, there is a group of soldiers called the Teutonic knights, and their origin is Germany. Originally, they were created to protect the Christendom, but they also protected German immigrants to Prussia and Lithuania. They built up fortification along the Baltic shoreline. They are loyal to the pope and closely related to the Holy Roman Empire and the Polish dukes—Conrad of Mazovia and Henry the Pious of Silesia. So, when we go into Poland, they will come at us together.

"Their characteristics are their armor and their helmet. They are using a full-coverage helmet shaped like a cylinder, and their armor, which covers them from their neck to their toes, weighs about 3 puus (100 pounds). They will hold a large, half-almond-shaped shield. On the shield will be painted the symbol of the Christian religion: a red-colored cross. Their movements are a bit slow due to the weight of the armor and, once they fall from the horse, it could be troublesome to get back on it. They could be good at close combat or inside the city."

Somebody in the other corner asked this question in a loud voice: "What are their weapons?"

Zorik answered, "Their major weapons are lances and straight swords, and they also keep maces and hammers."

Subedei intervened and said, "Our arrow can penetrate their armor. We are already using it. When our archers target the armored enemy, it is advised to use a long-range bow and an arrow to penetrate their armor. Our long-range arrowhead is reinforced with a very strong metal, so it can carry out the particular function of penetrating the armor."

At that time, the Mongol soldier's primary weapon was a bow and an arrow. Each soldier carried two bows—one for short range and the other for long range—and the long-range bow was more powerful.

Subedei added, "An armored knight's weak spot is his armpit because it is not protected. Even their necks are sword-proof because they are wearing a mail coif. Our soldiers should acknowledge that. The best way to handle them is to kill them by arrow or spear or pull them down from the horse and attack them with mace or a battle axe. We should train our soldiers in that regard."

Somebody asked, "Do they use bows and arrows?"

Subedei answered, "Yes, they use a crossbow, but they hold shields in their left hand. Mostly they use lances or swords with the other hand. Their foot soldiers carry cross-bows. It is a good combination. So, when we are on the field, we should separate their knights and foot soldiers. If this is successful, we can handle them one by one. Use a lot of the mangudai [fake retreat] tactic."

Zorik added, "The other military groups that would join the Polish are the Knight Templars and the Hospitallers. They are of French origin and part of the Crusaders, and their orig-inal function is taking care of the sick. But they are surely mil-itary powers."

After saying this, Zorik gave signals to the guards at the southern flap door. A group of Mongol soldiers moved in dummies dressed in Teutonic knight armor and helmets as well as those of the Knight Templars and the Hospitallers. They displayed them at one spot inside the tent for show.

The guards also displayed their weaponry and posted a large map, 6 feet by 6 feet, which was painted on thick paper and secured to a board. They handed out the woodcut print map in rolled paper. Subedei also explained how to handle enemy cavalry in case the whole cavalry was combined with foot soldiers. There were many discussions about every kind of situation, like how to handle each case and how to survive in unfavorably complicated moments.

Before the end of the council meeting, Batu gave a closing remark.

"Like my orlok said, the Hungarian campaign will be the pivotal battle of the whole European campaign. I want the Pannonian Plain. We could breed millions of horses there. I want to make Hungary the ruling center of all of Europe. If possible, capture Hungarian King Bela alive. If that happens, I will make him king of Europe under my rule."

Batu entrusted the northern European campaign to Prince Baidar and Prince Kadan. At the time, the Mongol army was counted as 130,000, but Batu had to leave 30,000 of them in Russia to maintain control. He gave 20,000 troops to Baidar and Kadan for the northern campaign, 10,000 to his brother Seiban for a vanguard, 40,000 for himself and the remaining 30,000 would be led by Subedei and Kuyuk for the southern campaign.

The master plan was formulated by Subedei. He mapped out every detail and explained clearly all the participants' roles until they were sure that complete victory was theirs.

Subedei's final remark was the highlight of the meeting.

"The war is cheating! The fake tactic works great! The final victor is the best cheater!"

He ended with a loud guffaw.

After the general meeting, Batu and Subedei got together and confirmed the espionage system in Europe, the pacifying units and the interpreters' corps.

Subedei said, "The Venetians' cooperation is praiseworthy. The basic information about the map was given by them, and the Chinese mapmakers finalized it."

The interpreters were essential for the conquerors when treading on different soil and dealing with different backgrounds of people. The Mongols were well prepared. At any place they went, they tried to save technicians, artisans, scholars and interpreters. In the Mongol army's interpreters' corps, there was an Armenian bishop who could speak six languages and one English prisoner who could speak seven languages. There were over 200 interpreters in the Mongol army.

Subedei told Batu, "Sein Khan, you are the main body to face the Hungarian major and their king, Bela. You'd better not move until you hear that Baidar and Kadan's northern flank destroyed the Polish army. At the same time, I and Prince Kuyuk will pacify Transylvania and Wallachia. Wait until that moment. We should make a three-pronged attack to the Hungarian main body. They could be strong and outnumber us."

Batu asked Subedei, "Orlok, do you think this is the right time to use the black powder?"

Subedei tilted his head a little bit and responded, "Maybe— but selectively. We did fine so far without it."

Batu nodded.

CHAPTER 37

Into Poland

In January 1241, Prince Baidar and Prince Kadan and their 20,000 Mongol cavalries marched toward Lublin, the first Polish city they encountered. The population of that city, which was taken by surprise and seemingly unprepared, was annihilated and the city was burned. Without delay, the Mongols moved toward their next target.

When they were leaving the main body of the army, Subedei gave them this piece of advice: "Move fast! Don't stay in one place too long. Don't give the enemy time to get help or a rescue army from the neighboring kingdom."

At the time, Poland had four dukes: Conrad of Mazovia, Miecislaw of Oppeln, Henry the Pious of Silesia and Boleslaw the Chaste of Sandomir and Cracow. Like Russia, they were concerned with inner conflicts among them and not from the outside. Even Duke Conrad was sheltering one of the princes of Russia—Michael of Chernigov—but he wasn't different from the other dukes.

In early February, Baidar and Kadan crossed the frozen Vistula River. They easily destroyed and sacked the city of Sandomir, and then planned their next step. They split their army into two groups: Kadan for Mazovia in the northwest direction and Baidar for Cracow in the southwest.

When Baidar's vanguard unit arrived at the gate in Cracow, they were carrying a significant number of Polish prisoners, including small children and girls. When Palantine Vladimir, the commander in chief of the Polish army at Cracow, saw this, he opened the gate and ordered his army to attack the small Mongol army. The Mongols began to retreat, and Palantine Vladimir ordered a full-scale attack. The Mongol soldiers occasionally sent shots of arrows and turned their back toward the chasers.

The chasing game continued until they reached Chmielnik, about 60 miles from Cracow. When the chasers arrived at the road, which had a thick forest on its sides, showers of arrows greeted them. The Polish chasers realized that they were trapped, but it was too late. They all collapsed from Mongol arrows and scimitars. Palantine Vladimir fell from his horse after being struck by several arrows.

A few survivors went back to the city and gave reports. The city of Cracow fell into big chaos. There was no army left to protect them—only a few gatekeepers. Upon the tragic news, Duke Boleslaw hurriedly packed his necessities and as many treasures as he could carry and rushed to Hungary with his family. He was married to Hungarian King Bela's daughter. The streets inside Cracow were crowded with loaded carts, horses and people who were seeking refuge in forests, mountains or other cities. It was hell.

A boy trumpeter climbed onto the balcony of St. Mary's church and began to sound an alarm. That sorrowful, somewhat exotic sound was loud enough to reach everybody's ears, even in the chaos, and it lasted for some time.

Before long, the Mongol reconnaissance unit arrived at the scene. One of them picked up an arrow from his quiver and carefully aimed it at the trumpeter. The arrow flew, making a horrible sound, and lodged on the side of the boy trumpeter's neck. He swayed on his feet, took a few tottering steps backward, and then fell down the balcony with the trumpet in his hand.

When the main body of the Mongol army arrived, they found a ghost city. They set a fire and burned it to the ground. Without much delay, they continued marching.

Baidar and Kadan were supposed to meet at the city of Breslau, the capital city of Silesia. Silesia was one of the principalities ruled by Duke Henry. Months before, Duke Henry had a war council with his voivodes and boyars (members of aristocracy next to princes) and made a war plan. Although Poland was divided into four principalities, Henry was the most powerful and was regarded as the king of Poland.

At the council, he remarked, "We will transfer our capital to Liegnitz. That is the rightful city to build up our defense line. Destroy all the bridges on the Oder River to delay the Mongol advance."

One of his boyars asked, "What about all of our properties and the 20,000 people here?"

Duke Henry said, "Just leave everything there like nothing has happened. Let the Mongols pillage and plunder the city. That will keep them here for some days. We need time."

CHAPTER 37

After these words, he fell into his chair and closed his eyes.

When Duke Henry learned that the Mongol army put its foot on Polish territory in January, he immediately summoned all the military lords and organized his army. At the same time, he sent messengers everywhere. First, he contacted the Teutonic knights to come to Poland as well as the Knight Templars and the Hospitallers. He hired Austrian and German mercenaries and sent urgent messengers to his brother-in-law Wenceslas, the king of Bohemia, for help.

Their meeting place was Liegnitz. The first group that showed up were the Teutonic knights. Their leader was Poppo von Osterna, Landmeister of Prussia, and he was with his 7,000 knights. They made a majestic, dramatic sight in their shining armor and glinting helmets in the sunlight with flying pennants. They even put armor on their horses and decorated them luxuriously.

In front of Duke Henry, Poppo von Osterna bowed, kneeled on one of his legs, and said:

> *By the order of Holy God,*
> *Punishment was ordained,*
> *For the evil pagans,*
> *To send them back to*
> *Tartarus.*
> *I, the servant of God,*
> *With my brothers of*
> *Teutonic knights,*
> *Will complete the task,*

INTO POLAND

On the collateral of
Our honor.

Ponce d'Aubon, grandmaster of the French Templars, made a similar pledge with his 500 men. Duke Henry's total manpower swelled to about 30,000, adding foot soldiers and 25,000 mercenaries to his own knights. He was waiting for King Wenceslas and his 50,000-man army.

Ponce d'Aubon asked one of his voivodes, "How long will it take for the Bohemian army to get here?"

One of his voivodes in charge answered, "Basically, we don't know. I presume it will be seven to 10 days."

Baidar and Kadan captured the city of Breslau without serious resistance. It was completely different than Cracow, which was a ghost city. Many people were still in the churches with their valuable properties, and all the gold and silver crosses and ceremonial utensils remained untouched. The Mongol soldiers became excited because the treasures were everywhere.

Baidar and Kadan said to each other, "This is a trap! We shouldn't stay here too long!"

Through their spy network, Baidar and Kadan found out that the main body of the Polish army was in Liegnitz, about 40 miles from Breslau to the west. They abandoned Breslau and continued marching in full speed.

When they arrived at the Oder River, they found all the bridges destroyed. They made temporary bridges by tying together large sheepskin airbags, and then tying flat, wooden boards on top of them. It took two full days to complete the temporary bridges.

When Duke Henry received the news that the Mongols had crossed the river, he realized that he couldn't wait any longer.

He asked his reporter, "What could be the size of the Mongol army?"

The reporter replied, "To my eyes, it looked like about 20,000."

Duke Henry murmured, "20,000? Maybe I can handle them!"

Duke Henry had an army of 30,000, including 7,000 Teutonic knights, which they nicknamed "the flowers of Europe."

On April 9, 1241, two armies met, face to face, on the plain of Walstadt. Duke Henry drew up his army in four divisions: the volunteers from Goldburg, led by Duke Boleslaw; the conscripts from all of Poland, led by Sudislaw; the army from Oppeln and the Teutonic knights, led by Duke Miecislaw; and the Silesian and Moravian main armies, the Knight Templars and the Hospitallers, led by Duke Henry.

Duke Henry saw a group of Mongol soldiers rapidly approaching his side. This Mongol vanguard unit looked like about 2,000 men. He immediately let out a similar number of his own Silesian cavalry and waited. It didn't take long for his soldiers to crush the Mongol army, making them retreat to their starting point. A quick inspiration hit his brain like lightning.

"This war is mine! I am the victor! I can see it with my own eyes!"

Henry immediately let out his most powerful weapon—
the Teutonic knights—as well as his own Polish knights.

He shouted, "Destroy everything in front of you!"

The Teutonic knights dashed to the Mongols in full speed.
The chasing game continued for a while. Even after 20 miles
of chasing, they could never catch up to the Mongols. It was
mangudai, the Mongol's tactic of fake retreat.

When the chasing Polish knights passed a certain spot,
numerous smoke bombs exploded, covering the whole area
with smoke. At the same time, a volley of arrows came from
every direction. The Teutonic knights began to fall back,
yet it created more confusion. The long, chasing line of
Teutonic and Polish knights began to collide with each other
in the thick smoke. It was only a few short moments, yet it
was enough time for the Mongol archers. Almost half of the
Teutonic and Polish knights fell from their arrow shots.

Then the Mongol heavy cavalry, which was hiding on the
back side of the hillock, showed up. They surrounded half-
dead Teutonic and Polish knights. A man-to-man fight continued, but the Teutonic and Polish knights couldn't move
as fast as the Mongols, and it became a one-sided game. The
knights could be strong inside the city but not in the field.

Soon, the dead bodies of the Teutonic and Polish knights
were strewn across the field. It was time to follow the Polish
infantry and crossbow men, who were still coming without knowing what had happened to the knight cavalries.
Separation of enemy cavalries and foot soldiers was the original plan of the Mongols. They used the same tactic of throw-
ing the smoke bombs to them, and they were easy prey for the
Mongol archers. It didn't take long for the Mongols to finalize

the battle. The Polish main power and their allies, including the flowers of the European knight, lay dead.

Duke Henry's impatient judgment might have brought irrevocable misery, but he tried to remain in the battlefield until the last moment; however, when he saw a group of Mongol soldiers approaching him, he began to gallop his horse at full speed in the opposite direction. Some of his guard soldiers followed him. The Mongol chasers shot down his guards, one by one, and finally caught up with him. They immediately cut off his head and carried it on a spear.

The Mongols cut off the right-side ears of all the dead Polish soldiers and their allies, and then put the ears into large sacks. Nine sacks of human ears were sent to Batu for proof of their complete victory.

The Mongols marched back to Liegnitz and put a siege on the citadel inside the city where all the remaining citizens took refuge. The Mongol soldiers circled the citadel with Duke Henry's head on a spear tip. It was just a matter of a time before the refugees inside the citadel walked out of their hiding places if they didn't have enough food and water.

Among the people of the city of Breslau, which could escape the Mongol onslaught, this rumor circulated throughout entire city: "The prayer of the chief priest worked. God put a strong, protective shield of light over the city, so the Mongols were scared to come into the city."

The chronicler Faqih Ashraf Aziz wrote:

I was with Batu Khan all the time. He was well aware of what was happening in the Poland campaign, just like he watched his own palm. The messengers were coming and going once or twice a day.

I asked him, "Do you think the Bohemian army of 50,000 will join Duke Henry?"

Batu stared into my eyes and said, "Fifty thousand is exaggerated. They don't have such a big number of armies—not even half. Even though they are coming, they will take a long, long time or won't show up at all. If Duke Henry was in the winning game, they might show up; otherwise, they will never join him. There is nobody in the world who would help others and risk themselves unless he is a fool."

The chronicler Chun Lee wrote:

I was with Baidar and Kadan. After their complete victory over the Polish army and their allies, they talked to each other.

Baidar said, "We still have time before we join our main body. What shall we do?"

They decided to sack the city of Breslau, which was untouched. They took all the valuable things in the city and massacred all 20,000 people. After that, they divided their army in half, and half began to devastate Bohemia, Silesia and a large area of Poland. They destroyed and sacked the towns of Heinrichau, Ottmanchaw, Bolatiz, Glatz, Hotzenpltz, Leoschutz, Trentschin, Neutra, Tyrnau, Troppsu, Magrave, Freudenthal, Hraditch, Unczove, Olmutz, Litta, Prerau, Gevitch and Brunn.

After all of these devastations, they joined Batu at the north end of the Danube.

CHAPTER 38

Into Transylvania

Batu's southern flank—an army of 30,000—was led by
Subedei, and Princes Kuyuk, Bujek and Buri joined
the campaign.

They started their advancement by raiding the towns of
Kamenetz and Chernovitz, and then arrived at the pass of
Rodna. After they successfully made it, they landed in the
town of Rodna, which shared the same name as the pass they
had just gone through, and entered northern Transylvania.

At the time, Transylvania was part of the territory of the
Hungarian kingdom. Rodna was a rich, much-populated town,
thanks to their gold-mining enterprise. In earlier times, this
area had been the target of many different groups of people due
to the presence of gold. It had been occupied by the Saxon colonists, but later the Roumans (Romanians) took it over and did
business with the Germans. They developed the gold-mining
industry with the Germans, and the area became an important
source of income for both groups. Most of the gold-mine workers and their garrison members were Germans.

Subedei and Kuyuk looked around the city from afar.
Subedei was surprised at the tight and threatening defense

structure of the town. The town was on a high hill in front of the foothill of the lofty mountain, and their defending wall looked quite robust. They had built up a tough defense and did not lose their source of richness: gold.

Subedei murmured, "We need to fake them. A direct attack will cost us a lot of soldiers."

Early in the morning on the following day, the Mongol vanguard unit attacked Transylvania while the other main body waited at another place, ambushed. Count Ariscald, the garrison commander, saw that the Mongols were coming and ordered his crossbow unit to attack. Some Mongols fell from their horses while others kept on coming. Encouraged by the small number of attackers, Ariscald ordered a full-scale attack on the invaders. The Mongols turned their horses around and began to run away. The chasing game continued for about 40 miles. They couldn't catch up, but they concluded that the invaders wouldn't come back. Finally, Ariscald and his 2,000 German garrisons returned in triumph.

In the evening, the 2,000 garrison soldiers and townspeople celebrated their victory. They enjoyed a feast and drank spirits in a wild manner. They were singing and dancing, and some of their soldiers wore Mongol helmets, which they picked up from the battlefield as souvenirs. They even discarded their weapons.

In the night, the Mongol commandoes climbed the town wall and opened the gate. The main body of the Mongol army was already out there. All of the garrison guard and townspeople were slaughtered except for the German gold-mine and weaponry technicians and a group of people who pledged loyalty and volunteered to be guides. Later, 600 German slaves were transferred to the city of Bolac through Talas—a one-month journey—to mine gold and manufacture weapons for the Mongols.

Subedei divided his army into many small units to cover areas of Transylvania and Wallachia. Subedei and Kuyuk went to the city of Wardein, which had a large population and a strong citadel inside the city. The city was surrounded by wooden towers and walls and was captured easily, even though there was some resistance. Many of the residents escaped to the citadel for safety and some went toward the outside of the city.

The Mongols retired for a few days. During their absence, many residents—with the false belief that the storm had passed—came back. This was their mistake. A big massacre in Mongol fashion followed. It seemed that depopulation was the main purpose of the Mongol onslaught.

Many times, they followed the conqueror's set rule: "Do not leave any prospective future enemies behind."

After this event, the Mongols brought seven catapults and began to bombard the citadel. In half a day, the stone wall of the citadel was breached, and the Mongols stormed inside. Many inhabitants had taken refuge inside the cathedral and the churches. Since the Mongols couldn't open the gate of the cathedral easily, they simply lit a fire. All the refugees inside perished in a miserable way. In the other churches, the Mongols ravished the women; outside the building, they slaughtered thousands of inhabitants. After they had their clothing stripped off, some defiant men and women were taken to an open space and impaled.

The Mongols continued to march, heading for Oradea. Guided by German captives, they crossed forests, hills and gorges and finally arrived at the spot halfway between Rodna and Oradea. From there, 100 miles to the south, there was a town named Frata. Though it was small, it was a big town for the churches. They had a big monastery, and they treasured the "holy wood," which was believed to be a real piece of the cross on which Jesus had been nailed.

Subedei dispatched 200 soldiers with two captains. Before their departure, he gave directions and guidelines on how to handle things in every situation. The 200 Mongol soldiers arrived in Frata and began to attack. Since Frata didn't have much defending forces, the head of the monastery immediately dispatched an urgent messenger to the bishop of Oradea for help.

Upon receiving the message, Bishop Benedict of Oradea jumped from his seat and headed for Frata with 400 soldiers. He couldn't afford to lose the invaluable "holy wood" because, if that happened, the blame would fall on him.

While on his way to Frata, Bishop Benedict encountered the Mongol invaders. Noticing that there were not many Mongols, he ordered a full-scale charge. The Mongols turned back and began to retreat; however, when they arrived at a certain spot under the hillock, numerous Mongol horse soldiers in armor slowly approached them.

Bishop Benedict exclaimed in frustration, "Alas! I have fallen into a trap!"

He turned around and tried to retreat to Oradea; however, it was too late. The Mongol main body had already surrounded the city of Oradea. Soon, Bishop Benedict had no place to go. He galloped to the north, toward the city of Pest, the Hungarian capital. He was tricked because the numerous Mongol soldiers that had been ambushed were not the real ones; they were dummies wearing Mongol armor and helmets. They were secured on saddles, and several servants were holding the reins of hundreds of horses and were moving slowly toward the approaching bishop's army.

The city of Oradea was a popular destination for nobles and ladies of Hungary. The citizens—nobles and commoners—enjoyed peaceful days though there were warnings that certain invaders were approaching. Their city wall wasn't protected very well, yet they had a strongly built citadel inside the city, which could accommodate hundreds or possibly a thousand people for a long time. The citadel was protected by a deep moat, high stone walls and towers, and many armored warriors guarded it.

Just after Bishop Benedict's flight, the Mongols surrounded Oradea. The citizens fled into the citadel, ran into nearby forests or just sat in place, not knowing where to go. The Mongols plundered the valuables, and then they started the killings. Their scimitars never spared anyone. They killed them all—nobles, commoners, men and women, even children and toddlers. Afterwards, the Mongols retired for five days. Most people were confident that they had withdrawn, so they came out of the citadel from their hiding places; however, the Mongols were just 5 miles away.

Then, one day at dawn, the Mongols showed up from nowhere, and the second phase of killings started. The victims were those who couldn't manage to return to the citadel or didn't have any place to go. The Mongols brought seven siege engines and bombarded them with rocks, day and night, toward the citadel. Soon, the stone walls gave out, and the Mongols stormed inside the citadel. That was the end of the city of Oradea. The entire population perished.

CHAPTER 39

Confessions of an eyewitness (story one)

M y name is Torre Maggiore, and I am an Italian who is staying in Hungary. I came into Hungary as one of a retinue with Cardinal Giacomo da Pecorara, who was sent to Hungary by the pope.

I am 37 years old and the archdeacon of the city of Varad (Oradea). I am the true witness of what happened in Hungary while the Mongols were here. I am going to tell the story of what I saw directly or heard from a very trustworthy source. I want to leave the true story for future generations.

Oradea is a peaceful city with many nobles and ladies as well as peasant women. The bishop wasn't in the city when the Mongols arrived. Many people refuged to the castle, but my situation was precarious, I decided to run away into the forest and stay there as long as I could. They took the city and pillaged, burned and left nothing outside of the castle. They killed everybody—men and women, old and young, nobles and commoners—in the houses, streets and fields.

One day, the Mongols brought seven siege engines and bombarded day and night. They didn't stop until the walls and towers were demolished. They captured the garrison soldiers and the canons and collected weapons from them. The ladies, damsels and noble girls refuged to the cathedral and locked all the doors. Knowing that it was not easy to break it open, they simply set it on fire. Many of the ladies and noble girls made a choice to die in the flames rather than have a shameful death.

In other churches, they dragged the women and girls inside and committed the evilest deeds. At the end, they took all the nobles, citizens and canons out to the field and ruthlessly beheaded them. They kept killing until they had nobody left to kill. After they destroyed everything, and an intolerable stench arose from the corpses, they left.

I stayed in the forest for a few days. I had two servants and three horses with me. I decided to take flight at night toward Tamasda, a large German village on the Cris River. I thought it could be a safer place. We had to move at night for safety.

Finally, when we arrived at Tamasda, the Germans did not let us cross the bridge to the village. The only way we could stay there was to volunteer as a laborer for town fortification. I wasn't sure about that offer, so I turned off to an island named Maros some miles away. I liked that island because of its well-built fortification. Later, I found many people from nearby towns like Adea, Voivodeni and Iermata.

On the same day that I arrived, the headman approached and told me that anybody could come into this island, but nobody can leave. He added that it was for safety measures. I stayed there for some days.

One day, our scout brought the bad news that the Mongols were approaching. I hired a guide and, on that night, I left the *island. My tentative destination was Cenad. All through the night, I rushed to the destination. When I arrived at dawn, I found that it was already taken by the Mongols and destroyed. A different Mongol army unit entered Hungary through a different route.*

I went back to the island. There was no other place I could go. On that night, one of my servants, who was guarding my horses, ran away with my horses, my money and my clothing. I heard later that he was caught by the Mongols and cut in half. Not much later, news arrived that the Mongols took the German town of Tamasda, and all the residents were killed with horrendous cruelty.

Upon hearing this, my hair stood on end, my body shivered with fear and my tongue stuttered miserably. I saw so many dying men at their last moments in their dreadful deaths. It was engraved in my memory and surfaced when I saw triggering images, heard words or saw actual things. I see my murderers in my mind's eye, and my body exudes the cold sweat of death. I saw human beings as they were expecting death, honestly. They were unable to grip their weapons, raise their arms, move their steps for safety or survey the land for an exit. They were half-dead with fear.

I moved back to the forest because the island was not any safer. The following day, at early dawn, the Mongols arrived and killed everybody there. I tried to stay in the forest as long as possible; yet, when hunger and thirst pained me too much, I was forced to go to the island at night.

I saw dead bodies everywhere—some cut into pieces and some not. I turned over the dead bodies in search of food. If I was lucky to find something, I consumed it immediately. I did

CONFESSIONS OF AN EYEWITNESS
(STORY ONE)

this for 20 days; after that, I could do it no more because the intolerable stench made me sick.

I will continue my story later, and forget me not.

CHAPTER 40

The battle at Mohi

One day, King Bela IV had a war council in the late afternoon with all of his nobles to plan for the incoming battle with the Mongol invaders. He was with Ugolin, the archbishop of Kalocsa; Prince Coloman, his brother; Raynald, the bishop of Transylvania; the bishop of the church in Nitra; Nicholas, the provost of Sibia; the archdeacon of Bacs; Master Albert, the archdeacon of Esztergom; and Mattias, the archbishop of Esztergom.

At the time, King Bela was staying in the town of Lent instead of the Hungarian capital Pest. In the council room, he got a note from his chief butler that an urgent messenger from the Carpathian front had arrived, and the king allowed him to enter.

His visitor was Palantine Dionysius, the chief commander of the defense unit at the Carpathian Mountains. Earlier, King Bela had sent Palantine Dionysius some troops to the most eastern border post, which they named the Russian Gate, to guard and watch for the Mongol invasion. All the attendants in the room were shocked and displeased with his appearance. He had blood stains all over his body and the look of extreme exhaustion.

"Your majesty, they are here!" Palantine Dionysius told them. "They destroyed the Russian Gate and killed all my soldiers! They are now entering Hungary."

King Bela nodded as a sign of acknowledgement and gestured him to leave.

All eyes fell upon the king as they impatiently waited for his words; however, the first one who opened his mouth was Archbishop Ugolin.

"Your majesty, leave all these to us! We can handle it, and we *will* handle it. Our God-blessed army of 100,000 will surely defeat the pagans. We will send them back to their original place: Tartarus."

At that time in Hungary, the power game between the monarch, the king and the nobles was serious. The nobles had the power to collect the taxes and recruit the troops, not the king. Without the nobles' consent, in many cases, the king was simply a puppet.

Ever since Bela became king, he tried to get back the sovereign powers but failed. One example were the Cumans, whom King Bela intended to recruit and nurture, making them part of his power, but the nobles didn't agree with the king's plan.

The nobles had all the powers and privileges, including residing in the castle or the palace, living lavishly, levying taxes on the peasants and maintaining and leading the army in the war. They didn't want to lose any of these things. If King Bela led the army and won, there might be a power shift in the king's favor.

King Bela reluctantly said, "My trust is in my noble lords. If things don't go as we expected, I will take the lead."

CHAPTER 40

Archbishop Ugolin bowed to the king and uttered, "So be it, your majesty."

Ugolin's almond-shaped mitre (headgear) was shinier, more luxurious and bigger than King Bela's crown.

King Bela immediately sent his family to a safer place: the border town close to Austria. Then he proceeded to encounter the Mongols. He had heard that the Mongols, after destroying the Hungarian garrison at the Russian Gate, were approaching Pest as fast as they could, burning the villages and massacring the entire population in their path.

King Bela, who stayed in Pest and waited for more troops to come, didn't move. The Mongols arrived at the spot, which was half a day's galloping distance from Pest. Every day, about 100 Mongols came close to the city and burned villages, killing the people with no mercy.

At the time, outside of the city or the castle, there used to be many villages, towns and farms around it, which belonged to the peasants. The Mongols kept coming and pillaging and slaughtering every day—sometimes twice a day—yet King Bela didn't allow anyone to engage them; however, when these things went on with no end, Archbishop Ugolin took it badly and thought that he should do something.

Without the king's permission, Ugolin put on his armor and, with his fully armored 200 knights, chased them. The Mongols turned their heads back and began to retreat. For a while, the chasing game continued.

At last, they reached the marshland, and the Mongols crossed it swiftly. The archbishop didn't notice this movement and continued the chase. Being weighed down by their armor, the knights became stuck in the marshland, and they couldn't cross or return. Seeing this, the Mongols, with contemptuous smiles, circled them slowly and showered them with arrows. Most of the Hungarian cavalrymen fell from their horses and were killed. Archbishop Ugolin, under the sacrifice of several of his men, managed to escape and came back to the city with embarrassment.

King Bela marched out of Pest and moved further north. He reached the Sajo River, which was a tributary of the Tisza River. The Sajo River was wide and muddy, so it seemed very unlikely that anybody could cross it except for one stone bridge.

King Bela and his 100,000 armed men crossed the bridge and encamped on the Mohi plain. He posted armed guards at the bridge and let them watch day and night. While building up camps, he went around and encouraged his men, handing out flags to as many soldiers as possible. Many of his soldiers were relaxed due to their great numbers.

Batu had been chasing them and dispatched his younger brother Seiban as a reconnaissance, who came back half a day later and gave a report.

"Big brother, I found them. Their numbers are enormous. Their soldiers are like stars in the sky or gravel on the river shore."

Batu stared into space and remained like that for a while. He and his 40,000 warriors moved to the opposite side of the Sajo River, near the Hungarian encampment. Batu stationed most of his army in the brushwood area, which had some distance from the river shore, where it was easy to hide.

CHAPTER 40

He sent out an arrow messenger to Subedei, who was still on his way to Pest. Batu knew that this battle would be a decisive and pivotal one in the whole European campaign. He gathered the Mongol shamans, the Muslim imams, the Christian priests and all the other religious leaders in his Mongol army and asked them to pray for victory with their soldiers.

Batu, believer of the eternal blue sky, went up to a nearby high hill with his two servants. He stayed there for a full day, meditating and praying.

Tengri,
The eternal blue sky,
The supreme God in heaven,
The creator of the universe,
The only one who is all powerful,
Talk to me,
Tell me if I am the chosen one,
To create a new world,
From the ashes,
Of the world, the product of evil,
Of the world full of disguise,
Of the world without soul,
Of the world contaminated with
Selfishness, ignorance and sympathy-lessness,
Of the world wrongfully variated from the purity,
Let the world be reincarnated!
Tengri,
My divine lord,
Listen to the words,

Not from the silvery tongue,
But from the pure heart.
Do not let the godlessness prevail,
Do not let the truth yield to falsehood.
Let the poison of misjudgment
Bypass me.
Allow me your mystery power,
So I can be your right hand,
To complete your master plan in
The mortal world.

On April 10, 1241, before dawn, the Mongol army commenced their attack. The stone bridge on the Sajo River between the two sides was narrow, allowing only three horsemen to pass side by side. At the western end of the bridge— the Hungarian side—the heavily armed guard unit held their position, seemingly not to allow the passage of a single enemy soldier. It looked like they could hold the bridge forever; however, from the Mongol side, very unusual things were happening.

The first line of the Mongol attackers moved the anti-arrow, protective, wheeled panel board; the second line carried something no human eyes had ever seen before. The Mongol soldiers called this newly designed weapon "po," which was a cannon that used black powder. The cylinder-type weapon was made of bronze, had a 10-inch diameter and was 4 feet long. It was carried on a two-wheel cart.

There were a total of six cannons, and three soldiers were assigned to each one. It was a very simple design with a black-powder chamber at the back (the closed side of the cylinder); on the front (open) side of the cylinder, the Mongol soldiers tightly pushed in accurately carved, 3-foot-long wooden projectiles, which were called "arrows" by the Mongol soldiers. At the tip of the projectile, they bound explosives, like club-shaped grenades. The Mongol soldiers filled the chamber with black powder through the opening and connected it with a fuse. They lit the fuses—one on the cannon and the other on the grenade—at the front side of the arrow.

The first cannon shot was made. Suddenly, a thunderous, explosive sound filled the space of the Sajo River basin. It was loud enough to wake up all the sleeping men and animals around the area. A projectile flew in the sky with a tale of smoke and a whistling sound. The projectile traveled and launched exactly in the middle of the Hungarian guard unit. There was another explosion when the projectile landed on the ground. It was like a thunder and lightning bolt. The astonished Hungarian soldiers were puzzled and scared, and their horses became wild; some of them ran into the open space after forcing off their reins.

The Hungarian stone-bridge guard unit had to retreat to their main camp. King Bela and all of his military leaders woke up and readied themselves for the incoming battle; however, the hurriedly recruited and assembled army of 100,000 men had trouble from the beginning. The sun had not risen yet, and the soldiers didn't know what to do in the darkness. They couldn't find their leaders and commanders, and the commanders couldn't find their soldiers.

While the Hungarian army was in chaos, the Mongols continuously poured into the Hungarian side with the help of the cannon firing squad. When all of Batu's army of 40,000 crossed the bridge, the day began to break. This was the moment that Subedei's 30,000 warriors were supposed to show up at the other side of the Hungarian army.

King Bela, flanked by his brother Prince Coloman, Archbishop Ugolin and Archbishop Mattias, began to lead his army. Since they were not very organized or ready, they swarmed around like grasshoppers or a school of fishes. Batu was waiting for Subedei's army to show up; nonetheless, he could see no sign of it. On the other hand, King Bela saw that the Mongol army was much smaller than his and, on the backside of them, there was a river!

King Bela gave an order of full charge.

"Push them to the river! They don't have any other place to go! Push them to the river!"

The 100,000 Hungarian cavalry began to push Batu's 40,000 men. The Mongol army was in danger because they had to fight with the river on their back, and Batu's army was gradually pushed back. Suddenly, Batu realized that his army had lost their free movement, which was the Mongol army's most-needed condition in field combat. The casualties among the Batu's soldiers increased. At this moment, Subedei's 30,000-man army emerged from behind the Hungarian army. They were a bit delayed due to the complexity of the temporary bridge construction at the downside of the river.

Batu's and Subedei's armies fanned out as planned, encircling the Hungarian army like they did in a hunting expedition. The situation was reversed, and the Mongols gained the upper hand. The Mongol archery units let out their lethally accurate arrow shots. In short time, numerous, unaccountable numbers of Hungarians fell from their horses and were killed.

The shocked Hungarian army retreated and took refuge into the fortress that they built up days ago. The chained connection of wagons—hundreds or maybe thousands of them—made a circle of half a mile in diameter, probably designed to create a safe zone from the Mongol horse soldiers' attack.

After careful observation, Subedei clicked his tongue and said, "What nonsense! They made their own trap!"

He gave an order to surround the circle of wagons but made an opening at one side, allowing escape. The Mongol artillery unit began to work. They bombarded their cannons, shooting numerous rocket explosives. The rocket explosives were composed of three parts: the body of a long, thick arrow of 3 feet; the black-powder cylinder, which was bound to the arrow; and a triangular-shaped explosive tip. They put the rocket explosives on the launching pad and lit the fire. It worked like fireworks. Inside the big, circled fortress of wagons, there were a lot of explosions, thundering noises, fire and smoke, which made it unbearable for both the men and the horses.

The Hungarian soldiers couldn't control their horses. They already knew that they were surrounded and that there was no hope of survival. They began to take off their armor and helmets to make themselves lighter and threw away their heavy weapons. They galloped out of the circle and ran toward the open field. This was the moment that the largest mass murder began.

The Mongol soldiers chased and shot them down, one by one. The chasing and killing game continued for almost a whole day, and the field of two day's walk-up distance (100 miles) was covered with the dead bodies of Hungarian soldiers. The earth was red with blood. The battlefield of Mohi was stacked with corpses, and the sky was covered with man-eating birds whose crowing and cawing noises were deafening. Almost 70,000 Hungarian soldiers lay dead.

The chronicler Faqih Ashraf Aziz wrote:

I never saw so many corpses strewn across the field. The earth was red with blood from horizon to horizon. Enormous numbers were killed and perished in the battle. Some were beheaded; some were dismembered. Many of the dead bodies were so damaged that they were beyond recognition. The fat tissue from the human body sometimes works well as fuel, and it takes a long time to be consumed. For days, the smoking continued from some dead bodies, and the smell filled the air around the epicenter of the battle.

The next day, the Mongol soldiers collected reusable weapons and valuables. In case they found a half-dead man, they confirmed the killing. After three days, it was hard to stay in the field because of the stench from the corpses, and the air was filled with toxic gas.

The dead bodies were on the river too. Numerous dead bodies floated and slowly moved downward along the stream. Probably they would be gnawed away by sharp-teethed fish and eaten by them instead of decomposing. The horses, still with saddles and bridles but no riders, looked like they had gone mad with panic and noise, roaming around the field and neighing as if crying.

CHAPTER 41

The survivors from Mohi

Most of the Hungarian military leaders fought bravely until their last moments:

Ugolin, the archbishop of Kalocsa, was speared on his waist and fell from his horse. He was cut into pieces while surrounded by three or four Mongol soldiers.

Archbishop Mattias of Esztergom was dead.

Bishop Gregory of Gyor was dead.

Bishop Raynald of Transylvania was dead.

The bishop of the church in Nitra was dead.

Nicholas, the provost of Sibiu, was dead.

The vice chancellor of the king of the noble hundred was dead.

The archdeacon of Bacs was dead.

Master Albert, the archdeacon of Esztergom, was dead.

Coloman, the king's brother, managed to escape from the battlefield. He took off all his armor and his helmet and galloped through the night in a southwestern direction. The following morning, when he arrived at the bank of the Danube River, he was so exhausted that he fell asleep at the riverbank.

When he woke up in the late afternoon, he could see a ferry boat and a group of people around it, far down below the river. He approached them to ask for a ride. The ferry boat was tiny and seemed able to carry a maximum of two to three people at a time, but there was already a long line.

Coloman approached the ferryman, who shouted, "Hey, you! Go back to the end of the line! These are all noble ladies, and you should wait."

There was no way that Coloman could prove that he was the king's brother and reveal his identity. He knew that the Mongol chasers were on his back.

Even though the water was still cold, he jumped into the river and swam across it. From there, he walked to a town named Somogy and then headed for Zagreb. He finally arrived there; however, due to the battle wound on his chest, he didn't survive. He died on the same day that he arrived at Zagreb.

King Bela was lucky to hide in the forest called Dios Gior. From there, he escaped to Szomolnok, then to Leutschau and finally at the castle of Piewnicza, south of Sandecz. He quickly realized that no place in Hungary was safe for him. He wouldn't stay long because he knew that the Mongol chasing unit would fall upon him at any moment.

He disguised himself as a pilgrim and continued his tormented march. He was accompanied by two servants, who were helping him carry the minimum necessities. His destination was Austria, although he was heading for the Carpathian Mountains to divert the attention of the Mongols. He changed his course and went to Oedenburg, the Hungarian border town to Austria, where his family was sheltering.

Batu appointed Baidar as the captain of the chasing unit and gave him 1,000 men. The Mongols already knew that King Bela was in the Carpathians, and Baidar began his chasing journey based on a very limited source of information. First, he went to Spisky Castle in the central Carpathian Mountains to no avail. By that time, King Bela had already left. The Mongols went to Auschwitz and Teschen with the same result. Baidar then realized that the king took a different escape route.

The chronicler Chun Lee wrote:

They celebrated the complete victory of the Hungarian campaign. I was invited to the feast.

I heard Batu say, "Now we can celebrate the complete victory over the Hungarian army! We destroyed the Hungarian army, but we can also say that we destroyed the major European army. From now on, there won't be any more major resistance. The rest of Europe is ours. I will give all this credit to our revered orlok, Subedei. He got 65 wins from 65 battles—still undefeated! He proved himself as the real god of war!"

After these words, all the attendants in the banquet room stood up and chanted in one voice, "Subedei! Subedei! Subedei!"

This chanting continued for a long, long time and echoed into the space of the Hungarian sky.

King Bela's escape journey

King Bela reached Nitra safely and was escorted by the German colonists to the Austrian frontier. At the border, the king was so tired that he decided to take a little rest at the bank of a small river while the meal was being cooked.

When he awoke, he found himself surrounded by a group of about 30 armed soldiers and their horses. When the king stood up, one man dismounted from his horse and approached him. He was wearing a lavishly embellished tunic, a cloak, leggings and trousers.

Standing in front of King Bela, he lowered his head slightly and introduced himself.

"I am Duke Frederick. Welcome to Austria! You are safe now."

King Bela replied, "It is a great pleasure and an honor that the ruler of Austria came directly to see me. I greatly appreciate your hospitality."

The duke, with a faint smile around his lips, lowering his head again. "There is a small castle across the stream, not far from here. Allow me to invite you there for your safety and comfort."

Without waiting for the king's answer, Frederick remounted his horse and stepped forward. The soldiers surrounding Bela offered him a horse and helped him to mount it. They surrounded the king, front and back, and took him to the nearby castle. In this small castle, in a medium-sized room, King Bela was surrounded by seven or eight people in addition to armed guards. A comfortable chair was offered to the king, and Duke Frederick walked around slowly, in front of King Bela, as if he were an interrogator asking questions to a criminal suspect.

The much-annoyed King Bela asked in a raised tone, "Where's my family? My wife and son?"

Duke Frederick answered, "They are in a safe place. Your wife Maria and your young son Stephen are receiving good care. As long as you answer 'yes' to all my questions, you will reunite with your beloved family. Please don't say 'no' to me because I don't want to see horrible thing happens to your lovely family."

King Bela stood on his feet abruptly and said, "What?"

He couldn't believe what he had heard. He was just standing there, staring at the duke. Ignoring this, Duke Frederick kept on talking, slowly circling the king.

"First, you must pay me 10,000 marks of protection money. With this money, you and your family's safety will be guaranteed."

Duke Frederick was asking for ransom. King Bela fell into his chair appalled. He was a prisoner of someone who approached him as a friend.

The bible says:

Beware of false prophets,
Which come
In sheep's clothing,
But inwardly, they are
Ravening wolves.

Duke Frederick continued, "The real thing is here. I want you to surrender three provinces of the Hungarian territory to us. They are Wieselburg, Oedenburg and Eisenburg."

After hearing these demands, King Bela closed his eyes, dropped his head and fell into deep sorrow.

Duke Frederick added, "Like I said, don't say 'no.' I really don't want to see a horrible thing happen to your lovely family."

King Bela knew that he had to agree to get out of this terrible trap. After a moment of pondering, he reluctantly nodded as a gesture of agreement.

Triumphantly, Duke Frederick said, "Smart decision! Now, let me see everything you have."

He ordered his guards to bring all the luggage that King Bela was carrying. There were some valuable items like gold and silver coins, crown jewels, additional jewelry and utensils.

After a careful inspection, Duke Frederick exclaimed, "Is that all? These won't be enough—not even half!"

Duke Frederick's eyes fixed on two rings that were on King Bela's fingers and asked, "Can I see your rings?"

Two guard soldiers approached King Bela and took off the two rings somewhat forcibly.

CHAPTER 42

Duke Frederick, after another careful inspection, said disdainfully, "These have poorer quality than I thought. I can count these at 500 marks each. So, the total count comes up to 4,000 marks. You still owe me 6,000 marks. All right! I will make a promissory note, and you will sign it."

They created a promissory note and one of acknowledgement, saying that King Bela owed 6,000 marks to Duke Frederick in the form of gold and silver and would surrender the three provinces of Wieselburg, Oedenburg and Eisenburg to Austria, by pure will, which would remain effective forever. King Bela and Duke Frederick signed the documents, along with seven witnesses.

King Bela was ordered to make this oath on the bible: "I, King Bela of Hungary, make an oath in the name of the Father, the Son and the Holy Spirit. If I am the one who breaks this oath, I will burn in hell forever."

King Bela hastened to the queen and his son, who were not far from there, and moved to Agram in Croatia. From there, he heard that the Mongol chasing unit was following his steps and chasing sharply. The Mongol chasing unit of 2,000 cavalry, led by Prince Kadan, made their base camp in Verbacz, where pasturage was abundant. A relatively small unit of 500 chased King Bela through the barrens and mountains of Croatia.

King Bela decided to separate from his family in consideration of potential bad luck. He sent his wife Maria and son Stephen to Clissa and then later to Spalatro; however, in Spalatro, Queen Maria was very uncomfortable because she frequently met with unfriendly gazes from the women in the town and heard some rumors. Most of the town's women were widows whose husbands were killed in battle by the Mongols, and some of the town's hoodlums thought that she was carrying a lot of the king's treasures.

After hearing this, King Bela moved his wife and son to the island of Lesina and then later to Brazza on the Dalmatian coast, and he moved to Trau. The Mongol unit arrived at Trau and searched around but quickly found that the town was unassailable with their limited manpower and lack of equipment.

Prince Kadan sent a messenger, who could speak Slavic, saying, "I, Kadan, the captain of the unconquered army, bids you to know that if you do not wish to share the penalty earned by the one who is believed to be there, just deliver him to our hands."

Nevertheless, there was no answer from inside the town.

On that very day, deep in the night while the Mongols were not available, a few dark images slipped out of town—one being King Bela—and headed for the shore. A small boat was waiting for them and, before daybreak, the boat was already far from the coast and heading for the island.

The fate of Pest, Vac
and Esztergom

Batu and his Mongol army advanced to the city of Pest, which was situated on the right bank of the Danube River. It was the capital city of Hungary by that time. Pest was the commercial center correlated with Kiev, Novgorod and Constantinople along with many other areas.

All the merchants from these areas (Frenchmen, Lombards and Greeks) claimed that Pest was their hometown. The normal population of Pest was about 30,000; however, people from towns and villages in the vicinity of the capital swarmed into the city in search of safety, doubling the population. Many of them escaped individually or with their families into the forests and mountains outside of the city; others, who felt safe in the middle of a big group, remained.

When the news arrived that the battle had been lost, all of the citizens hurriedly tried to reinforce their defense walls, moats and battlements, but they didn't have a garrison, and all died in the battle of Mohi. The citizens had formed a poorly armed militia, which was next to none. The defense line had been easily broken, and enormous numbers of people tried to swarm into churches and the palace. Those who couldn't enter the churches or the palace were killed by swords, and the ones in the buildings or houses were killed by fire. The Mongols burned the whole city. It took three full days to completely burn it down, and the cloud of smoke could be seen 100 miles away. Most of the citizens and refugees were perished in the flame.

Almost simultaneously, another branch of the Mongol army attacked the city of Vac, which was just half a day's walk from Pest. Similar things happened in Vac. The city's defense couldn't hold their resistance for long. Countless citizens and refugees perished. Before they burned everything, the Mongols picked up all the treasures and valuables from the churches and the palace.

Days later, Batu and his Mongol army move to the city of Esztergom, which was also on the right bank of the Danube River and about 30 miles from Pest in the northwestern direction. Esztergom had been the capital city of Hungary for about 200 to 300 years until King Bela moved the royal seat to Pest.

Esztergom was more populated, bigger and more luxurious than Pest with numerous historical monuments from earlier centuries. The lords of the city were Hungarian, French and Lombards and, upon the arrival of the news that the Hungarians had lost the war, they began to reinforce the city's defense system. Together, the nobles, burghers, knights and commoners built up tall walls and wooden towers, fixed the moat and organized the city's garrisons. They felt like they could keep the city safe for many years. Like many other big cities, numerous refugees from nearby towns and villages swarmed into this city, making it overpopulated. The Mongols knew that they reinforced their defense walls and there were many stone structures in the city, so they brought 30 catapults.

Before the attack, Batu sent a messenger to tap the possibility of their surrender. There was no answer from inside. After day and night bombardments of rocks from the catapults, the defense wall gave in. Next, the Mongols brought about 4,000 levies, mostly Hungarian captives who pledged to serve the Mongols on the collateral of their lives. They filled the bags with dirt and filled up the moat. The garrisons inside the wall shot arrows to kill the levies. Hungarians were killing Hungarians for their own lives.

After the collapse of the wall, the citizens fell into chaos and horrible panic. Once the city leaders and elders realized that they could not hold the city, they set fire to the wooden houses and burned and destroyed thousands of expensive garments and valuables in the warehouse. They killed the horses, buried gold and silver and carried whatever they could hold and then bring to the stone castle. They thought they could be safe there, but they could not.

Before the complete annihilation, about 300 ladies and damsels—beautifully dressed—gathered in one corner of the palace and appealed for an audience for Batu, begging for mercy. They volunteered to be slaves in return for their lives, but the answer was cold.

"We don't give out chances twice!"

They were beheaded right on the spot.

Most of the citizens were dragged into the field and beheaded; some remained in the building structure and were burned to death. Only 15 people survived out of about 40,000 to 50,000.

After this event, the Mongols swept over the rest of Hungary. During this period, half of the total population had perished, which came to 2,000,000 Hungarians out of 4,000,000.

CHAPTER 44

Confessions of an eyewitness (story two)

I was tricked by a ruse created by the Mongols. The Mongols found the king's royal seal from the dead body of a chancellor and took advantage of it. Some Hungarian clerks, who were left alive, created a letter to nobles and commoners as well, in the king's name, with these words:

"*Do not fear the ferocity and cruelty of the Tatars (Mongols), and do not dare to leave your houses because, although on account of some unavoidable circumstances, we had to leave behind the camp and our tents, yet by the favor of God we intend gradually to recover them and fight a valiant battle against the Tatars; therefore, do nothing except pray that merciful God may permit us to crush the head of our enemies.*"

The letter was stamped with the king's royal seal and carried around by the hands of Hungarians who joined the Mongols. At the same time, the created rumors circulated that, if they return before the deadline of a certain day, they would be bestowed with certain incentives; otherwise, they would be chased and killed by the Mongol's hound dogs.

CONFESSIONS OF AN EYEWITNESS
(STORY TWO)

Many people came out of their hiding places and returned. I was one of them. When this news arrived to me, I subjected myself to one of the Hungarians who became a Tatar in deed. He gracefully accepted me as his servant. Anyhow, I was on the verge of death from starvation.

It seemed that they would try to rebuild Hungary for their own way. They tried to reorganize the society and economic system. They divided Hungary into many districts and posted a king (governor) in each district. They were all Mongols. Then, they posted a knes, who functioned as a judge or an administrator as well as the tax collector. They were all Hungarians. They began to mint new coins, making the coins of the previous king Bela fall into disuse.

Since the harvest season had already arrived, they needed labor desperately. All the village people were called in, gathered in one place and were to the farms, fields and orchards. They cropped the barley, oats, wheat, onions, grapes and some other fruit. The Mongols and Cumans were everywhere, supervising and watching the laborers. At any time, they raped the girls and women on the field in front of their parents, brothers or husbands, and they didn't care who watched them.

My master was one of the kneses, and sometimes I went to their meetings, which were held once a week. There were about 100 of them, and they were controlling and supervising thousands of villages. They rendered justice and distributed necessities like horses, sheep and clothing based on what they thought they deserved. In some way, they were popular, so people sent them their most beautiful girls as gifts. On the other hand, if they were unhappy with a certain group of village people, they summoned them and killed them ruthlessly. They were Hungarians yet they were truthful Tatars in deed.

Sometimes, new villages formed naturally without permission or knowledge of the Mongol authority. These new villages were the gatherings of Hungarian refugees in some locations as they built their own communities. They built houses and a defense system and even produced weapons.

Once these communities were known to the Mongols, they sent out army units to root them out. Once they surrounded a new city or town, they first sent Hungarians to fight with Hungarians. If they were all dead, they sent the Russians next, then the Muslims and then the Cumans. The Mongols always worked as a supervising unit, standing behind and killing anyone who retreated.

CHAPTER 45

A letter to Frederick II, the Holy Roman Emperor

After the battles of Liegnitz and Mohi, western Europe's psychology had fallen into deep disparity and hopelessness. Feelings of doom and an apocalyptic atmosphere covered the whole region like dark clouds, like lost souls roaming on the barren or roving in a dark valley, simply because they didn't know what to do.

These feelings are shown in the letter of Count Henry, the ruler of Lorraine (an autonomous region in 13th century on the border of central and western Europe) to his father-in-law (a French monarch):

The dangers foretold long ago in the Holy Bible are spring-ing up, erupting and looming, which is owing to our sin. A cruel tribe of people, lawless and savage beyond our imagination, is now invading, occupying and sweeping our borders. Now, they reached our land too, after roaring through many other lands and exterminating the people there. It seems that the servants of

Satan have finally been let loose, that the apocalypse is at hand and retribution for the sins of mankind will soon follow. The collapse and extinction of our world, our value system and our Christendom is obvious, if not the end of time itself.

In France, in earlier times after the loss of Liegnitz but before the battle at Mohi, King Louis IX received a letter from the master of the Knight Templars, saying, "If, by the will of God, the Hungarians are defeated, these Tatars will find no one to stand against them as far as your land."

Queen Blanche, who was King Louis's mother, was horrified and asked her son what would happen.

"Mother, if we die, we will be in heaven. Otherwise, they will be in hell: Tartarus. So, anyway, we will be good."

In Germany, this rumor of unknown origin circulated the whole territory: "Tatars are the lost tribes of Israel, and the Jews are smuggling arms to them."

Based on this rumor, they slaughtered many Jews around the border town.

Every day, churches were filled with terrified congregations and numerous flagellants traveled across the nation, shouting, "Repent! The end of the world has finally arrived!"

After the conquest of Hungary, the Mongol Empire bordered with the Holy Roman Empire. The Holy Roman Empire inherited its name in the 8th century, yet it was not a centralized nation. It was far from the Roman Empire, which existed about a thousand years before. Medieval Europe was under the control of Christendom. The pope was the most power-ful figure, and he could control every district, country and monarch.

Holy Roman Emperor Frederick II didn't get along with the pope, and there were seen and unseen conflicts between them. Frederick II was well educated, could speak many languages, understood well and respected the much-advanced Islamic culture. He was a disobedient child to the Christian world and to the pope, so he was excommunicated by Pope Gregory IX three times.

Frederick II had the title of the master of Sicily and Naples, yet he didn't possess any major military power. Even the Teutonic knights in Germany pledged loyalty to him; nonetheless, it came after the pope. If the pope formulated new crusaders against the Mongols, then he would lead the army. The truth was that, when the pope proclaimed to regroup the crusaders, nothing happened because there was no army left in western Europe. Even Frederick, the duke of Austria who shared the same name with the Holy Roman Emperor, refused to join, saying that he didn't want to be blown away in front of a tornado. Because of this, some ignorant souls within the European courts created rumors that even the pope was in league with the Mongols to control his rivals.

At about this time, Batu sent a letter to Frederick II, the Holy Roman Emperor:

I, Batu, am the captain of the all-powerful God, who bestowed on us the land from the sunrise to the sunset. We are on the way to the final destination, the Great Ocean, and the ones who submit will be saved and allowed to exist till many generations to come; otherwise, they will be perished into eternity.

You, Frederick II, are just an eagle without wings or a tiger without claws. Where is your army? Your Teutonic knights were annihilated on the field of Liegnitz, and your enmity with the pope will prevent you from obtaining a Christian army, if any.

I plan to post you as a real emperor after I fulfill God's mission, under my suzerainty; however, this will be possible only after your heart is filled with submission. Do not make an enemy out of me. That will be the beginning of your dooms-day. Look what happened in Hungary. Almost half of their population has perished. Do not follow the foolish footsteps of the Hungarian king!

Frederick II sent out this very short reply: "I want to be your falconer. I know birds, and I am happy when I am with birds."

CHAPTER 46

Into Germany

In the winter of 1241, Batu was ready to cross the Danube River. It was almost the end of December, and they said that winter had arrived earlier than usual. It was a harsh winter, which was what the Mongols were waiting for.

Batu and Subedei went up the hill where they could oversee the flow of the river from the faraway northwestern upper end to the southeast. The river was serpentine and wound through the plain, yet some areas were hilly banks that stretched on either side of the river.

Batu, looking at Subedei, asked, "Orlok, do you think the river has frozen strong enough to cross over?"

"It looks like it has, but we will make sure."

Batu and Subedei knew that the Germans and Hungarians, who were on the other side of the river, were breaking the ice every day to stop the Mongols' advance. Nonetheless, the weather was on the Mongol side. The biting winter cold turned the river into an unbreakable, strong bridge.

On the same day, the Mongols left about 50 oxen on the riverbank and retreated 20 miles. During the first and second days, nothing happened. On the night of the third day, a group of about 40 to 50 people showed up on the other side of the bank and approached the Mongol side. They took all 50 oxen and hurriedly returned to their side on the frozen river.

The following day, the Mongol army began to cross the river with a more relaxed pace. It had been proven that the ice was strong enough to withhold 50 oxen and 50 people at the same time. They advanced toward the west, annihilating towns and villages on their way. Their destination was Vienna.

Until they arrived at the town of Neustadt, they massacred almost 20,000 peasants, villagers and townspeople. In Neustadt, they found a small castle, but it was easily captured. All the houses and buildings were destroyed and leveled to assure that future enemies would not use them. Around the town, there were many grape orchards, and a small tributary of the Danube River covered them. Batu and Subedei discussed a plan to encircle the city of Vienna.

That night, Batu and about 50 of his usual dinner group members were served a slightly different menu including a variety of drinks, such as kumiss, wine, old mead and a fermented barley drink by their own choice.

Batu picked up a goblet with the barley drink and, after taking a sip, asked, "What is this?"

The chef replied, "That's the drink they are using a lot in this area, my lord. Even the children drink it every day."

Batu asked, "Even the children?"

"Yes, the water around here is probably not so good. That's why. I learned that they can keep it safer and longer."

After drinks, the first course was an elongated tube of meat.

Batu asked again, "What is this?"

"That is a cleaned and cooked pig intestine stuffed with meat. This is the favorite choice for the people here. They use it a lot—I mean the Germans and the Austrians."

Batu put this meat aside.

Finally, Batu picked up the rabbit and ate it all. The final course that night was honey cake, which was made of mashed black beans, pine nuts, raisins and honey.

After dinner was the entertainment time, and a very unusual guest showed up. He was a priest at a local church in Neustadt, and he wore a dark brown, long dress with a belt on his waist. He was also wearing rosary beads on his neck with a silver cross hanging down. He seemed to have tonsured (shaved off the hair on top of his head), showing that he was in his priestship.

Batu told him, "Introduce yourself, and tell us what you believe."

The priest bowed with his two palms together and said in Latin, "In the name of the Father, the Son and the Holy Spirit, I greet you. My sincere appreciation goes to the Great Khan for giving me a chance to confess my belief. My name is Gerhard, and I have been serving God as a plain priest during the last 40 years in the church and monastery in Neustadt. While I was serving God, I experienced enormous amounts of love of God, his warm and touching hand and many miracles that come through him. God is always with me."

The interpreter translated the priest's words from Latin to Mongolian.

At this moment, this question came up: "Did you ever see God?"

"No. I can see him only through my mind's eye. You cannot see him, but he is everywhere."

Another question: "Who is Jesus?"

"Jesus was God's son sent by his father on this earth to take over the original sin of the human beings."

And another: "What is the original sin?"

The priest replied in a calm voice, "In the beginning of creation, God created one couple of human beings and allowed them into paradise. They disobeyed God by eating an apple, which was a forbidden fruit. They became smart but had to pay the penalty of not being allowed to live in paradise anymore. So, Jesus took away their original sin in exchange for his own life."

Another question: "So, after his death, the paradise came back on Earth?"

The priest didn't answer for some moments, and then mentioned, "One of the key obligations of Christian believers is to believe what the bible says as it is—not to ask any questions about it. Once Jesus said that, if you want to go to paradise, you should be like children."

After a short, silent moment, another question popped up from the corner: "Did you know that one of the three wise men from the east in the bible was a Mongol?"

Gerhard raised his head and regarded the seat where the question originated.

The questioner continued, "I am a descendant of Naiman—one of the Mongol tribes with Christian belief. I have been told that one of the three wise men in the bible was a Naiman."

At this point, Batu interrupted and asked, "Do you believe that Jesus was born without sexual intercourse between a man and a woman?"

The priest answered, "Yes. Maria, Jesus's mother, was impregnated by the Holy Spirit."

At this point, Prince Bujek, Batu's cousin, intervened.

"No. My mother is a Christian, and my mother's father was a Christian. I have never heard them said such things. I have been told that Jesus was just a man, simply imbued with the Holy Spirit. They don't believe in Holy Mary and deny the belief that Jesus is God himself. They believe in the Holy Spirit only, which is the real God."

Bujek's mother, Sorqoqtani Beki, and her father, Wang-Khan, were Nestorian Christians, who defy Jesus as God itself.

Gerhard bowed and said in a calm voice, "The ultimate goal of our Christians is to build paradise on Earth through our belief."

At this time, Batu declared, "That is enough! Every religion should be respected unless it makes a social problem."

Batu gave an order not to harm the priest, the monks or the nuns.

CHAPTER 47

A letter from Karakorum

One morning in late January 1242, on the eastern horizon of the plain of Neustadt where the Mongol army was stationed, two images emerged. As time went on, the images became clearer: They were two men on their horses. Seeing this, the Mongol guard soldiers at the post were on alert.

As they approached, the two men shouted, "Urgent message for Batu Khan! Urgent message!"

They had small pennants on their shoulders, indicating that they were arrow messengers. Nobody was allowed to stop them until they got to their destination—even the noyans. Two of the guard soldiers immediately got on their horses and escorted them, from the front and back, to Batu's camp. They were the arrow messengers from Karakorum, the capital of the Mongol mainland.

In front of Batu, one of the messengers knelt and handed him a wrapped package. It was a letter written on a paper roll, carefully wrapped with leather, sealed and tightened to avoid damage. The letter was written in Mongolian script and stamped with the imperial seal.

After reading the letter, Batu raised his head and stared into space. He dropped his head and remained that way for a while.

After a few moments, he murmured, "The great khan has died ..." Then he raised his head and asked the messengers, "When did you leave Karakorum?"

One of them answered, "About 15 days ago, my lord. At the beginning, there were three of us, but one couldn't make it. We had to leave him behind in one of the Yam stations (relay stations that provided food, shelter and spare horses for Mongol army messengers) in the middle part."

It was about 5,000 miles from Karakorum to the spot where Batu was stationed. Batu praised them highly for the amazing mission that they completed.

"You two did a great job. Take a good rest while you are here. I will let you know when you will return."

Batu summoned Subedei and showed him the letter. Batu and Subedei decided to limit the news to the princes and noyans.

Batu, looking directly into Subedei's eyes, said, "Orlok, I want to complete the European campaign."

Subedei turned away and remained silent for a while.

When he was ready, he said, "Sein Khan, remember the Yassa? It says that all the princes should be back in the Mongol mainland to elect a new khagan. This great empire cannot go without a khagan for even a single day. Now, the letter shows that the khagan's widow Toregene Khatun is the regent, which means that you need her agreement to continue. Do you think all these things will be possible in the way you want?"

CHAPTER 47

That night, Batu remained alone in his tent to think. He knew that Kuyuk was his political enemy and rival, and the regent Toregene was Kuyuk's mother. It was plausible that Toregene would do anything to make her son Kuyuk become the next khagan. She could also recall the imperial army at any time, which was the backbone of his European campaign. He asked himself if he could become the khagan, and the answer was "no." Batu knew his father Juchi's history of suffering all through his life and of illegitimacy in Genghis's blood line.

Batu also tried to recall Genghis Khan's expectations of him as the firstborn grandson. Genghis never mentioned them to Batu directly; however, Batu could feel it. It was the Mongol unity. The biggest fear of the Great One was that the empire he built would split into many small pieces after his death.

If Batu became the khagan, Kuyuk would surely challenge him with all the princes and the power of Ogodei's and Chagatai's lineage. If Kuyuk became the khagan, he would surely try to remove him politically or by force. The war between Batu and Kuyuk was inevitable. It became clear to Batu which way to go. He decided to support his cousin and best friend Monku as the next khagan.

As the news of the khagan's death spread among the princes and noyans, the first ones who took action were Kuyuk Khan and Buri Khan. Again, they left their positions and returned to the Mongol mainland. It was plausible that Kuyuk wanted to take preparatory steps to become the next khagan.

Batu didn't stop them.

CHAPTER 48

Back to Russia

Hungary was abandoned. By that time, Hungarian King Bela still could not be found because he was hiding in one of the remote islands in Croatia.

Batu and Subedei discussed the return route.

Subedei said, "Let's take the southern route. We'd better not take the same route that we took when we came in. There are still many areas that our Mongol horses haven't treaded yet."

They decided to take the route passing Croatia, Dalmatia, Albania, Bulgaria, Wallachia and Transylvania. The destination was Sarai, north of the Caspian Sea.

The chronicler Faqih Ashraf Aziz wrote:

For two to three months, the Mongols concentrated on pillaging and plundering all the nearby areas and systemically depopulated the places where they stayed. When there was nothing left and no human forms remained, they left Hungary. Then, they slowly moved to the south. Another huge tempest or tornado swept away the whole area on their pass. In the areas that the Mongols had passed, no living creatures of human form were left. They killed everybody on their way. Almost all the villages and towns were erased from the map.

The chronicler Chun Lee wrote:

I think their purpose of massacre and depopulation was to give safety to their newly born empire. It could be the same philosophy that the farmers use when they remove all the weeds around the farm that are newly plowed. I think it will take at least 100 years to regain the same population after the devastation.

When Batu reached Bulgaria—then a rich and powerful country—they recognized Batu as their overlord. Shortly before Batu's arrival, the Bulgarian king, Ivan Assen II, had died. Koloman I became the new king, but he knew that he could not match Batu. He surrendered to save his people and himself.

Batu finally arrived in Sarai and was welcomed by his younger brother Sinkur, who had been left there to command. Batu liked Sarai very much. Near the Volga River, it was in the middle of an enormously large and high-quality pasture, more than any other area.

Nestled in the center of his realm, Batu's empire began to be known as the Golden Ordu because he frequently used his favorite golden color for his royal tent. Batu's new empire stretched from the west of the Ural Mountains to the east of the Carpathian Mountains, which was bigger than any other ulus. He accumulated immense riches, and most of the generals made their choice to remain with Batu. Now his richness and power grew almost equal to or more than Karakorum.

CHAPTER 49

Confessions of an eyewitness (story three)

I *am not telling this story without a purpose because he*
who has fallen into the hands of the Tatars would have
been better not to have been born. He will feel that he
is not the prisoner of the Tatars but Tartarus. I can say this
because I was there. I have been the prisoner of the Tatars for
over a year. During that time, death would have been a solace,
for life was nothing but torture.

On the command of the king of kings (Batu), we retreated
across the wasteland with our carts loaded with booty, arms
and herds of cattle and sheep. They searched all the hiding
places and the darkness of the forest for their safety and to
find anything missed when they came in.

We reached Transylvania where many people left and some
castles were still standing, even though the Tatars had been
there already; however, this time, they left the country deso-
late and empty as they passed. Then they left Hungary and
stepped into Cumania. I was informed by an interpreter that,
once we step out of Hungary, we will all be slaughtered by their
scimitars.

CONFESSIONS OF AN EYEWITNESS
(STORY THREE)

As I had no hope of survival, and a bitter and cruel death awaited me at the door, I thought it would be better to die here than to be tortured by the sting of the fear of death. I left the highway as if following the urgent call of nature and rushed into the dense forest with my only servant.

We hid ourselves in the hollows of a creek, covering ourselves with leaves and branches. My servant hid himself at the faraway location, to lower the chances of an unlucky moment in case one was detected. Scared, we stayed there for a full two days.

During that time, I even limited the number of times I raised my head, but finally the moment came when I couldn't hold this position anymore. We crawled like snakes with our arms and legs and approached each other. We mournfully wept and groaned that it would have been easier to be killed by a sword than be tormented mentally and physically. Fear and the pain of starvation pushed us to the verge of a cliff.

While we exchanged words of consolation, a man appeared. As soon as we set our eyes on him, we took flight without seeing if he was coming nearer or falling behind. Finally, when we confirmed to each other that we were all fugitives and unarmed, we sat and exchanged sincere and friendly conversations about what to do. Even though the sting of death numbed us and the pain of hunger was torturing, we found hope in our escape, which gave us strength and mental powers to withstand it. Thus, taking confidence and strength in God, we excitedly reached the edge of the forest.

We walked across the wasted and abandoned land that they had destroyed while retreating. Church towers were our markers from one place to another because the roads and paths had vanished. We were lucky to find a garden of peasants with leeks, purslane, onions and garlic. When I put them in my mouth, they tasted like the choicest delicacies. We filled our hungry stomachs, and the spirit of life was revived in our drained bodies.

In the nighttime, we slept under no roof, and we had nothing to cover our heads. Finally, after eight days, we left the forest and arrived at a ruined city named Alba Iulia. In that place, we could find nothing but bones and skulls of the dead, the destroyed and broken walls of basilicas and palaces, soiled by the blood of enormous numbers of people. The earth did not show the blood of the innocent for it had been absorbed, but the stones were still cloaked with crimson blood, and we could not hurry through them without continuous groans and bitter sighs.

Ten miles from there, we found a ruined village and, not far from there, we discovered a mountain where a great number of men and women had taken refuge. They received us with joy among tears and inquired about the perils we had passed through. We could not keep our answers to just a few words.

Finally, they gave us black bread baked with flour and the ground bark of oak trees, and it tasted sweeter than any other simnel cake that we had ever eaten. We stayed there for a month and dared not to come out. We only sent out scouts among ourselves to find out the whereabouts of the Tatars. Although we came out from time to time in need of food, it was never safe until King Bela returned and reclaimed the kingship.

CHAPTER 50

Consolidation of the empire

To effectively rule Russia, Batu needed two main areas to be sure: first, enforce obedience of all the Russian princes to his will; second, organize the system to collect tributes and taxes.

Russia was a vast land with many populations, so it was difficult to put every city under Batu's direct control. He put three important areas—Kiev, Chernigov and Podolia—under his direct control, and all others appointed darughachis among the Russian princes. He summoned all the Russian princes to his court.

During this time, these princes showed up and pledged their allegiance to Batu: Vladimir Constantinovitch of Uglich; Boris Vasilkovitch of Rostov; Gleb Vasilkovitch; Vasili Vsevolodovitch; Yaroslav, the grand duke of Vladimir, with his sons and nephews; and Ivan Sviatoslav and his male descendants—the sons and nephews of Vasilko of Rostov. Later, Yaroslav came to Batu's court and pledged his alliance. Soon after this, the allegiances of his sons Alexander Nevsky and his brother Andrey followed.

CHAPTER 50

Batu paid special attention to two men: Daniel of Galicia and Prince Michael of Chernigov. Daniel was a strong man among the princes for he was the winner of conflict among them. He complied with Batu's order and pledged his vassal allegiance. When he showed up in Batu's court, he kotowed three times in the Mongol fashion, which pleased Batu.

When Daniel was ushered into his seat, Batu asked, "Have you ever tried our kumiss?"

"Until now, I have never tried it. But, if it is your order, I am happy to try it."

A goblet of kumiss was offered to him. When he emptied the goblet in one breath, Batu let out a loud guffaw and said, "You are now one of us! I know that you are not familiar with kumiss, so have some wine."

Daniel became a powerful man under Batu's suzerainty.

Later, an unknown Galician chronicler gave a severe criticism for Daniel:

Oh! Eviler than evil itself!
In the Tatar honor.
Daniel, the great prince,
The lord of Russian land,
Now kneels,
And calls himself,
The khan's slave.

Months later, Prince Michael of Chernigov showed up in Batu's court. Batu didn't trust him because of his previous misbehavior. He abandoned Kiev and its people, sneaking out in the middle of the night when the Mongols were about to attack the city. Michael was accompanied by his son and one of his boyars in Batu's court; however, before he entered the court, he was asked to walk through two columns of fire. It was a Mongolian belief that fire purified any thoughts of evil intentions.

Michael walked through the fire without any trouble. Next, he was required to kowtow three times onto the tablet of Genghis Khan, but he hesitated.

"In the case of a living person, I am willing to do this. But how can I bow to a dead person? It is against my belief. I bow only before God."

His son, who was next to him, shouted, "Father! Do it!"

However, his boyar said, "If you bow, you will win the earthly crown. If you refuse, you will win the crown of martyrdom."

Michael refused, and Batu sentenced him. He was surrounded by 10 Mongol soldiers who kicked him to death.

The boyar got the same treatment, but his son was released unharmed.

CHAPTER 51

The regent Toregene

It goes ill in the house
Where the hen sings,
While the cock is silent.
The hen sings
With her bosom,
The cock sings
With his head.

Toregene was not a woman of great beauty, but she was masterful in nature, crafty and extremely shrewd. She was Naiman born and married to Dair Usun of Merkid. When Genghis Khan conquered the Merkids, he gave Toregene to Ogodei because his first wife Boraqchin couldn't have any sons.

Toregene gave five sons to Ogodei: Kuyuk, Koten, Kochu, Qachar and Qasi. Ogodei favored his third son Kochu as his heir and successor, but he died early. His first son Kuyuk was unpopular even to his father, so the heirship eventually went to Shiremun, who was the firstborn son of Kochu as well as the grandson of Ogodei. Shiremun was extremely smart;

however, Toregene wanted her own first son Kuyuk to be the khagan instead of Shiremun, who was the son of Qadaqach from a different womb. Among the list of Ogodei's descendants who joined the European campaign, Kuyuk and Kadan were outstanding, but Kadan was born from a concubine and was out of line.

After the khagan's death, Toregene began to eclipse all the other wives and increased her influence in the court. She persuaded many others to support her son Kuyuk as the next khagan. She didn't hesitate to replace all the important positions with her sycophants. There was a rumor inside the court that the khagan Ogodei was poisoned. Nobody knew the origin of the rumor, yet it was a good pretext for the new regent Toregene to put the blame on Ibaqa, who was the cupbearer for Ogodei.

Ibaqa was originally the third wife of Genghis Khan; yet, when her father Jagambu was blamed for the rebellion, she was forcefully divorced and given to General Julchedai. She remained influential in the court because of her two sisters—Bebtutmish, who was chief wife of Juchi, and Sorqoqtani Beki, who was the chief wife of Tolui. Toregene was always jealous of these three sisters and didn't look at them with friendly eyes. Ibaqa was prosecuted, but the well-respected Jalair general, who had deep relations with the Ogodeis, protested strongly.

"Please do not make me an innocent victim! It is well known that the late khagan had a bad habit of uncontrolled drinking. The blame should go to someone who didn't help him control it!"

These comments were condemning even to Toregene, but the Jalair general was so respected that no one could challenge his reasoning. Ibaqa was saved; however, another person was prosecuted with Ibaqa—Il Alti—who was Genghis Khan's daughter from an unknown, low-class concubine. Il Alti was very close with Ibaqa and, on many days, they were together. Toregene hated to see her and gave an order to execute her. She needed a scapegoat to divert the blame.

Next, Toregene gave an order to arrest Chingai, who was the chief vizier for Ogodei Khan. Having been offended by Chingai during Ogodei's reign, and with feelings of resentment rooted in her heart, it was time for revenge. Chingai learned about this order and sought refuge under the protection of Koten, the late khagan's second son.

Toregene had a retainer called Fatima, who was a Persian slave woman practicing witchcraft and sorcery. She was believed to have supernatural power and the ability to foresee the future.

One time, when Toregene had a bad dream of falling into a bottomless, dark abyss and soon after became ill, Fatima gave a helping hand. After Fatima touched Toregene's forehead with her palm and remained there for a while, she vividly described the nature of the scenery that Toregene saw and experienced in her dream. She also gave Toregene an amulet, which she advised her to put under her pillow for the complete elimination of an evil spirit. It worked, and Toregene recovered.

On another occasion, Fatima foretold the exact date of Ogodei's death. She also practiced astrology and, one night, after careful observation of the sky, she foretold that Ogodei

Khan would die on December 11, 1241, which was 15 days late. Ever since then, Toregene became an ardent admirer of Fatima. Fatima also became a close spiritual advisor to Toregene.

Fatima had an old grudge with Mahmud Yalavach, who was the sahib-divan (minister of finance). Toregene gave an order to Oqal Qorchi, the guard captain, to arrest Yalavach. When Oqal Qorchi arrived at Yalavach's residence with an ambassador and nokers (guards), Yalavach quickly noticed that it was for his arrest.

Since Yalavach and Oqal Qorchi were friends, Yalavach said, "It has been a while since I shared a nice talk with you, so tonight, let's have a drink. Tomorrow, I will hear the terms of the decree."

Yalavach plied them with drinks until they became intoxicated and snuck out while they were in a deep sleep. Yalavach also went to Koten for protection.

When Koten received the ambassador from his mother Toregene to surrender the two refugees he was hiding, he answered, "What crime did they commit? Soon, we will have Kuriltai for election for the next khagan, and it won't be too late to put them on fair trial after that."

Toregene appointed Abd al-Rahman as the minister of finance in place of Yalavach. Abd al-Rahman promised Toregene that he would double the taxes from northern China. By that time, they were collecting 1,100,000 ounces of silver annually, but Abd al-Rahman promised 2,200,000.

Yelu-chuchai, the chancellor of the nation, strongly opposed.

"It is impossible! They are already suffering a lot to make the current taxes on time! It will put them into a miserable situation!"

His opposition was ignored. Since then, Yelu-chuchai couldn't hold his sorrow, and he became sick and died. The great man who helped Genghis Khan build up the great empire died in despair.

Toregene gave an order to search his house with the belief that he might have accumulated a large fortune since he had been the chancellor of the empire for such a long time. They found a lot of books in his library, maps, some artwork, stone collections, some musical instruments, daily necessities and three servants. Later, Yelu-chuchai was bestowed with the posthumous title of "the king of northern China."

Toregene then replaced Kurguz, the Persian viceroy (governor) who had been obnoxious to her for a long time, with General Arghun Aqa. Kurguz was discharged from his position and arrested. When all these events happened, Massudbey, the governor of Turkistan and Transoxania, didn't trust Toregene's regime, and he escaped to Batu and joined him.

Toregene did all these things without consulting Aqa and Inis (her elder and younger brothers, respectively) but was simply guided by advice from Fatima. Toregene wooed her kinsfolk and emirs with gifts and presents to endear her to them.

This behavior lasted for four years until the next khagan was elected because all the princes couldn't get together for the election. One of the men who couldn't tolerate what was going on in the empire was Ochigin Noyan, who was the younger brother of Genghis Khan. He came to Karakorum with his eight sons and a large army, but his actions couldn't change anything in the regime. Rather, his actions were regarded as a rebellion and, at a later time, he had to face an inquiry and a trial.

Finally, there was an election, and Kuyuk was elected as the next khagan—all done without Batu's presence or consent.

CHAPTER 52

Kuyuk, the new khagan

I n the early summer of 1246, on the plain near Koko-nur Lake and the Orkhon River, just a few miles from Karakorum, a new tent city had emerged named Sira Ordu. About 2,000 white tents erupted for guests from every part of the world. It was a magnificent display of Mongol imperialism for the enthronement of the new khagan Kuyuk.

The honored guests were: Yaroslav, the grand duke of Russia; two ambassadors from Pope Innocent IV and the council of Leon; ambassadors from the caliphate of Baghdad; ambassador brothers of the Egyptian sultan; two brother kings of Georgia; the brothers of the sultan of Aleppo; the Ismailia prince of Alamut; Far and Kernan, the princes of Mosul; the Sempad brothers from the kingdom of Cilicia; Argun, the governor of Persia; Massudbey, the governor of Turkistan and Transoxania; Rokn-ud-dn, the Seljuk sultan of Rum; Constable Sempad from Armenia; ambassadors from Korea; ambassadors from northern China; and ambassadors from Tibet.

The ceremony lasted for four days, and they followed the traditional culture of nomads. Each day, the attendants had to change their ceremonial costume with one of a different color, which signified the four directions of the empire harmoniously combined.

Kuyuk declared that the world was finally under one nation, which had been God's ordainment since the beginning of creation.

Following the official ceremony of enthronement, there were celebrations and feasts for one week. After these events, the new khagan had an official audience with the individual subject kings, princes, grand dukes, sultans, governors and ambassadors from every corner of the empire with whom he discussed current issues.

During these individual meetings, the khagan often made many important decisions and immediately issued decrees. For example, two brothers from the Georgia Kingdom, who both shared the name David, also shared their kingdom. Henceforth, Georgia had two kings—one for northern Georgia and the other for southern Georgia.

The new regime began to handle the internal affairs.

First, the sorceress Fatima was prosecuted for false accusations and the practice of illegal occult art. She was found guilty, but the sentence couldn't be carried out while Toregene was alive. After Toregene's death, Fatima was thrown into the river with her body orifices sewn up with a needle and thread. Some superstitious Mongols believed that the evil spirits would come out when she died. Her intimate family members were punished together.

Then they got down to Ochigin Noyan's case, and the questioning, judgment and sentencing jobs were given to Monku and Orda. Monku was careful because Ochigin Noyan's case was very sensitive. The inside stories of the descendants of Chigisides and his prestige and image as the Great One's brother were not light.

Monku asked, "What is your motivation for moving such a large army?"

Ochigin Noyan answered, "I wanted to give some lessons to Toregene and her regime. I couldn't tolerate the direction into which she was taking the nation. The longer she was holding the power, the weaker the nation would be."

Monku accepted this explanation and gave the death penalty order for seven of his close advisors. For Ochigin Noyan, the punishment was to limit his living space within 100 miles.

On the last day of the celebration of enthronement, the outgoing regent Toregene kindly invited Yaroslav, the grand duke of Russia. Yaroslav wondered why he got a personal invitation from the regent, but he was not in a position to say "yes" or "no." He had to be there. He was ushered into Toregene's official yult (a Mongolian dome-shaped tent), which was luxuriously decorated and carpeted with the finest Persian products. Between the lacquered dining table, two people sat facing each other.

With a smiling face, Toregene said, "Welcome to Mongolia! I really appreciate your coming from such a long distance. From now on, Mongolia and Russia are like sister countries. We are now one! I will tell my son to lower the taxes for the Oruss people."

Yaroslav got on his feet and bowed to Toregene, saying, "Your generosity has touched my heart! My people and I will never forget your kindness."

Toregene gave a hand signal to her servant, who was standing behind her, to hand over a small box wrapped with silk.

She said to Yaroslav, "Please hand this to Batu Khan when you get home. This is my gift for Batu." (The box was empty and only designed to give the impression of a good reason to summon Yaroslav personally.)

They shared a friendly conversation and, after tea, they enjoyed dinner together. At the end of the dinner, just before the dessert course, Yaroslav stood up and groaned, holding his belly with his two palms. His face turned green and numerous beads of sweat stood out. Within a short time, he fell to the ground.

Toregene had used a very powerful, fast-acting Persian poison. Showing ridicule and a contemptuous image on her face, she slowly stood on her feet and approached the already dead body of Yaroslav. Kicking the body, she spoke in a scornful manner.

"Batu's dog! Batu will soon join you! You won't be lonely!"

Toregene suppressed the news of Yaroslav's sudden death from spreading throughout the tent city, so many of the other honored guests left the city without knowing.

The journey of John
of Plano Carpini

Italian archbishop John of Plano Carpini (Giovanni da Pian de Carpine, in Italian) left Lyon, France, in April 1245. He was on a mission to the Mongol mainland to deliver the letter written by Pope Innocent IV to the Mongol khagan.

Ever since Pope Innocent IV had been elected, he realized that the most urgent issue he had to face was the Mongol onslaught, which they frequently referred to as "the punishment of God." Their main concern was whether they were coming back again. The pope decided to dispatch envoys for a direct communication with the Mongol khagan.

Among all the possible candidates, Carpini and Friar Stephen had been chosen, yet Stephen had been left behind at Kiev in the middle of the journey. Carpini had a new travel companion named Benedykt Polak, who also was a monk with fluency in many different languages. Carpini had two missions: checking the possibility of the conversion of the khagan's religion into Catholicism by handing over the pope's letter and spying to find out the Mongols' possible next movement and the size of their military power.

Carpini was about 60 years old when he left Lyon. After leaving Kiev, he crossed the Don River and arrived at Batu's Golden Ordu in Sarai near the Volga River. He had to pass between two columns of fire to remove possible injurious thoughts and poisons. When he mentioned that he was bringing the pope's letter to the supreme leader of the Mongol Empire, Batu allowed them to pass through his domain.

Several days later, they restarted their journey to Karakorum. It was early April in 1246, almost a year after he left Lyon. Their journey was a very difficult, troubled one, yet possible thanks to the Yam system. Every 50 miles, there was a station where they could get rest, emergency supplies and information about the next Yam stations. They couldn't get the paiza from Batu, yet the travel itself was very safe under the Mongol rule.

Their main meal during the journey was millet, barley and some salt, which they carried in their bags. They had to find every possible way to endure the excessive fatigue of this enormous ride of thousands of miles. They crossed the Syr Darya River, went along the shores of the Dzungarian lakes and finally arrived at Sira Ordu, the imperial camp. It was early July and about 100 days after they left Batu's Golden Ordu.

First, they had to register the guests for Kuyuk's new khagan enthronement ceremony. They were guided to the registration office and stood in front of the clerk, who was sitting in front of a desk.

The clerk asked, "Where are you from, and what are your names?"

Carpini answered, "We are from Lyon, France. My name is Giovanni da Pian de Carpine, and his name is Benedykt Polak. We are the messengers from Pope Innocent IV. We are on a special mission."

The clerk wrote down the names and all the other information, and then asked, "What gift did you bring?"

The question was unexpected, and Carpini didn't know how to answer it.

"We didn't bring any gift."

The clerk looked at Carpini and his companion and asked again with a look of surprise, "You didn't bring any gift? If you didn't, I cannot put your name on the list of guests. You must go back to the place you came from."

Carpini was astounded, and there were some arguments. The clerk stood up and went into another tent. Moments later, he came out with a man who looked like someone in charge.

The man said, "It is our culture that you must bring a gift to be considered as a guest."

"I have the pope's letter to the new khagan," Carpini replied.

After a moment, the man, who was a chief clerk, said, "You breached the etiquette. It is a humiliation for our khagan. A letter cannot be the gift. We will put your name on the list of the guests and hand your letter to the khagan, yet you cannot be considered as our honored guest. You won't be provided with a tent or any supplies. You must go back, now!"

After these words, the chief clerk went back to his tent.

Carpini and Benedykt had trouble ever since this encounter. First, they didn't have a place to sleep or anything to eat.

They had to sleep on the street and, for a few days, could manage with leftovers of millet and barley. After that, they had to check the trash to find anything to eat, like stray dogs. All they could do was pray.

One day, a miracle happened when a man showed up in front of them.

The man introduced himself by saying, "My name is Cosmas. I am a Russian. I am a goldsmith for the khagan, and I heard that two ambassadors of the pope arrived here, so I was looking around. I am a Christian. I think it's my obligation to support someone on God's mission."

Cosmas invited Carpini and Benedykt to his tent and allowed them to stay there. He provided hot meals and comfortable beds.

He told them, "I have been here since I was 17 years old. Now I am 37. My father was a goldsmith in Russia, and I inherited his skills and craftsmanship. I married a Mongolian woman and now have two sons. I have some connections with the high Mongol aristocratic society because I make them a lot of jewelry, like rings, bracelets, necklaces, bangles—you name it. I am even making the khagan's royal seal."

Carpini couldn't attend Kuyuk's enthronement ceremony and couldn't get an audience. The only thing he confirmed was that the pope's letter had been delivered to the new khagan. Actually, Kuyuk was upset with the content of the letter, which accused the massacring of millions of Christians in the pope's territory. Kuyuk ignored this letter and didn't pay any attention to Carpini, who was anxiously awaiting an audience.

CHAPTER 53

Carpini had to wait until early November, which was more than six months after he had arrived.

Finally, thanks to Cosmas's efforts, the audience was allowed, and Carpini could finally stand in front of Kuyuk. By that time, Chingai, who had been disposed by the regent Toregene, was reinstated by the new khagan Kuyuk. Toregene died about three months after Kuyuk's enthronement. In Kuyuk's official tent, Chingai read the pope's letter, which was in Latin and which the interpreter translated into Mongolian.

Kuyuk said, "I cannot accept your pope's invitation to Catholicism. My answer is 'no.' Hand this letter to your pope. You must leave tomorrow."

Kuyuk gave the letter to Chingai and let him read it in front of all the attendants. It was in three languages: Mongolian, Latin and Arabic. Chingai read the one in Mongolian:

The Mongol Empire is not just another nation. It is a supreme, universal monarchy that is destined to rule all other nations under the heaven by the order of God, himself. Any nation and any people who understand this and follow God's order shall survive and thrive; otherwise; they shall perish with no trace. Though you are the great pope, with all the princes and nations, you must serve us. If you do not observe God's command, and if you ignore my command, I shall know that you are my enemy. Thereupon, I shall make you understand. If you do otherwise, God knows what I know.

The letter was stamped with the royal seal, which read, "The khagan, God's power on Earth, ruler of all mankind."

Carpini and Benedykt left Karakorum and arrived in Lyon through Batu's Sarai and Kiev. They traveled through the depth of cold weather, and it was a harsh winter. Their journey took almost two and one-half years.

Once they got home, they received a warm welcome from the pope and the council of Lyon.

CHAPTER 54

The death of Kuyuk

The year had changed and then another. It was early springtime in 1248 (Hijri 645 and the year of the monkey in the Chinese zodiac). The air was still chilly, and the faraway mountaintop was covered with snow.

On the vast plain of Kipchak, thousands of tents spread out in a very organized way, making a big tent city. It was north of the Caspian Sea and very close to the Volga River. Batu Khan's royal golden tent was at the northern end of the city, which was the reserved spot for the great khan. His own royal tent was flanked by another 20 tents for his wives and concubines. Outside of this group of tents, another 500 to 600 tents encircled in an oval shape, making about a mile in circumference. Those were for Batu's 1,000 night-guard units.

It was late in the morning, and Batu had just gotten up from bed in his major wife Boraqchin's tent. The captain on duty shouted from outside the tent, making a report. Even in an urgent situation, nobody could come into the khan's tent; if they did, the punishment was severe: death.

"My lord, an urgent messenger from the house of Sorqoqtani Beki. What shall I do?"

Batu heard the report and answered, "I will see the messenger in front of my official tent very soon."

Batu met the urgent messenger and immediately recognized him. He was the retainer of the house of Tolui for a long time, and his father was also a retainer.

Batu said, "I remember you. What is the message?"

The messenger knelt on one knee and made a verbal report. At the time, when the Mongols tried to deliver secret messages, they preferred a verbal report rather than a written one. It was mainly for security measures and to not leave any evidence. They picked up someone very trustworthy, had him memorize all the lines and deliver it verbally. This method was only possible between two trusted parties, and usually the messenger was selected among someone known from both parties. Usually, the messengers carried out their jobs on their lives. If they were captured, they never talked.

The messenger made a report by saying, "Great Khan, this message is from Sorqoqtani Beki, the widow of the Great Khan Tolui. She is letting you know that the khagan Kuyuk has left Karakorum with a large army, heading for the west. His main target is believed to be the ulus of Juchi, which is you. He wants to consolidate his empire to subjugate the ulus of Juchi. Be prepared for that."

After hearing this report, Batu raised his head and stared into space for a while, murmuring, "The civil war is inevitable. Many Mongols will die, and the Mongol Empire will be shattered. This is not the way the Great One, Genghis Khan, wanted it to be."

Batu immediately summoned the war council. All his brothers and generals gathered in Batu's war tent. At the time,

Batu's military power was almost equal to the mainland's imperial army.

Batu announced, "The civil war is inevitable. How can we handle this?"

First, no one came forward to speak freely, but then Batu's younger brother spoke.

Seiban carefully said, "Big brother, we must find a way to stop this. The war with the Ogodeis and the Chagatais will ruin us even though we will win. Same thing goes to them. If that happens, the Mongol Empire is destined to decline."

Batu replied, "Everybody in this tent knows that. But how? How can we bypass the war? Soon, Kuyuk will summon me. If I refuse, then he will have a good pretext to attack me. That's treason. If I was there …"

Seiban interrupted, "Big brother! Don't go there. You will be assassinated. If Kuyuk summons you, I will be there on your behalf. He might not kill me because I have been keeping a good relationship with him. There should be someone between you and him. Otherwise, nothing will happen—only war."

Batu stared into Seiban's eyes for a while; eventually, he shook his head and said, "It won't work. But I won't stop you either."

A general asked, "Will Subedei join Kuyuk?"

Batu answered, "No. He retired. He is now in his hometown near the Selenga River."

Batu was ready. He mustered his army and set out for the incoming civil war, heading east. When he arrived near the Aral Sea, he received the envoy from Kuyuk as expected.

Kuyuk was stationed in Samarqand and demanded that Batu personally show up in Kuyuk's court. As planned, Seiban left for Samarqand.

When Seiban showed up in Kuyuk's war tent, Kuyuk got on his feet and shouted, "Where's Batu? I asked Batu to come here, not you!"

Seiban, standing in front of Kuyuk, tried to convince him about the importance of unity. By that time, Kuyuk firmly made up his mind to remove Batu and his brothers. Kuyuk already put about 30 ax men around his tent and 150 archers at a nearby place.

Seiban raised his voice and said, "Kuyuk, you are wrong! You shouldn't bring a large army just to remove my brother."

Determined, Kuyuk angrily said, "What? I am wrong? I will remove Batu and all his brothers! It is too late for you."

Kuyuk picked up the dagger from his waist and approached Seiban. At that time, nobody was allowed to keep any form of weapon in the khan's tent—except the khan himself. Seiban had to leave all of his weapons before entering Kuyuk's tent.

Seiban exclaimed, "Kuyuk, you are wrong! You will be damned too!"

Kuyuk brandished his dagger to cut Seiban's neck. It cut Seiban's jugular, yet it didn't kill him. Seiban tussled with Kuyuk and snatched his dagger. Seiban, with the dagger in his hand, put it deep into Kuyuk's heart. A short, loud, piercing cry burst from Kuyuk's mouth. Both men fell on the carpet, immediately staining it with a flood of blood, and both met an instant death. It happened in such a short moment that nobody inside the tent could do anything.

CHAPTER 54

Batu received the news that Seiban and Kuyuk had killed each other.

A general approached Batu and said, "My lord, this is a good chance to defeat the Ogodeis and the Chagatais. Let's proceed!"

Batu responded, "No! That would not be the will of the Great One. We will go back. Let them return. We will stay here until we retrieve Seiban's body."

CHAPTER 55

Oghul Quaimish, the regent

From the beginning, at the time of Genghis Khan, women's lives in a nomadic society weren't easy; however, they had equal rights with men, which was unusual compared to other cultures. War was a man's job, and all other jobs were left for women, who were tough, resilient and independent. In a feudal society, like Mongolia, a woman often had to marry and bear children with the man who killed her father. Women on the steppe needed both physical and mental toughness to face these ugly and horrible situations.

After Kuyuk's death, his major wife Oghul Quaimish became the regent. She was born of the Merkid tribe and, when Genghis Khan put down the rebellion of her clan, she was given to Kuyuk as a wife. She bore Kuyuk two sons—Quchar and Naqu—and moved them to her appanage Emil and set up the royal encampment. She was not a political woman like Toregene, but she had a strong sense of obligation to elect one of her sons or Shiremun as the khagan. She understood that her major obligation was to keep the line of khaganship limited to the house of Ogodei.

CHAPTER 55

From an early age, Oghul Quaimish spent much of her time with shamans and was fantasized by the world of the supernatural realm, which was the belief of the steppe people and a strong or weak point for them. Like her mother-in-law Toregene was to the sorceress Fatima, Oghul Quaimish was to shamans. When she took over the empire as a regent, due to the sudden death of Kuyuk, she wasn't ready. She was an accidental leader. She could manage with the help of Kuyuk's three chief officials—Chingai, Qadaq and Bala—yet she had to depend largely on shamans for her spiritual support. She was supported by the houses of Chagatai and Ogodei, but there was no outstanding man in those two families after Kuyuk's death.

At the beginning, Oghul Quaimish tried to recover the financial difficulties in the empire caused mainly by her mother-in-law Toregene, who spent extravagantly. It wasn't an easy job for her. Even in Kuyuk's time, he spent a lot more than he could collect.

As time went by, it went from bad to worse, so Oghul Quaimish sought to prop up her waning image through diplomacy. She received a group of ambassadors from the French king Louis IX, who sent a fabulous gift of a sumptuous, highly decorated tent, which was a portable chapel of scarlet cloth. It was an indication of the French king's submission to Mongol rule on the expectation that the Mongol Empire would crush the Islamic power of the Abbasid caliphate of Baghdad and the sultan of Egypt.

Oghul Quaimish welcomed Friar Andrew Longjumeau and six other friars and treated them well. In return, she sent her own envoys with a fine brocade to confirm the French king's submission. Even with this diplomatic victory, her image didn't improve due to political unrest and financial hardship.

At this time, Sorqoqtani showed up as a rival, pushing Oghul Quaimish to open the kuriltai as soon as possible for the new khagan. She had long desired that all her sons be leaders of the Mongol Empire.

Sorqoqtani was the daughter of Jagambu, who was the younger brother of Wang Khan, who was the chief of the Keraits. When Genghis Khan conquered the Keraits, he took the policy of amalgamation; instead of removing them, he accepted them. Many of the Kerait royal girls married Genghis Khan's sons, and many of the Kerait generals were absorbed as regular Mongol army members. They became core members of the Mongol aristocrats and the army.

Sorqoqtani differed from Oghul Quaimish and Toregene. Sorqoqtani had many connections with aristocratic society and even in the army. She was a Nestorian Christian like her uncle Wang Khan. Sorqoqtani was married to Tolui, who was Genghis Khan's youngest son, and had four sons: Monku, Hulegu, Kubilai and Aribog. When Tolui died during the northern China campaign, Sorqoqtani was asked for her hand by Ogodei by levirate rule, which allows a widow to remarry her late husband's brother.

Sorqoqtani refused and said, "I will devote the rest of my life to my four sons. I will raise them as the leaders of the empire."

Sorqoqtani sent Monku to visit Batu. After the second generation had gone, Batu was the most senior member of the third generation. Batu was pleased to see Monku since they were very close friends beyond cousinship.

Over a cup of tea after dinner, Monku said, "Batu, we need a new khagan. It is quite sloppy out there. If things keep going on like this, the empire will be weakened."

"That's right! It has been years since Ogodei Khan died. We should not delay anymore."

For a few moments, there was silence between them.

Soon, Batu said, "Monku, you are the next khagan. I am pretty sure that you are the right one."

Monku, with his eyes wide open, said, "What about you? *You* are the right one! You are the Great One's firstborn grandson."

With a smiling face, Batu replied, "Monku, I like it here in Kipchak. I wouldn't leave here."

After another silent moment, Monku said, "What about the Chagatais and the Ogodeis? They will reject us. How can we handle them?"

"We have to find a way."

A few months later, Batu proclaimed the kuriltai. He used his seniority among all the princes to qualify his proclamation. The location was Ala-Qamaq in central Asia, which was 2,000 miles from Karakorum. Most of the princes from the houses of Juchi and Tolui attended, but not many from the houses of Ogodei and Chagatai were there. The regent Oghul Quaimish sent Bala, her secretary, to represent her.

Before her departure, Oghul Quaimish asked Bala, "Who do you think I have to support for the next khagan—one of my sons or Shiremun?"

"I think it should be Shiremun. He has a better position and better chances than Quchar or Naqu."

Oghul Quaimish concluded that keeping the khaganship inside the house of Ogodei was the most important thing. She had a very good relationship with Shiremun's mother too. She agreed that Shiremun would be the candidate.

At the kuriltai, Bala spoke in a loud voice, "The next khagan should be Shiremun. He is the handpicked successor of the late khagan Ogodei. I must remind all of you that the khaganship should be continued through the descendants of Ogodei Khan. All the princes agreed on that condition before Ogodei Khan accepted the khaganship and was enthroned."

Bala's comments were accurate, and no one offered any negative comments. When Ogodei accepted the khaganship, he set a condition that all the other khagans must come from his descendants from generation to generation. At the time, all the other princes had to agree with this condition.

Batu stood up and said, "Commissary Bala's theory seems quite right; however, I must also remind you that if Shiremun is Ogodei Khan's rightful successor, why has Kuyuk became the khagan instead? Regarding the legitimacy of the house of Ogodei for the inheritance of the khaganship, if it was agreed and confirmed by all the other princes at the time, then why did the house of Ogodei kill Princess Il Alti without the consent of Aka [the elder brother] and Inis [the younger brother]? The house of Ogodei has already broken Genghis

Khan's Yassa and our traditional law of Yosun, which says, 'When you punish your own princes or princesses, you need the consent from most of the other princes and princesses.' The house of Ogodei is no longer qualified to produce khagans anymore."

Il Alti, Genghis Khan's favorite daughter from one of the concubines, was killed by Toregene because she was too close to Ibaqa and Sorqoqtani. This information silenced Bala.

Batu continued, "I strongly recommend Monku, who is intelligent and brave and has already proven to have great leadership in the military campaigns in Russia and Europe. He is the only one who will complete the mission of a world conquest."

Monku won the election, and Batu proclaimed that Monku would be the next khagan.

Oghul Quaimish immediately claimed that the kuriltai was illegitimate because it was held outside of the Mongol mainland. Genghis Khan's Yassa clearly stated that the kuriltai should be held inside Mongol land; otherwise, it would be considered illegitimate.

CHAPTER 56

Monku, the new khagan

In the middle of summer of 1251 (648 Hijri and the year of the pig in the Chinese zodiac), the second kuriltai opened. The location was Kodeu Aral by the Kerulen River in the heart of the Mongol mainland. A gigantic tent was erected, which could accommodate nearly 2,000 people. It was for a joint event of a kuriltai and an official enthronement ceremony. There had already been a preliminary kuriltai; this time, it was just for confirmation.

For this kuriltai, Batu sent his brothers, including Berke and Toqa-Temur, along with 2,000 soldiers for protection. Of course, all the princes from the house of Tolui were there as well as the descendants of Ochigin Noyan; the descendants of Genghis Khan's half-brother Belgutei; and the descendants of Khan Kulgan, who was the son of Genghis Khan from his fourth wife Kulan.

Many other Chigisides attended; however, many from the houses of Ogodei and Chagatai didn't come. Kadan and Melik from the house of Ogodei attended and realized that the power game had already been shifted in favor of the house of Tolui and was no longer in doubt. They were the sons of a concubine, so they were out of line for any candidacy. Other attendees were Mongetu and Qara-Hulegu, who had personal reasons to join Monku.

The kuriltai was successfully completed, and Monku was elected as the next khagan. Immediately, they commenced the official ceremony of enthronement. Monku, the new khagan, wore armor, a helmet and military boots. A scimitar hung on his left-hand side waist and a dagger was on the right.

Guided by four other princes, Monku walked through the new carpet from the southern entrance to the northernmost khagan's seat. At all enthronement ceremonies, the new khan or new khagan always wore armor and a helmet, which signified that the Mongols were born soldiers and would die as soldiers. Monku sat on the chair, which was luxuriously designed by the Russian artisan Cosmas.

Batu's younger brother, Berke, declared, "Monku Khan, the descendant of Tolui and the descendant of Genghis Khan now proclaims that he is the new khagan. Nothing on this earth is above him, and all living creatures belong to him. His power comes from God himself. Obey him!"

All the attendants in the tent took off their helmets and belts and kowtowed nine times toward Monku, which was the traditional Mongol ceremonial gesture meaning complete obedience.

In the afternoon, they discussed the national ideology, which would guide the direction of the empire. They decided to continue the completion of the world conquest and discussed this plan in detail.

Monku appointed his younger brother Hulegu as the commander in chief of the southwestern expedition army and ordered him to conquer the Assassins, the caliphate of Baghdad, Mesopotamia and the sultanate of Egypt. For the southern Sung conquest, he appointed Kubilai, who was Monku's other younger brother, as the commander. Until that time, southern Sung never had been conquered by any other people.

After making all these plans, they began a seven-day celebratory feast. Almost 10,000 people gathered on the vast plain by the Kerulen River and consumed enormous amounts of food and drink, including 2,000 carts of kumiss and wine, 300 horses and oxen and 2,000 sheep.

CHAPTER 57

The last strike of Oghul Quaimish

When Oghul Quaimish talked to General Eljigidei Noyan for counseling, she asked, "Noyan, how can we stop the march of Batu and Monku's joint force?"

General Eljigidei had been the commander of Ogodei's kheshiq (night guards) and was posted to the Persian governor by Toregene and affirmed by Kuyuk. He belonged to the house of Ogodei.

The general said, "Khatun, it is too late now. They had a kuriltai yesterday and Monku became the khagan. They completed everything with lightning speed. They are on the feast now, and it will last about a week. What can we do at this point?"

"We must do something. I can't just sit down here and get killed!"

Eljigidei kept silent for a while because he didn't know how to answer.

He then said, "The only way we can try now is here. First, declare that the kuriltai is invalid because the houses of

Ogodei and Chagatai didn't participate. Then we can send the assassins to kill Monku. Once we successfully get rid of Monku, many of the other princes and noyans will change their mind to support us."

They set this plan into motion. Eljigidei selected 200 commandoes from the house of Ogodei and disguised them as congratulators. Many of them were Uighurs disguised as congratulatory ambassadors from the Uighur Kingdom. Since they couldn't carry weapons on their bodies, they hid them in a cart and covered them with rolls of silk, damask and Persian carpets. The house of Ogodei had a marriage connection with the Uighur Kingdom, and its iduqut (king) Salindi was always loyal to the house of Ogodei. Oghul Quaimish immediately dispatched an arrow messenger to Besh-Baliq, the capital of the Uighur Kingdom, to summon the army and get ready for battle.

The 200 assassins arrived outside of the feasting ground, waiting for permission to enter. It was the last day of the feast. Monku received a report from the guard captain that a group of ambassadors from the Uighur Kingdom had arrived and were waiting for an audience. He also received another urgent report from one of his house servants who said that he accidentally caught sight of a group of people approaching, hiding weapons in their cart.

The servant said, "My lord! I was looking around for one of my lost sheep. Suddenly, I saw a group of people approaching, and I quickly hid under the bush. They were all in white kaftans and were carrying a cart driven by a horse. They suddenly stopped in front of the bushes where I was hiding and were repacking the cart. It contained stacks of carpets and silk rolls but, underneath them, I saw all kinds of weapons."

Monku immediately mobilized 2,000 armed guardsmen and ordered them to get ready. The 200 fake congratulatory ambassadors were invited to a large guest tent, which could accommodate well over 200 people. Soon, they were attacked by 2,000 armed guards and massacred with only a few survivors. These survivors were questioned to find out who sent them and were left alive for living evidence.

Salindi, after receiving Oghul Quaimish's letter, said, "I cannot abandon my former supporters and benefactors by simply moving to Monku's side."

He decided to remain loyal to the house of Ogodei. He mustered his army and got ready to advance.

The following day, two men appeared in front of Oghul Quaimish and asked her to accompany them, but she refused to follow. The next day, 20 soldiers bound her with rawhide and forcefully dragged her. Shiremun's mother Qadaqach met the same fate. They were taken to their rival Sorqoqtani's camp and tortured with burning brands in front of Sorqoqtani.

Sorqoqtani ordered the torturers to take off her whole dress, which symbolized khatun (queen).

Oghul Quaimish yelled at Sorqoqtani, "How can you do this to me? Nobody has seen my naked body except the emperor!"

The trial court, which was ruled by the chief judge Menggesser, found both women guilty and sentenced them to death. Oghul Quaimish was wrapped in a carpet and thrown into the river. When someone was wrapped with carpet and thrown into water, they could not move their arms and legs because of its weight, so death would come soon due to asphyxiation.

After the plot failed, Eljigidei fled to Iraq. The manhunt began, and there was no place to hide from the Mongol chasers. He was captured in a small town close to Herat and taken to the court. He was sentenced to death and killed by boiling water from a large pot.

The purging process continued. During this period, many princes, high-ranking officials and generals were wiped out, including Oghul Quaimish's two sons Quchar and Naqu, Shiremun, Buri, Chingai, Qadaq, Bala and Eljigidei's two sons.

Salindi, the Uighur iduqut, was captured by the Mongol expeditionary troops and executed. He was dragged into the center of a busy marketplace and beheaded by his own brother Ogunch. Ogunch remained loyal to Monku from that moment. The Mongol Empire needed strong unity.

The master of the past, present and future

The purging process lasted for a while to consolidate the unity of the empire. Many of the main house members of Ogodei and Chagatai perished with the exceptions being the ones who were cooperative and loyal to the Batu-Monku line. They were allowed to have their own appanages and could join major events. Otherwise, they were degraded to commoners and had to pay taxes. They were completely blocked from any chance of resurgence.

A few months after Monku's enthronement, Sorqoqtani became sick and died. The superstitious Mongols exchanged whispers that she was cursed by the spirit of Oghul Quaimish.

The Mongol Empire once again was handed over to the expansionist Monku. In 1253, Monku gave a 200,000-man army to his younger brother Hulegu to conquer the Nazari Ismaili State (Assassins); Abbasid, the caliphate in Baghdad; the Ayyubid State of Syria in Damascus; and Bahri Mamuluke, the sultanate of Egypt.

Hulegu truthfully and successfully carried out Monku's order to destroy and conquer all of those states with the utmost cruelty for several years. Monku also gave a large army to his other younger brother Kubilai to conquer the southern Sung of China, which had never been conquered by any other people. Kubilai had to face the Sung's newly developed canons and improved black powder, yet eventually he completed his mission.

Ever since Monku became the khagan, the friendship and cooperation between Batu and Monku deepened on a personal level as well as in state affairs. They shared the same key for the imperial treasure warehouse in Karakorum, and Monku's officials could visit Batu's domain for censors without Batu's permission. Eventually, Monku acknowledged Batu's independence and it remained that way.

In the early spring of 1255, in the magnificent tent city of Sarai near the bank of the Volga River, the air was still chilly and frosty. It was evening, and the dusk was falling rapidly. In Batu's main tent, about 10 people were gathered. In a normal situation, nobody could enter this tent except Batu or an allowed person.

Batu's main tent was humble, unlike a typical conqueror. The only exceptions were high-quality Persian carpets and lacquered Russian chests on which a couple of incense burners were placed to add a fragrant smell. On the wall, numerous furs of white wolves and snow leopards hung, which seemed to be the hunted game of Batu himself. The servant woman lit a few Baghdad lamps since it was becoming dark inside the tent.

CHAPTER 58

Around his death bed, Batu was surrounded by his sons Sartaq and Toqoqan, his brother Berke, his chief wife Boraqchin and a few grandsons.

Batu opened his mouth and clearly said, "I am going to tell you what I heard from my father just before he passed away: 'Know who you are. Then you will see the way.'"

Batu died in Sarai, the capital city of his domain. He was 50 years old. His ulus—the Golden Ordu that ruled over the Kievan Rus, Volga Bulgaria, Cumania and Caucasus—lasted for 270 years, which were the longest-lived ulus.

The Russians used the title "tsar" when they addressed him:

Tsar Bati
The ruler of
Heaven and earth.
The master of
Past, present and future.

About the Author

S am Djang writes novels and poems. He is a historian specialized in Genghis Khan and his Mongol Empire. He studied literature, history and dentistry at the University of Southern California in Los Angeles. He won the **Irwin Award** for Best Historical Fiction Campaign in 2011 for his first book, *Genghis Khan the World Conqueror Volume 1 and Volume 2.*